Incident
at the
Pink Beach House

Kay Williamson

ISBN-10: 1493742531
ISBN-13: 978-1493742530

OTHER BOOKS
BY KAY WILLIAMSON

Ghostly Whispers
The Bridge to Nowhere
Listen to the Heart
Time After Time
Murder at the Starlight Pavilion
The Mysterious Woman on the Train
Murder on Star Route 1

Chapter 1

Brandon Sterling is my name, and teaching is my game…along with a bit of amateur sleuthing.

It was a year ago on Friday, April 29, that I was enjoying my late afternoon jog on a secluded area of the beach and approaching an intriguing two-story, pink beach house that held an aura of mystery. I've never considered myself even remotely psychic, but on my jog that day, I would find that my interest in the house indicated that I'd had some precognitive vibes.

As always, I turned to look at the interesting two-story house surrounded by a high, pink stucco wall with wrap-around porches and stairs that lead to the cupola. Up until then, I'd never observed anyone in the cupola, so I was excited to see the silhouette of a person, turned towards the ocean, using binoculars. Jogging in place, I stopped to take a better look. The person appeared to be a petite woman. A few seconds later, another, taller, person appeared directly behind the woman. My heart, already racing from my jog, picked up a few more beats when I heard a piercing scream. Horrified, I watched the woman plunge to the ground.

Though I realized I could be placing my life in jeopardy, I ran up the sand dune and onto the boardwalk that led to the beach house. I pushed at the ornate iron gate with all my strength, but it was locked and the gate wouldn't budge. I could see through the widely spaced bars and noticed someone lying prone on the immaculate lawn. I decided to climb over the gate, and after dropping to the ground on the other side, I rushed over to the motionless form. I had been correct in my assessment. She was a young, petite female with dark shoulder-length hair, wearing a yellow blouse and matching shorts. She was totally still. I was afraid her neck might be broken, so I didn't dare move her. I assumed she had been pushed through the open space of the cupola by her assailant. I reached for her wrist and felt no pulse. But *my* pulse was pounding a fast, steady beat in my ears.

I'd left my cell phone in my car approximately three miles away, so I couldn't call 911. Unless the assailant had run down the stairs and disappeared while I was running up the sand dune and boardwalk, I figured he or she must still be in the cupola. I made a quick decision not to pound on the front door to ask for help because the assailant might be the owner of the beach house. I had no choice but to run back to my car and call the police.

I sprinted to the iron gate and lifted the hinge-lock that slid into the wall from the inside. At least I wouldn't need to climb it again. Turning around to take another look, I almost drowned in my adrenaline when I observed a tall, blond male wearing sunglasses and a white shirt and shorts, running down the cupola stairs. Of course, he must have been watching me as I bent over the dead body.

I flew down the boardwalk and sand dune, not having run that fast since I'd won my high school's five-hundred yard dash, but this time I'd need to run approximately three miles. I had a vision of the local paper's headlines: *Young Teacher's Heart Gives Out While Running on the Beach.* As I ran, I glanced back several times to see if he were following. Thankfully, I saw no one.

I was gasping for breath when I finally reached my car. I now understood what Einstein meant by "time is relative," for it seemed I'd been running for hours. Pulling my keys from my shorts pocket, I opened the car door and slid into the seat. I grabbed a bottle of water (wishing it were a stiff drink) and took a large swig while taking out my cell phone from under the seat. My heart was pounding so hard, I felt like I was listening to it with a doctor's stethoscope.

When I punched in 911, my words must have sounded jumbled when the dispatcher answered.

"My name is Brandon Sterling, and I want to report a murder." I was shocked to hear myself saying the words.

"Where are you, Brandon?"

Trying to calm myself, I pulled in a deep breath, but it didn't work. Still huffing and puffing, I gave what I hoped was enough information to get one or more officers of the law out here to my car. I didn't know the address of the pink beach house.

In all the excitement, I'd forgotten to check the time. I'd read enough murder mysteries to know the time line is important. I glanced at my watch and saw it was 6:10. It probably took five minutes or so to climb the gate, check out the victim, and run back down the boardwalk and sand dune. I estimated twenty-five or so minutes to run back to the car. So roughly speaking, the crime was committed around 5:35, give or take five to ten minutes.

Though it didn't appear that the murderer had followed me, understandably I felt uneasy. When I noticed a car pulling up, my fear held me captive. Perhaps the assailant, thinking I might have a car in the parking lot, decided to look for me here. The car windows were up, but if he had a gun, a bullet would probably break through the glass. It seemed an eternity since I'd called the police – Einstein's theory again. I watched as the man pulled into a parking space a few spaces down. If I started up the car for a quick getaway, the policemen wouldn't know where to find me.

It appeared the man was making no move to get out of his car, but I turned on my ignition in case he opened his door and came in my direction. If he started coming towards me shooting, I wondered if I could drive scooted down in my seat. But why would he come looking for me here, when he'd already had the chance to come after me at the beach house? I guess fear had caused my reasoning faculties to turn to mush.

Suddenly, I heard the wail of a siren. Relief spread over me like a hot shower on sore muscles.

When the police car drew up beside me, I jumped out of my car, gave them my name, told them I taught high school English in the area, and gave a quick run-down on what had happened. "It's a two-story pink house about three miles south of here," I told them. "I think I can recognize it from the frontage road since it's the only pink house on my three mile jog. I'll lead the way." I felt braver now with the police protection of one Captain Sean Delaney and his sidekick Sergeant Erin O'Grady.

As I pulled out of the parking space, I noticed the car I'd been watching hadn't moved. The occupant appeared to be looking straight ahead at the ocean. Sometimes people would park and relax after work, but I wondered how long it would be before I relaxed again. If I'd been detained at school for just five minutes, I'd have missed the entire scene and wouldn't be in this dire predicament. I'm sure my girlfriend, Amberly Raine, would say it was synchronicity – a favorite word of hers. A sense of foreboding swooped into my psyche.

Chapter 2

I've lived in Lo Verde Beach for five years, but I'd never been down this frontage road, so I made a quick calculation of approximately three miles. Though the cupola wasn't visible from the back, I knew I'd found the correct house when I spied a two story pink house with wrap around porches surrounded by a high wall with an iron gate. Luckily, there were enough parking spaces for two cars in front of the gate. I jumped out of my car and nodded at the two policemen who had followed me. Of course, the gate was locked, so I vaulted (*sans* pole) over the gate. Feeling a touch of déjà vu, I unlocked the gate from the inside and pulled it open for the two policemen. The captain looked to be in his fifties, black hair speckled with gray, nice looking but not movie-star handsome, and around six foot two or three. The sergeant was considerably younger – maybe in his early thirties, of medium height with dark hair, and a pleasant face.

"Hey, looks like you've done that trick before," Captain Delaney said sarcastically, referring to my vaulting talent. "Are you sure you're not in our files?"

I ignored his question. "Quick, this way." I led them to the front lawn and to the area where I'd seen the dead woman. To my astonishment, the body had disappeared! I felt a rush of heat to my face and turned to the policemen who were observing me skeptically.

"I swear," I said, stunned at the turn of events, "a young woman with dark hair wearing a yellow blouse and shorts was lying about here. See, you can tell the grass is flatter." I pointed to the grass then got down on my knees searching for signs of anything that would show the woman had been there. I found nothing. *Now I know how Bush must have felt when no weapons of mass destruction were found in Iraq,* I thought. "The assailant must

5

have moved her. Let's check the cupola."

The two skeptical policemen followed me up the porch stairs. If there was no evidence of her being there, I hoped I'd not be arrested for mischievous conduct. Not too long ago I'd been frightened out of my wits because I'd observed a murder; now, still witless, I was scared no one was going to believe me.

While Captain Delaney and Sergeant O'Grady scrutinized the small area, I braced for what was coming.

Captain Delaney stared at me not too kindly. "So you say you witnessed a murder around thirty-five to forty minutes ago, huh? I don't see any evidence of any murder on the ground or up here. How about you, O'Grady? Do you see any evidence of a murder?"

Sergeant O'Grady shook his head. "Can't say as I do, Captain. But it doesn't make much sense why a teacher, of all people, would want to make up a lie and get himself in trouble."

"You're so right, Sergeant," I said quickly and with a bit of hope. "What possible motive would cause me to call 911 and waste your valuable time with a ridiculous made-up story of murder?"

Captain Delaney was not so easily persuaded. "Just because you're a teacher doesn't exclude you from a wacko list, Mr. Sterling. Our jails are full of people who do crazy things just to get attention."

I'm in big trouble and in grave danger of losing my job. "Look, Captain, I get plenty of attention from five different classrooms full of spirited, high school students. And while we're standing here discussing my sanity, a man is getting away with murder. Please let's at least try to get into the house. Perhaps he's in there hiding. It's a huge house, and he could have been smart enough to know that I, as witness to the murder, would most certainly call the police."

Sergeant O'Grady nodded. "Yeah, if Mr. Sterling here is telling the truth, what he just said makes sense."

"Oh, all right," the captain commented begrudgingly. "But we'll need a search warrant."

"And just how many hours or days will that take?" My fear of being arrested was replaced by impatience.

"Don't be a smart-ass, Mr. Sterling, or we'll haul you off to jail right now."

"I'm sorry," I said. "I didn't mean to sound impertinent. But if we don't search the house right now, the assailant could leave while we're downtown waiting for the warrant – that is, if he hasn't already left. Isn't there some kind of law that permits you to do an emergency search without a warrant?"

The captain rolled his eyes upward and sighed. "I suppose there is. Listen, Mr. Sterling, if we break into this house, the owner might very well sue us if we don't find any evidence of a murder."

"Who is going to know, Captain? I'll certainly never tell."

He glared menacingly at me for a moment. "Come on, Sergeant. We'll ring the doorbell and knock at the door. If no one answers and the door is locked, I'll be damned if we're going to break it down."

"Fair enough," I replied, rushing down the cupola stairs before he could change his mind. If someone did come to the door, I prayed it wouldn't be the murderer holding a weapon.

I reached the door first and rang the doorbell while knocking on the door with the heavy, gold-plated door knocker. As expected, no one answered. I turned the doorknob and found it to be unlocked. I allowed the captain and the sergeant to go in, and I followed. I wasn't a coward, but I didn't have a gun, and they did. Too bad I didn't have on a coat. I could have stuck my finger in my pocket and made it look like a gun like the characters in the old movies.

The foyer seemed dark, so I flipped on the light switch and a forged, iron chandelier flooded the area with light. "Some pad," I whispered and then wondered why. We'd made enough noise ringing the door bell and banging on the door to wake the dead (the murdered woman, that is, if she were indeed dead and on the premises). The terra cotta floor, the wicker console table holding a tall vase of colorful silk flowers, and the upholstered wicker bench next to the table shouted in unison, "expensive, expensive." I felt sure the rest of the mini-mansion furnishings would not be a disappointment to any fine-furniture connoisseur. Considering my modest teacher's salary, I would have had to live many lifetimes to pay for the beach house plus furnishings.

"I wonder what business the owner is in," the sergeant commented, while glancing around.

"Yeah, the dude must make a bundle," the captain replied. "And I bet this is just his winter home. He could have a few more up north or maybe a couple in Europe." He pulled out his cell. "Perhaps it was an accident, and the man you saw running down the steps took the young woman to the emergency room at the hospital." Punching in the numbers, he muttered, "If there ever was a body."

After speaking to an emergency attendant for a few minutes, he closed his cell. "No one has been admitted of your description, Sterling."

I knew the captain thought I was a kook.

Feeling a bit more secure, since no one had started shooting when we entered, I ventured into the living area. The blinds were drawn, and once again I flipped on a switch. I was impressed with more gorgeous furnishings.

We went over each room on the first floor carefully and checked each closet but found nothing out of order; however, as we started to exit, my attention was drawn to a large family portrait sitting on a console in the large living room. Six solemn faces stared at us from the portrait. The oldest, most likely the father, was a handsome man, probably in his late fifties, with dark hair. His face was unlined, and his complexion olive. The lovely woman sitting next to him had dark, medium-length hair. Like her husband, she had a youthful face and olive complexion. *Good genes or excellent cosmetic surgery,* I thought. They appeared to be of Spanish or South American descent. Standing behind the couple were four young people – two boys and two girls looking to be in their twenties or early thirties. One of the young men appeared to be a perfect combination of both parents, but the taller of the two was blond and had no resemblance to the parents. Could he be adopted? Perhaps he was the child of a previous marriage. The two girls, who were dressed alike, looked identical.

I pointed to the girls in the portrait. "Obviously, the girls are twins. And I believe one of them could well be the murder victim. Remember I told you she was lying on her stomach, and I only saw her profile. But her hair looks the same as these two girls, and she'd be about the right size."

The captain stared at the portrait. "They look like twins all right. One of them could have been staying here by herself." He glanced around. "But everything looks so closed up…you know, like no one is living here."

"That's true," I sighed. "But remember, the front door was unlocked. If the murderer was staying here with one of the twins or at least knew she was here, he could have thrown her into his car after he pushed her from the cupola. He would have had thirty-five or so minutes before we arrived, so perhaps he took all her things, straightened up, and made it look like no one had been here. I think that's what I'd have done."

The captain shot me a mean-eyed, distrustful look. "Oh?"

I cut him off at the pass. "We haven't checked the top floor yet. We might find something there."

We climbed the beautiful, winding staircase in silence, and I began to experience a few serious palpitations while wondering what I'd do if the murderer suddenly jumped out of a closet and began shooting wildly.

At the top of the stairs, we entered what I supposed was the master bedroom. Certainly it was large enough and elegant enough with an adjoining bath and Jacuzzi. Scattered on the top of an armoire, a lingerie chest, a triple dresser and bedside table, there were more photographs of the family enjoying various sports activities. Once again, nothing seemed to be out of order.

When we stepped into the next bedroom, I recognized a lovely fragrance permeating the air. "*Nuit Jardin*," I said, inhaling deeply. "It's an expensive French perfume – my girlfriend wears it. I know it's expensive, because I bought her a bottle for Christmas." I perused the room. "I bet this is the bedroom the murdered girl occupied. The king-sized bed has been made up but wrinkled, and the pillows are askew. Perhaps the young woman had taken a nap, or she could have had an afternoon tumble in the hay with a lover." The two officers nodded.

Feeling a bit depressed that the unfortunate victim might have had her last sexual romp, I refocused and opened the closet door and found a few dresses, blouses, and cropped pants hanging on silk-covered hangers. Three pairs of heels were placed next to a few pairs of casual shoes, and a white, silk bathrobe and gown were hanging on a large hook. It was obvious the shoes and clothes had not come from K-Mart. Hanging next to her clothes were several men's shirts of various colors, trousers, and a cream-colored coat. Three pairs of men's casual shoes and two pieces of expensive-looking luggage completed the items in the closet.

I walked into the adjoining bath bathroom deep in thought. The man who shoved the victim from the cupola must have been her husband or lover. If so, she would have been shocked when she realized what he'd done as she fell to the ground. I noticed another Jacuzzi and a large mirrored dressing table reflecting jars and bottles filled with creams, lotions, and make-up. I was awakened from my reflections by the voice of Captain Delaney who was peeking around the door.

"You've been in there a long time, Sterling. Are you planning on taking a shower or perhaps a soak in the Jacuzzi?"

"Sorry, I guess my imagination is working overtime. Are you now convinced that a woman was staying here?" I pointed to the dressing table.

"Hey, I figured that out when I looked into the bedroom closet. I think you must have been looking at too many dumb cop movies. Give me some credit for deductive reasoning. Okay?"

His comments surprised me. "If I gave you that impression, please forgive me, Captain."

He crossed his arms. "Even though it's obvious a woman was staying here, and also a man, we haven't proved she was murdered. We still don't have a body. Maybe the woman is out shopping or something."

"I see I haven't convinced you that I witnessed a murder. Can you at least consider the fact that a murder may have taken place, and the murderer placed the body in a vehicle and took off to parts unknown?"

His eyebrows furrowed. "Yeah, I can picture that scenario."

I sighed. "Good. But don't you think that just in case the murderer is still hiding somewhere in this palatial home, we'd better finish checking out all the rooms and closets?"

He glared at me then walked back into the bedroom. "Okay, let's get to it."

Fifteen minutes later, the two policemen and I had checked every nook and cranny in the huge house. We were impressed with our surroundings but had found no dead body.

"We haven't checked the garage. Maybe he left her there before he took off," I offered.

"All right, but I think we're wasting our time," the captain snapped.

When we entered the three-car garage through the kitchen door, we found a shiny, silver BMW.

"I expect that belongs to the victim," I said. "I don't think she'd be driving a beat-up old hot rod."

"Yeah, it must be nice," Sergeant O'Grady said. "But look where all this...this beautiful home, clothes and car got her...that is, if she was murdered."

I didn't think that her money and lifestyle had anything to do with it, but then maybe it did. I looked closely at the floor. "Hey, come over here. It looks like blood." I pointed to four red spots each about the size of a nickel. "She could have been bleeding internally, and blood was dripping from her mouth. He could have placed her in the trunk of his car, and in his hurry, he didn't notice these blood spots. The concrete wall is high and conceals the area around the house. He wouldn't need to go through the house at all and carried her body straight to the garage."

"So you've got it all figured out, eh Sterling? I'll have to hunt up a junior detective badge for you."

I ignored the captain's sarcasm and continued with my deductive reasoning. "I believe the perpetrator was her husband or lover. Remember the rumpled bed?"

Captain Delaney spat out the words. "Yeah, I still have my memory. I ain't *that* old!"

Boy is he sensitive. "Well, Captain. Where do we go from here?" I wanted to tell him my plan, but I could see Sergeant O'Grady's eyes moving frantically back and forth from his superior to me. I had a strong hunch that the sergeant was getting nervous because I kept giving suggestions to a man who didn't like to be told what to do.

Much to my surprise, the captain said sardonically, "Well now, Mr. Sterling, you've been trying to run the show so far; just where do *you* think we should go from here?"

I couldn't believe he was asking me what I thought. "I'd call the station and have someone find out the names of the people who live here. Then I'd get someone from forensics to come out and lift the woman's DNA from her bedroom then check the DNA with the blood on the garage floor. If the blood does belong to the woman who lives in this house, it would help substantiate my story of the murder. Do you agree, Captain?"

"Yeah, if the blood checks out, it does give some evidence that a murder was committed." Once again, he stared at me mean-eyed. "But maybe the blood came from a knee scrape or something." He pulled out his cell phone. "We'll stay here and wait for the guys with the DNA lab."

I couldn't tell if the captain was taking my account of the murder seriously, and I had to give him credit for the comment about the knee scrape. Where in hell had the murderer hidden or taken the body?

When the captain pulled out his cell phone, I told the sergeant I wanted to take another look at the family portrait in the living room.

Having more time to observe my surroundings, I walked more slowly through the kitchen. The large breakfast-room area was furnished with a richly detailed-carved iron forged table and armchairs. A baker's rack stood against the wall filled with colorful pottery. My entire bachelor pad could fit right into the kitchen area. Though I had little knowledge of antiques and fine furniture, I felt the décor throughout the house was South American or Mediterranean. But wherever the furniture came from, it wouldn't take a Fifth Avenue decorator to know that the furnishings were expensive and of the highest quality.

Upon reaching the living area, I once again reached for the family portrait. I'd always been fascinated by identical twins, and though I didn't know too much about the subject, I did know that they had the same DNA. I remembered an old movie I'd seen with an evil twin vs. good twin plot and thought, *Wouldn't it be crazy if the wrong twin had been murdered?* I scrutinized the photograph. The twins were quite beautiful. They were wearing heavy eye make-up, which emphasized their exotic beauty. I felt great sympathy for the parents and siblings – especially the twin of the deceased. I would not want to be the person who would deliver the sad news, but I would soon find out I'd been selected, by whoever does the selecting, to be the messenger. Deep in thought, I jumped when I heard the phone ring. If it was the parents of the murdered girl or any of her family, what should I say? I knew I had to pick up.

"Hello," I answered a bit hesitantly.

"Hello, Alberto? This is Eduardo. You sound half asleep. Have you been keeping my daughter up half the night?" He talked with a slight Spanish accent.

He's probably the victim's father. I can't tell him his daughter has been murdered.

"Hey, Alberto, are you still there? Is something wrong?"

"Eduardo, this is not Alberto. My name is Brandon Sterling. I'm…I'm afraid there's been an accident."

"What? What kind of an accident, and who the hell are you? Are you with the police? Is Alberto there?"

I could feel my stomach knotting. "Alberto is not here. I'm working with the police, sir. I…I witnessed the accident."

"Would you kindly tell me what kind of accident you're talking about? Is my daughter hurt?"

"Sir, please describe your daughter."

"Please describe my daughter? Rosalia is slim and has dark hair. She's around five feet four inches tall. She's a beautiful girl. She has an identical twin, Maria. Rosalia and her fiancé, Alberto, have been staying in the beach house for almost a week. She was supposed to call me an hour ago for a business conference. Now please tell me what is going on!"

"I'm so very sorry to have to tell you sir, but the young woman staying in this house was pushed from the cupola and seriously if not fatally injured. From the way you described your daughter, I strongly believe she is the victim." I wished I had not been the person chosen to deliver the shattering news. I prayed Eduardo would not have a heart attack.

"Oh, my God! Is this some kind of joke?"

"No, it's not a joke, sir. I only–"

"Is Rosalia still alive? Is she in the hospital?"

"Sir, it's a…a strange situation. Your daughter was pushed from the cupola then someone took her body…in other words, she's been kidnapped."

"I'm having difficulty taking this in," he said.

"Yes, sir, I'm sure you are."

"Are the police there?"

"Yes, sir."

"My wife and I will fly out immediately. We're in New York. How can I reach you?"

I could tell by his voice he was holding back tears. I gave him my cell number and asked for his. I wanted to get off the phone as soon as possible, for I knew he needed time to pull himself together.

Feeling as miserable as a half-drowned cat, I headed for the garage. At least I'd spared the captain and the sergeant from having to inform Eduardo the terrible news about his daughter, Rosalia. Somehow knowing her name made it all the worse.

When I opened the kitchen door and walked into the garage, I was surprised to see the policemen talking to a young man. As I approached, my knees threatened to buckle when I noticed his hair seemed to be about the same shade and length as the man I'd seen running down the porch stairs, and he was about the same height. He was also wearing a white shirt, but his shorts were dark blue. Perhaps he'd gotten blood on his white ones, and he changed them. Too bad the assailant had been wearing sunglasses and was too far away to see his face clearly. But surely he wouldn't have returned to the scene of the crime, would he?

"Sterling, this is Alberto Cardoza," the captain said.

For once I was speechless.

Chapter 3

"Alberto Cardoza?" I finally managed. If he were the murderer, surely he would recognize me, but he looked straight into my eyes without flinching. "I've just been talking with Eduardo, your future father-in-law," I told him. "He and his wife will be flying down as soon as possible."

The captain broke in. "Mr. Cardoza arrived just a few seconds before you entered, Sterling. We've not had time to explain why we're here."

Alberto's expression was a study of uneasy puzzlement as he glanced from the captain back to me. "So, just what are you doing here? Why are Eduardo and Estrella flying down? Where is my fiancée, Rosalia? She's not hurt is she?"

"If Rosalia is the name of the young woman who was staying here, I'm afraid she's been murdered," the captain answered gravely.

"Murdered? What the hell do you mean?"

The captain turned to me. "Give him the details, Sterling. You're the one who witnessed the murder – that is, if there really was a murder. As you know, we still don't have a body."

And he still doesn't quite believe my story. And the coward has given me the job of giving the terrible news to a man whose fiancée has been murdered. I closely observed Alberto's expression as I gave a rundown of what I'd witnessed. I was especially interested in his reaction as I described the man running down the cupola steps, but his expression was one of bewilderment and grief.

"But why would anyone take her body?" Alberto asked, tears streaming down his cheeks.

"We don't know, unless the murderer plans to ask for a ransom," the captain commented.

Since the Captain gave me the responsibility of telling Alberto

15

what I'd witnessed, I decided to ask a few questions. "So where were you an hour ago, Alberto?"

Shaking his head, Alberto closed his eyes. "Give me a minute, will you? You've just told me that my fiancée was murdered and her body has disappeared. To say I'm in shock would be an understatement. Do you think we could go inside? I'm desperate for a glass of brandy."

"That's a reasonable request," the captain answered. "Sergeant, wait here for the DNA lab."

Hoping I was going to be offered a drink to calm *my* frayed nerves, I was feeling a bit better.

The captain and I followed Alberto into the house. Though I did wonder if he'd deliberately put off answering my question about where he'd been for the last hour so he could have a few minutes to think up a convincing story. So far he'd been a cool character reacting exactly like an innocent person, but I was more than a bit suspicious. Too bad the assailant had been wearing sunglasses and I hadn't been closer. But even at that, Alberto's resemblance to the man I saw was uncanny.

In a few minutes, we were back in the living room. Alberto flipped a switch, and all the lamps in the room popped on, swathing the room with a soft, velvety light. I watched in anticipation as he approached a liquor cabinet (expensive looking, of course). He reached for brandy snifters and what I perceived to be an expensive bottle of brandy sitting on a large silver tray.

"Mr. Sterling," he said, pouring brandy, "since you're not a policeman, would you join me."

I forced myself not to appear too eager. "Yes, thank you," I said.

He placed the snifter in my outstretched hand. "By the way, I didn't catch your first name."

"My name is Brandon – Brandon Sterling." I was standing under the air conditioner and felt a cold blast of air threatening to freeze my naked torso. Too bad I hadn't taken time to put on my shirt while in my car waiting for the police. But at that time, I was hot from running. I also had other things on my mind. I tried not to gulp the brandy that was pleasantly burning my throat – talk about needing a drink!

Alberto twirled his brandy snifter then took a swallow. I took a

16

lesson in brandy twirling while waiting for his explanation of his last hour.

He stared at the family portrait and began, "Rosalia and I arrived last Wednesday for a brief working holiday. I work for her father who owns one of the United States' largest and most prestigious, furniture manufacturing companies. He also has numerous showrooms and furniture stores in every state and also in Europe. Rosalia and I work in the same department in the head office in New York. I'm in sales, but she's head auditor of the firm." He paused, twirled, and sipped his brandy.

He was giving a lot of valuable information, but he still hadn't said where he'd been for the past hour. Getting the hang of it, I twirled and sipped.

"I won't bore you and the captain with the details of our agenda for today," Alberto continued, "but around two, I left for Orlando, where I had scheduled a meeting with the salespeople at the store there. Since Rosalia and I had reservations for dinner at the Chart House for seven-thirty, I finished my business around five and came straight here. As usual, the business rush traffic was heavy. That's about it. You were here when I arrived."

His alibi will be easy enough to check, I thought while watching him amble towards the sofa. He placed his drink on the coffee table, sat down on the luxurious sofa, put his hands over his face, and began crying uncontrollably. "God, I can't believe this is happening," he sobbed. "Who would want to harm Rosalia? I don't understand."

I figured the shock had worn off, and he appeared to be genuinely heartbroken, but even though we were drinking buddies now, I wasn't totally convinced. I'd done a bit of acting in college and knew a good actor could turn on the facet at will. My feelings were ambivalent when, still holding my drink, I sat down next to him and patted his arm. "I know this has been really tough on you, Alberto. I wish I could say something to make it better for you. If it's any consolation, I'll stop at nothing to find the murdering bastard who killed Maria." I guess that last statement sounded like something from a movie, but it was the way I felt. Though the captain had been silent, I knew he was listening intently to our conversation. I bet he'd love to have a drink. He remained standing.

Alberto nodded and pulled out a handkerchief from his shorts pocket. Swiping at his eyes he said, "Since there is no evidence of a body, if you hadn't witnessed the murder, we wouldn't know that there had even been a murder." He smiled slightly through his tears. "I guess I would prefer not to know there had been a murder."

"Yes, but if you came home and Rosalia was nowhere to be found, you might think she'd run away with an unknown lover, or something to that effect."

Alberto appeared distracted for a few moments. "You don't suppose…no, I'm sure that would not be possible." He reached for his brandy glass.

"What would not be possible, Alberto?" the captain asked.

"Rosalia and I were very much in love. I can't conceive of the idea that she'd have a lover, but if she did, it could explain what happened. She knew in advance that I'd be gone for a few hours. If that were the case, and if she broke off with him, he could have killed her in a fit of anger. But as I said, I can't conceive of the idea that she'd have a lover. Just forget that theory."

Perhaps she told you that she had a lover, and you killed her in a fit of anger! Of course, I didn't voice my thoughts. But a new thought popped into my mind. "Alberto, do you have a brother?"

His left eyebrow raised a fraction. "Yes, I do have a brother. His name is Emilio. Why do you ask?"

I ignored his question and asked another. "Describe Emilio. Is there a strong resemblance between you?"

"Yes, most people say there is. Emilio and I both have blond hair and are about the same height and weight. He's two years older than I."

"And are you close? I mean do you get along?"

"Yes, I'd say we get along most of the time. Like most brothers, we've had disagreements along the way. But we're not close. I don't believe Emilio is close with anyone. He's always been a loner. Mom is always saying that if we didn't look so much alike, no one would believe we were brothers. I'm an extravert, and he's very much an introvert. Emilio has always had expensive tastes, even as a teen, but having money has never been as important to me as it is to my brother. Our family is far from rich, and often Emilio would pressure Mom and Dad into giving him things they couldn't really afford." He glanced around the room. "Not that I have anything against money." He paused a few moments. "I don't like to bad-mouth him, but he's self-centered and often not considerate of others. Yet he's quite charming if it's to his advantage. As I know of, there's never been any problem with his business contacts. Where are these questions leading?"

I pulled in a deep breath thinking that Emilio must be quite the narcissist. "Alberto, when I was giving you the rundown of what I'd witnessed at the murder scene, I don't think you realized you fit the description of the man who pushed Rosalia from the cupola. Though I only had a quick glimpse, I could see he was wearing sunglasses, a white shirt, and white shorts. He was blond and about your height. The only difference is you were wearing blue shorts when you returned from Orlando. We both know you could have changed if you had blood on them. That's why I asked if you had a brother who looked like you."

Alberto shook his head. "I can't believe you consider me a suspect. It's just as unbelievable that you think my brother could have harmed Rosalia. Why would he? And he's not even in the area."

I tried to sound lighthearted. "Don't take it personal, Alberto. Everyone involved with Rosalia is a suspect until they can produce an alibi. If the time of your meeting in Orlando checks out, you'll have no problem. Right, Captain?"

"That's right, Alberto."

Alberto slapped his forehead. "I'll have no problem, the man says. My fiancée, the love of my life, reportedly has been murdered, and her body is nowhere to be found! Wouldn't you say that's a problem?"

I nodded. "Yes, yes, of course you have a problem. I'm sorry. I didn't mean to sound flippant. So tell me, does Emilio work for Eduardo's company?"

He took another sip of brandy before answering. "Yes, he does. Emilio is head of the sales department in Europe. He lives in Spain and travels from there through Europe. I heard from him, I guess, around two weeks ago. His vacation was coming up, and he said he was planning on flying home to New York for a few weeks. Our parents' home is in New York State. He said he'd meet Rosalia and me at our parents' house this Sunday."

"So he hasn't made contact since that call?" the captain asked.

"No, if he's going to be in the states for a few weeks, there's no hurry. He shot the captain furtive look. "Are the police even trying to find Rosalia?"

"We really don't have much to go on. We don't know what kind of vehicle the killer was driving, do we? When I called the DNA lab, I sent out the details to all the Florida police and even the surrounding states, but no one knows what to look out for – unless the perpetrator dumps the body, and the police can identify it to be Rosalia."

Alberto let out a strangled cry. "Oh, my God!"

The captain apologized. "I'm sorry. I didn't mean to be insensitive."

Alberto made another swipe at his eyes. "I know you're just telling it like you see it. I feel like I'm in the middle of a horrible nightmare."

If this guy is acting, he ought to go to Hollywood. "I'm sure you do, Alberto. Among other things, you must feel quite helpless." I began rubbing my arms trying to get warm. The brandy had not helped all that much.

Alberto gave me a feeble smile. "I can see you're freezing. If you'll pour us another brandy, I'll run upstairs and bring you one of my shirts."

"That's a deal," I said gratefully.

"Keep a close eye on him," the captain instructed after Alberto exited. "I have more calls to make."

I nodded then picked up the snifters and walked over to the liquor cabinet. While pouring brandy, I glanced up and caught my reflection in the mirror. Except for our height, as we are both tall, I am the opposite of Alberto. His features are finely chiseled and mine rugged. We both have thick, wavy hair, though his is blond and mine dark brown.

The thought did occur to me that he might try to run away if he was guilty, but I quickly dismissed it. Where would he go? The police would be on his tail in seconds. He seemed like a really nice guy and one that would give you the shirt off his back – well, at least a guy who would lend you his shirt. I'd be disappointed if the shirt was a cheap one. My ruminations were interrupted when Alberto entered carrying a light blue polo shirt. I wasn't

20

disappointed; it looked warm and expensive.

"Thanks so much, Alberto," I said putting down my glass and reaching for the shirt. "I don't think it would have been long before this shirt and my skin would have been the same shade of blue!" Not that it mattered, but the shirt was a perfect fit.

"What happened to the captain?" Alberto asked, looking around as though the burly policeman might be hiding.

"He had some calls to make."

We took our places back on the sofa. After a few sips of brandy I said, "Tell me about Rosalia and Maria. I've read that identical twins are usually closely bonded."

Alberto's eyes took on a faraway look. "From what Rosalia has told me, she and Maria have always been close and pick up on each other when they're in trouble. They even roomed together in college. Sometimes one would start a sentence, and the other would finish it. The twins and I attended Greenwood University in Greenwood, New York. I met them in a psychology class. At first, we just hung out together as friends, but by the end of the semester, I was feeling much more than friendship for Rosalia. I had the feeling that Maria was a bit jealous when I started asking her twin out, because they had been inseparable for so long. But she adjusted and started dating a few guys on campus.

"After we graduated, Rosalia introduced me to her family. We hit it off immediately, and I began working for her father. I'm sure the fact that I was of Spanish descent and spoke the language had something to do with my acceptance from the family. Emilio joined the company soon after. That was two years ago. Rosalia and I have been engaged for a little over a year, and we were planning a June wedding. I can't believe she's gone," he said in a quavering voice. He reached for his handkerchief and blotted his eyes.

"I know that answering my questions has not been easy on you, Alberto. Would you prefer to be alone?"

"No, it's rather a comfort to have you here, though I don't why since you told me I'm a suspect."

"Hey, maybe you haven't picked up on it, but the police have a suspicion that I made up the entire story just to get attention! So in a way, we're both suspects."

"But Rosalia is missing. Doesn't that substantiate your story?

And didn't the captain say he'd notified the police all over Florida."

I nodded. "Yeah, that's true. But it's difficult to know what the captain is thinking. And speaking of the police, I think I hear them coming through the kitchen." I stood, and sure enough, the captain and sergeant were coming towards us accompanied by two men carrying lab equipment.

"The lab guys just finished taking samples of blood on the garage floor," the captain informed us. "We're on our way upstairs to get DNA from Rosalia's hairbrush. Have you received any more calls?"

I shook my head. "No more calls, Captain."

"I'm sure Eduardo and Estrella are taking the company jet," Alberto interjected. "They should be here in a few hours."

The captain held out his hand. "We'll need your keys, Alberto, so we can move your car into the garage. The light will be better there for the lab work."

Alberto reached into his pocket and pulled out his keys. "I had to park the car on the side of the road because your cars were parked in front of the gate."

"Yeah, we know that, Alberto," he said, impatiently. He took the keys. "Okay. We've got some men talking to the neighbors on each side of the house. Even though the houses are few and far between, someone might have been looking out of his window or backing out of his garage at just the right time. My feeling is the killer would have been breaking the speed limit to get away as fast as possible. It would certainly help to know the make of the perp's car."

"Yeah, well good luck," I said. I watched as he and the lab guys disappeared. At last, feeling warm and cozy from the excellent brandy and the borrowed shirt, I sat back down on the sofa.

"So you found blood on the garage floor?" Alberto asked.

"Yes, around four nickel-sized drops."

"What do you think that means?"

"It could mean that the murderer placed the body in the trunk of his car and a few drops spilled on the floor. I didn't notice any blood when I examined Rosalia briefly, but she certainly must have hit the ground hard. Perhaps it somehow caused blood to spill out from her ear or mouth. As I told you, she was lying on her stomach and her head was turned to one side. I didn't want to move her in any way, in case her neck was broken. Yet the blood in the garage could be from a knee scrape or something like that."

Alberto's face was a study of desolation. Copious tears slid down his cheeks. He didn't bother to wipe them. "She must be dead then; Rosalia is dead."

"Yes, that's probably true, Alberto. But there's a slim chance that's she's not. Why else would the body be moved?"

He took a sip of brandy before answering. "Nothing makes any sense. I've been searching my mind. There is no one who would want to harm Rosalia."

I decided to change the subject. "Do you think Maria will be flying down with Eduardo and Estrella?" I asked Alberto.

Alberto shook his head. "No. Maria doesn't work for the company. She's in Spain. Though she's not a model, she went to work for a modeling firm right out of college, and like Emilio, she travels all over Europe. She helps her firm find new prospects, both men and women, and then hires them. Rosalia told me that recently she's become involved with one of the male models. She has apartments in New York and in Spain. Only this morning, Rosalia was talking to Maria over the phone about her maid-of-honor dress." He reached for his handkerchief and blew loudly. "Maria is going to take all this very hard."

I nodded. "I'm sure she will. But didn't you say Emilio also lives in Spain?"

"Yes, they both live in Madrid."

"Hmm. That's interesting. Are they good friends?"

Alberto seemed to be mulling over my question. "I would say they're friends but not good friends. I mean they seem to get along okay, but I don't think they see each other socially. As I mentioned, Emilio is rather a loner. A few times Rosalia and I have flown over and made sure it was at a time both of them were not traveling. We stayed at Maria's place, because she and Rosalia were so close. We'd all get together for dinner and a bit of sightseeing. Maria and Emilio always seemed cordial enough to each other."

"Do you know why Maria chose not to work for her dad's firm?"

Alberto leaned his head back on the sofa. "According to Rosalia, Maria always wanted to be a model since she was a little girl. She's certainly beautiful enough in my opinion, but for some reason she didn't make the grade. I guess she wanted to be in the modeling business so badly that she took another position. She must be good at what she does because she climbed the ladder quite fast."

"My friends who are identical twins have quite different personalities. Is that the case with Rosalia and Maria?"

"Yes. Rosalia is practical, sweet, and compassionate, and she thinks things through. Maria is playful, enjoys playing practical jokes, and kind of jumps into things without thinking of the consequences. Yet, she seems to have made good business decisions."

I noticed an indecipherable expression in Alberto's eyes while he was describing the twins.

The phone's sudden ring caused us both to jump. Alberto hurried over to the desk and lifted the phone. "Hello, this is Alberto."

As I needed a bathroom break, I left Alberto so he could talk in private. I could see that I was not making a good detective. Alberto was still a suspect, and I was feeling far too considerate and sympathetic. I wondered if other policemen and detectives ever ran into that problem.

A few minutes later, after finding a gorgeous bathroom and watching myself take a pee (there was a wall-to-wall mirror behind the commode), I ran into the captain, sergeant, and lab guys. "Alberto is talking to someone now," I told them. "I expect it's someone in the family."

"Well, stick with him, Sterling," the captain instructed. "Right now, he's the prime suspect. And if he did commit the murder, he might try suicide."

Gosh, I never considered that. "Captain, I'm just wondering…I've never had any training as a medic, do you think there's a chance the victim's pulse was beating so faintly that I couldn't feel it?"

He chewed on his bottom lip for a second. "Yeah, I do recall an incident that happened a few years ago. A woman was actually pronounced dead in an accident and sent to the morgue. An attendant passed by a few hours later and saw the sheet moving. You might know it would be a woman attendant. Of course, she screamed loud enough to wake all the other dead people in the morgue."

I didn't laugh at his terrible, male-chauvinist joke. "So what happened? Was the accident victim in a coma?"

He nodded. "Yeah, it seems a person in a coma can have a pulse that's so faint that it can go undetected. Are you having second thoughts about the woman you *say* you saw lying on the ground?"

So he still doesn't quite believe me. I wish he'd make up his mind. "I'm not having second thoughts about what I witnessed, but I am having second thoughts about her pulse. It's at least possible I couldn't feel it. But if she was not dead when I knelt next to her, if her neck was broken, I believe she would have died really soon after. The killer would have needed to get her to a hospital quick, and I don't think he would want to expose himself as a murderer, do you, Captain?"

"I certainly wouldn't want to, and you might not want to, but it's pretty hard to guess what a murderer is thinking. It will be interesting to see what we find in the trunk of Alberto's car."

I nodded. "In my opinion, the perpetrator hadn't planned on killing her, but if something happened that frightened him enough to make him want to kill her, or he got really angry with her over something, he just gave her a push from the cupola. But why did he feel he had to move the body?"

Walking towards the kitchen, the captain stopped and turned. "There are many unanswered questions. Oh, did I mention that Alberto's car is a rental? Doesn't it seem strange that he'd drive the rental when there's a BMW parked in the garage."

"He and Rosalia probably picked up the rental when they landed at the airport in Orlando. Maybe he left the BMW in case Rosalia wanted to go shopping. I read somewhere that the rich keep a car at all their homes, but it seems such a waste to keep a BMW idle for weeks. I'll ask Alberto," I told him.

"Yeah, you be sure and do that," he smirked.

"Yes, sir," I answered while watching him swagger down the hall. The captain was getting on my nerves big time. He'd better watch his step or I might lose my temper. He didn't know that when I was in high school, I was a boxing champion. My mom used to say, "Brandon, guard your mouth; if you don't, you'll be keeping your teeth in a glass every night like your Grandma Katie." Luckily, I didn't lose any teeth. A vision of me knocking out the captain's front teeth floated across my imagination. It took some of the sting out of my anger. I turned to focus on more important things.

"Maria is flying out of Madrid in an hour," Alberto told me when I returned to the living room. "She was so hysterical we could hardly communicate. I guess I should call my parents. Emilio, should be there by now also. But I really dread going through explaining it all again. I feel so emotionally drained." His eyes filled again and threatened to spill over.

"I'm sure you do, Alberto. Perhaps if you ate something you'd feel better. I'd be glad to fix you a sandwich or something." I was beginning to feel quite hungry myself.

"Thanks, but I couldn't eat a thing. My stomach feels like I've been in a hotdog-eating contest."

"The captain said your car was a rental. Did you land at the Orlando airport?"

"Yes, we rented the car there. I drove it this afternoon in case Rosalia wanted to go out for something."

"Look Alberto, I don't want to get your hopes up, but a few minutes ago I had a discussion with the captain. I wondered if I'd been mistaken about Rosalia's pulse. I asked him if he knew of any situation where a person had such a faint pulse that it couldn't be detected. He said yes, and then he told me that sometimes when a person is in a coma, it's possible not to feel a pulse."

His face took on a sudden glow. "You mean there's hope? Rosalia could be alive?"

"I'd say there is a very slim chance, but it's something to hold on to. It's all so strange. Why would Rosalia be abducted if the killer thought she was dead?"

Alberto pursed his lips. "Unless…unless he plans to ask for a ransom and wants us to think she's still alive."

"Yes, we did discuss that earlier. The perpetrator certainly must have seen me bending over the body and taking Rosalia's pulse. If she was dead, he would know that I would know that. But if he could feel something that I couldn't, and he thought she was alive, then it would make sense that he'd abduct her so he could ask for a ransom. But it does seem awfully farfetched, don't you think?"

Alberto was silent for a few seconds. "After you've given me a ray of hope, I hate to say this, but even if he thought she was dead, maybe he took her in case she was still alive and she could identify him, that is, if she knew who he was. But I can't believe anyone who knew Rosalia would want to murder her."

I picked up my snifter and twirled. It seemed to be therapeutic. "Though I feel in my gut she knew the man who pushed her, perhaps she didn't. Maybe it was a planned kidnapping all along. Knowing she was a wealthy young woman with an even wealthier father, the perpetrator could have been watching her and waiting for a chance for an abduction. When he saw her going up to the cupola, he followed her and made his move. She could have surprised him by fighting. But then she wasn't fighting when I first saw her. She was looking through binoculars facing the ocean. Someone shoved her while her back was turned. That's why I believe it has to be someone she knew and trusted."

Alberto appeared pensive for a minute. "If the perpetrator does call and ask for a ransom, of course, we'll ask to speak to Rosalia. If he declines, we'll know she's dead." His eyes were glistening again.

"This is all hypothetical, but we can certainly hope and pray she's alive."

Alberto nodded and walked over to the desk. "Would you please pour me another brandy while I make this call to my parents?"

"Sure." I figured we'd be looped before the family arrived, but under the circumstances it would be understandable. Suddenly, I remembered I had a date with my girlfriend, Amberly, at seven. I glanced at my watch. I was fifteen minutes late already. I knew she'd be more worried than angry. I poured two brandies and held on to one of them then placed the other on the desk next to the phone, gave Alberto a little wave, and high-tailed it to the hall.

Right after I punched in her number on my cell, Amberly answered. "Hey, Brandon, where are you?"

I visualized my lovely girl with flawless skin, perfect features, and long hair the color of amber. Her expressive, brown eyes denoted exactly how she was feeling. They were particularly expressive when we were making love. She would probably be wearing one of her many sundresses that showed off her voluptuous body. She's beautiful on the inside, too. She teaches sixth grade, and I think she's totally suited for her job. "Hey, sweetheart," I said, feeling a surge of new energy just hearing her voice. "I'm sorry I haven't called sooner. I'm in an unbelievable situation right now."

"Brandon, you're not in any trouble are you?"

My girl is quite perceptive. "I don't think so," I told her, chuckling. "It's a long and complicated story, but the bottom line is I witnessed a murder at that pink beach house you've heard me speak of. I'm at that house with the police and a suspect. I'll explain it to you later, though right now I have no idea when that will be. It may be too late to go out to dinner, so go ahead and get something to eat."

"Good grief! No wonder you didn't have a chance to call. Take your time. I'll pick up your favorite pizza, and we'll eat when you get here."

"That's my girl! 'Bye now." As intriguing as my situation was here, I wished I was with Amberly anywhere eating almost anything!

I switched off my phone just in time to see Captain Delaney, who was fast becoming my least favorite person in the world, walking towards me accompanied by the lab guys.

"We need to swab you and Alberto for DNA purposes," he said in a commanding voice of authority.

"Why me?" I asked. "I didn't realize I was a suspect."

"Your ignorance is showing, Sterling," he said, his mouth crimping in annoyance. "We need to take DNA from everyone in order to eliminate the good guys from the bad. See, you don't know as much as you think you do."

So the captain thinks I'm a smart ass. Perhaps I am — he brings out the worst in me. "I won't dignify that statement with a reply," I mumbled.

He gave me one of his mean-eyed looks. "What did you say, Sterling?"

"Nothing of importance, sir. Are the guys going to swab the inside of my mouth?"

"Yeah. We'll go into the living room and do yours and Alberto's at the same time."

I led the way into the living room to where Alberto was sitting on the sofa. I noticed his eyes were puffy and red. He'd probably been crying again.

"Stand up and open your mouth, Alberto," the captain barked. "We're going to swab your mouth for DNA."

Noticing the startled look on Alberto's face, I came and stood beside him. "Hey, don't let it bother you; the boys are going to swab my mouth also." I opened my mouth and stuck out my tongue wondering why I was always feeling so darn protective of Alberto.

After the lab boys left, the captain, with his arms folded across his chest, glared at us and addressed Alberto. "So, have you been able to contact the rest of the victim's family?"

Alberto nodded. "Yes, I've talked to all of the immediate family, and I just finished a conversation with my mom and dad, who are not Rosalia's family, but they know and love her. After all, they were to be her in-laws next month."

"Was your brother, Emilio, at your parents' home?" I asked.

"No, Emilio was not there. Mom said he arrived from Spain last week and left most of his luggage at their place. He visited with them for a few days and told my parents he wanted some time by himself in order to totally unwind. He said he'd be back this Sunday." Alberto paused then added, "You remember I told you that he knew Rosalia and I would be returning to Mom and Dad's house on Sunday."

Once again the phone's sudden ring startled me. I wondered if the kidnappers, if there had indeed been a kidnapping, were calling to ask for a ransom. I started to ask the captain if he'd thought about hooking up tracer apparatus on the phone, but since he was acting like he thought I was a smart ass, I decided against giving him any more suggestions.

Alberto picked up the phone. I could make out enough of the conversation to know he was talking to his mother.

The captain turned to go. "Keep an eye on Alberto. I've got people doing background checks, and I'm interested in seeing what they've found so far. And I'm looking forward to reading *your* background profile, Sterling."

I clenched my fists. "I think you'll be quite bored with my profile. I've never even received a speeding ticket. But to my credit, I did graduate with honors, was an Eagle Scout, and I saved an eleven year old boy from drowning last summer. Oh, let's see...there are no criminals in my family either. We're all upstanding citizens. In fact, my grandfather was a captain on the Jacksonville police force. He was killed in the line of duty when I was sixteen years old."

The captain stopped and turned around. "Really? That's interesting. I hope for his sake that we don't find anything in your profile that would cause him embarrassment," he pointed upward, "up there in another dimension."

It took great will power, but I held my tongue. I shot him a mean-eyed look of my own and walked back into the living room. If my grandfather *was* looking down at this moment, he'd probably also like to take a punch at Captain Delaney.

Alberto was hanging up the phone. "That was my mom. She said she'd contacted Emilio on his cell phone. He told her he'd decided to rent an isolated cabin at the lake. You see, my brother likes to read and hike. She said he was quite upset over Rosalia's disappearance and possible murder, and he'd be in touch."

"Did your mom say where Emilio's isolated cabin was located?"

"No, actually she didn't. Would it make any difference?"

I nodded. "I should think it would if the cabin was located somewhere in Florida, for instance."

Alberto's brow furrowed. "Florida? I guess I've never thought of isolated cabins being located in Florida, which is pretty dumb I guess."

"Sure, we have a lot of fishing camps and hunting camps around. I'm sure many of them are isolated."

We returned to the sofa and picked up our drinks. I took another sip. At the rate I was drinking on an empty stomach, I wouldn't be surprised if I had a sudden urge to dance on the coffee table with the proverbial lamp shade on my head.

"So, Alberto, tell me about your family. From your name, I assume you're of Spanish descent like Rosalia and her family."

Alberto leaned back on the sofa and closed his eyes. "My grandfather, Alfredo Cardoza, came over from Spain in the late

1920s and landed in New York City. He attended Columbia and majored in history. He met my grandmother, Belia Diaz, also of Spanish descent, who was majoring in history. After graduating, they married, and both were able to obtain positions in a college in upper New York. Three years later my father, Esteban, was born.

"My father followed in his mother's and father's footsteps. He teaches at the same college, though my grandfather and grandmother are now retired. By the way, my grandfather taught my dad Spanish, and my dad taught Emilio and me Spanish, and we took the language in high school and college."

"Your family history is interesting. Is your mother also of Spanish descent?"

Alberto sat up. "No, Mom is of French ancestry. Her name is Annette. Her parents, Claude and Brigitte Arneau, are retired and live in south Florida." He shook his head. "They also think the world of Rosalia. I can't believe that the man who killed her knew her, because everyone who knew her loved her."

"I'm sure we'll find the answers soon, Alberto. What about Rosalia's grandparents? Are they still living?"

"Estrella's parents are deceased, but Eduardo's parents are still living and are quite well for their age. They live in New York State in a small town not far from my parents' home. Their names are Antonio and Delores Vargas. Needless to say, they both dote on their twin granddaughters."

I suddenly remembered someone in the family portrait I wanted identified. I walked over and brought the photo back to the sofa and pointed to the tall, blond male. "So who is this, Alberto? He doesn't look like anyone in the family."

Alberto nodded. "That's Rosalia's adopted brother, Andre. His parents, who both worked in one of the showcase furniture stores in France, were killed in a terrible car accident. Andre was twelve when it happened. None of his relatives seemed to want him, so Eduardo and Estrella adopted him when the twins were thirteen. According to Rosalia, everyone in her family showered him with love and tender care, but the times I've been around him, I get the feeling he's sort of a misfit and seems to have a chip on his shoulder. He's in college in Miami and is taking business courses."

I studied the photo closely. I imagined him wearing sunglasses and a white shirt and shorts. His hair was blond, and he was the correct height. Yep, now we had three males in the family who could be suspects. I wondered where he was at approximately five-thirty this afternoon. No doubt we'd find out.

There was still another brother I hadn't asked about, but he was not blond like the man I saw running down the steps. "This young man strongly resembles his dad, Eduardo, doesn't he?" I asked pointing to a tall, handsome, young man with dark hair.

"Fernando is very much like Eduardo in many ways. He's charming, intelligent, and considerate, and he's an astute business person, though Rosalia said he wasn't very happy with his job. He took it because it was expected of him. He's the firm's PR man and takes care of advertising here in the U. S. He's very close to Rosalia and Maria." His eyes were brimming over again, and he made a swipe with his handkerchief. "My guess is Eduardo has been in touch with all the family by now." He pulled in a deep breath. "I really should call him and see if he and Estrella are on the way."

"Yeah, I guess you'll need to pick them up at the airport."

Nodding, Alberto walked over to the phone. "I'll ask them if they're going to touch down in Orlando or our small airport here. I think he usually puts down here."

"While you're talking, I'll go out to the garage and find out what's going on with the group out there."

I left as Alberto punched in some numbers. I didn't want to even try to put myself in Eduardo's and Estrella's situation. Losing a child has to be the most difficult thing that could happen to a parent. I hoped it would never happen to me.

A few minutes later, I entered the garage and saw that the trunk, of what I surmised to be Alberto's rental, was open. I walked over to the captain and sergeant who were talking to the lab guys.

"So have you found anything?" I asked the captain.

"Nope," he answered, "this car is as clean as my mother's white, bleached sheets."

"If Alberto had killed her and then disposed of the body somewhere, my guess is he would have stashed the body in the trunk first," I suggested.

The captain shook his head and rolled his eyes upward. "You don't say! What great powers of reasoning you have, Sterling." His voice dripped with sarcasm.

Clenching my fists was becoming a habit whenever I had a conversation with this man. At least I was getting good training in holding my temper. "Don't guess you've had a chance to check Alberto's alibi, have you?" I waited for another sarcastic reply.

"No. His Orlando office closes at five like most offices across the nation and will most likely be closed tomorrow, since it's Saturday. When we get to it, we'll ask Alberto how to get in touch with the people who were working in the office yesterday at the time he was there. If you remember he said he left the office around five. It's sixty or so miles from here to Orlando. He'd have a hell of a time getting here by five-thirty to murder the victim and then dump her body and return here by six-fifteen – unless he's Kent Clark in disguise."

"And if Alberto did push her from the cupola, where would he have hidden the body?"

"We're going to check the vacant lots on each side of the house."

I couldn't visualize Alberto, or anyone else, carrying Rosalia's body to an empty space on either side of the house and burying her in broad daylight. In my opinion, even though the houses are not remotely close to each other, the murderer would not want to take the chance that someone would see him. And he'd need a shovel, though he could have found one in one in the garage. I kept my mouth shut. No point in aggravating the captain any further so I changed the subject. "Since I've had a chance to question Alberto about his family, and to scrutinize Rosalia's family portrait, you might be interested in knowing that there are two more possible suspects."

The captain's eyebrows climbed toward his hairline. "What? What do you mean?"

"Alberto's brother, Emilio, is one possible suspect. Though I haven't seen a photo of him, Alberto described his brother as looking very much like him. He said they were the same height and had the same build and hair color. Of course, I'd need to see him in person. The other possible suspect is Rosalia's adopted brother, Andre. From looking at the photo, he's tall and blond, and has the same build as the man I saw running down the cupola steps. I visualized him wearing sunglasses and shorts, and he could pass for the assailant."

He nodded. "You'll need to take a good look at them in person."

I leaned against the car. The stress of being a witness to a murder and near starvation was catching up with me. "From my understanding, Andre is majoring in business at a college in Miami. Emilio, who lives in Spain and works for the company, is vacationing somewhere in the states at a remote cabin."

The captain's eyes narrowed speculatively. "Hm-m. By that remark, you must mean that Emilio's whereabouts is unknown. Right?"

"That's correct, though he did call his mother, Annette, to touch base."

"Does Alberto have his brother's cell phone number?"

"I would assume so."

"You go tell your friend Alberto to get in touch with Emilio and also Rosalia's stepbrother, Andre. I want them to come in for questioning no later than tomorrow afternoon. Of course, you'll have to come to the station also. Got it?"

"Okay. But after I give Alberto those instructions, I'm going to have to take off and get something to eat. I haven't eaten since eleven-thirty this morning, and I'm about to fold." (After all, I'd put in a full day of teaching energetic, hormonal high school students, jogged a few miles, witnessed a terrifying murder, then ran back a few miles, plus playing detective with a mean-eyed captain who couldn't seem make up his mind if I was a pathological liar or just a plain smart-ass).

The captain's smirk returned. "You'd never make it on the police force, Sterling. Sometimes we have to go hours past meal time before we can take a break."

"Oh yeah...I thought all policemen kept a box of doughnuts in their vehicles just for emergencies." I could be sarcastic, too. I left quickly before he could answer.

Walking down the hall, my thoughts were twirling as fast as a majorette's baton, (or perhaps as fast as I'd twirled my brandy.) I hoped my drinking buddy would not be crying when I entered the living room. I also hoped he would not ask me to go with him to pick up Eduardo and Estrella. I really just wanted to go over to Amberly's for pizza, a good back rub, and go to where the back rub would lead. I was tired, hungry, and beginning to feel sorry for myself.

I entered the living room and found Alberto sitting on the sofa holding his half-filled snifter and staring at the wall with a far-away expression. I immediately felt ashamed for feeling sorry for myself. This man had just lost the love of his life. Even though he looked like the man I saw running down the cupola, every fiber of my being told me he couldn't have done it. I didn't want to startle him, so I sat down and touched his arm gently. "How's it going, Alberto?"

He turned, but he seemed to take a few seconds to focus. "Oh, hi, Brandon. I've been reminiscing about my day with Rosalia before I left for Orlando." He smiled. "She fixed us a wonderful lunch. We ate on the porch while looking at the ocean. As you know, it was a beautiful day." He sighed. "Afterwards, we went upstairs to the bedroom, undressed each other, and jumped into the Jacuzzi. A little later we made love. Rosalia told me that she was the happiest she'd ever been, and if anything ever happened to her that she'd always love me even if she were in another dimension. Can you believe that, Brandon? It was almost like she knew something might happen to her."

I nodded. "I guess that statement seems a bit precognitive, yet sometimes people do say things like that when they're very much in love. But to change the subject, did Rosalia make a habit of going up to the cupola every afternoon at the same time?"

"Yes. She loved to watch the dolphins. They usually swam by close in around five-thirty every day."

I smiled. "That's one of the reasons I like to jog at that time. I'm on the lookout for them, too. But I was just thinking…if the murderer knew Rosalia would be standing in the cupola at a certain time, and he knew you were going to be in Orlando, then that might be why he chose that time to try and kidnap Rosalia or talk to her or…you know…whatever he meant to do."

Alberto pulled in a deep breath. "That's a good theory. I guess I'm still clinging to the hope that she was kidnapped by a stranger, and by some miracle she's still alive."

"I'm also hoping that, Alberto. Look, the captain wants you to get in touch with Emilio and Andre. If possible, he wants them down at the police station by tomorrow afternoon. You see, they both may fit the description of the assailant."

He drew back in surprise. "What?"

"I hate to remind you, Alberto, but you are a prime suspect. Personally, I'm keeping my fingers crossed that your alibi checks out. I like you, and I can't imagine that you'd kill anyone, but you do closely resemble the man I saw running down the cupola steps. And you were the last person to see Rosalia alive. Since you told me Emilio looks very much like you, and since Andre is also tall, blond, and at least from his photo appears to fit the description of the man I saw, then he also will have to come up with an alibi."

Alberto slapped his forehead. (It seemed to be a habit). "As I said before, why on earth would Emilio want to murder Rosalia? And now you're adding Andre to the suspect list. It's insane and just as preposterous as me wanting to murder her."

"I'm sure it appears that way to you, Alberto. If you three come up with alibis, then you have nothing to worry about."

Alberto placed his snifter on the coffee table. He appeared even more distressed, and that's big-time distressed. "I suppose I don't have any choice. Emilio and Andre aren't going to understand why they would be suspects."

"I think they'll understand perfectly when you explain the situation."

He stood. "I hope you're right, Brandon."

"And when you talk to them, you may also want to mention that most murders are committed by family members or someone close to the victim. That's why police are always interested in checking those people out thoroughly."

"I didn't know that."

I stood and faced him. "I've got to go and get something to eat. Did you find out when Eduardo and Estrella are arriving?"

He glanced at his watch. "It's eight-thirty now. They should be here in a couple of hours. They're landing at our local airport and want me to pick them up."

"Alberto, if you keep putting those brandies away with no food, you won't be in any shape to pick them up. Won't you at least let me make you a sandwich?"

His eyes were pleading. "If I eat something, will you go with me to the airport? I need some emotional support. I'd rather walk over hot coals barefooted than face them. I mean, along with

Rosalia's disappearance and possible murder, I now have to tell them that Emilio, Andre, and I are suspects!"

I felt nearly hysterical. Holding back my laughter and tears I said, "Yep, and you're asking your accuser to go with you to give you emotional support. I've never been in such a weird predicament."

Alberto chuckled. "Touché! So are you going with me?"

I shrugged. "Sure. I guess the captain would want me to go anyway, just to make sure you didn't make a run for it – you know, in case you're guilty."

"And for sure, I'd rather have you accompany me than the onerous captain."

"You make your calls, and I'm going to check out the fridge."

Alberto walked to the desk. (I thought the carpet might be getting worn between the sofa and desk.) "Hey, Brandon, I don't think you're going to find much to eat anywhere in the kitchen. We ate out a lot."

"Don't worry; I'm sure I'll find something. If not, I'll pick up a couple of burgers."

A few minutes later, I opened the refrigerator and peered in. Alberto was right, not too much in there. I reached for what could have been the remains of lunch. Now if I could find the bread to go with the ham, pickles, and mustard, we could stave off starvation. Luck was with me. I found whole-grain bread and tea bags in a cabinet. I put on the teapot and quickly made the sandwiches. I was so starved I started working on one of my two sandwiches while the tea was brewing. I rooted around in another cabinet and found chips and cookies. I could not have been more excited than if I were preparing a gourmet dinner.

The door to the garage opened, and the captain entered. "Making yourself at home, huh, Brandon?"

"Yeah, it was either finding something here, or going out for a burger. I'm also making something for Alberto before he gets looped on brandy; that is, if I'm not already too late. He's asked me to go with him to the airport to pick up Eduardo and Estrella."

For once he didn't make a snide remark. "That's a good idea. We don't want him driving under the influence and causing an accident. He's in enough trouble already. I'm on my way in to ask him for those names of the people in his office in Orlando. By the time we get the family together tomorrow afternoon, I want to know if Alberto has an air-tight alibi. Then we'll start to work on Emilios and Andre's alibis."

"Okay. I'll be in there in a few minutes." I grabbed a few chips and munched away. Food had never tasted so good. The teapot was hissing as I reached for two mugs and two plates. I spied two trays at the end of the counter, but Alberto's remark about his last lunch with Rosalia zapped some of the elation I was feeling. I poured the tea, placed the sandwiches, chips, and cookies on the plates, hunted up two napkins, and put everything on two trays. I'd take his tray in first then come back for mine.

When I entered the living room, I noticed the captain was in one of his usual positions, standing and rocking on his heels. He was alone.

"Where's Alberto?" I asked, placing the tray on the coffee table.

"He's upstairs working on his laptop. He's getting me the names and phone numbers I asked for. I hope those employees won't cover for him about the time he left this afternoon."

I folded my arms and rocked along with the captain. It *was* a bit soothing and kind of like rocking in Grandma's rocking chair. "Oh, I don't think you need to worry about anyone covering for Alberto. I'm sure you can threaten them with how people are sent to prison if they lie to the police. And if Eduardo thought any of his personnel were covering for his daughter's murderer, they would really be in trouble."

"I guess you have a point, Sterling." He glanced towards the hall. "I think I hear Alberto coming now."

"Good. I'm going back for my food."

The captain shook his head. "Like I said–"

"I know, I know; I wouldn't last long on the police force." At this point I couldn't care less about anything he said. My main focus in life was on eating as I headed for the kitchen.

I returned quickly with the tray and set it on the coffee table. I dug in while listening to the captain's lecture.

"Alberto," he was saying, "you are sure you left the Orlando office at five. Right?"

"Yes, sir; I remember looking at the time, because we had a reservation at the Chart House."

The captain shot him one of his mean-eyed looks. "So these four people on this list would be able to substantiate that you left the office at five."

Alberto glanced up at the ceiling for a few seconds. "Well, now that I think about it, a couple of those employees might have left before five. Since it's Friday, I think a few may have sneaked out a little early."

I nearly choked on a chip. If all the employees left before five, then Alberto's alibi would not hold. I noticed a vein in the captain's neck pulsing and swelling dangerously.

"Okay, now let's get this straight, Alberto. You're now telling me that some of the employees may have left before five. I don't understand the 'may' word. They either left or they didn't. Are you sure they didn't *all* leave before five? It will be better for you if you tell the truth than for me to find out you've been lying." His mean-eyed look shot up a few notches.

Alberto pursed his lips. "When I was upstairs working on the laptop, I suddenly remembered that the office personnel had cleared out around four-thirty. I still had paper work to finish, so I left around five. I've been so upset over everything, the whole time-line thing simply slipped my mind."

As hungry as I was, I stopped eating. I didn't like the implications. If Alberto had left at four-thirty instead of five, he would have had time to commit the murder and abscond with the body. But where in hell could he have taken it? Surely, he wouldn't have buried it in one of the large empty areas on each side of the house. I felt sick with disappointment.

The captain's eyes scoured Alberto's face. "The fact that everyone in the office left at four-thirty simply slipped your mind, huh? Are you sure you didn't leave with them? You know I'm going to find that out, don't you?"

Alberto drew his shoulders back. "No, I'm quite sure I didn't leave with the office personnel."

The captain snapped, "But you could have left two to five minutes after four-thirty and no one would know. Isn't that correct?"

With a look of defeat, Alberto nodded. "That's correct, sir. And when I left at five, there was no one in the elevator. Actually, I didn't see anyone even in the parking lot. I think every person in

Orlando leaves before five on Friday afternoons."

The captain looked like a bear getting ready to devour his young. "How very convenient." He turned towards me. "Not one soul saw Alberto, here, leave. What do you make of that, Sterling?"

"Well...well...it's certainly possible, sir."

"Sure," the captain retorted, "it's possible, but not probable." He turned back towards Alberto. "You're in big trouble, Mr. Cardoza. Mainly because you lied, and when you realized we were going to check with the employees, you cooked up another story. You have no alibi, and right now, you're at the top of my list of suspects."

Alberto shrugged. "What can I say? You've already condemned me. But I'm innocent, and sooner or later you'll find that out."

The captain's stare was as frigid as a day in the Klondike *before* global warming. "Yeah, I've heard that story before." He turned to me again. "Be sure you accompany him to the airport, Sterling."

I licked my dry lips. "Yes, sir." At least the captain was off my back for a change. I half-heartedly reached for my sandwich. My appetite had sorely diminished.

Alberto sat down on the sofa and reached for his snifter, and I gently took it out of his hand. "You must force yourself to eat, pal," I told him. "You don't want to be wobbly on your feet when we meet Rosalia's parents at the airport, do you?"

He picked up his sandwich. "No, of course not." He looked at me, his face etched in desperation. "Do you believe I murdered Rosalia, Brandon?"

I pulled in a deep breath. "I'm not sure what I believe, Alberto. Let's say I don't want to believe you murdered Rosalia. I'm going to postpone condemning you for the time being."

Alberto shot me a wavering smile. "Thank you, Brandon. As my mother is fond of saying, 'the truth will out.' And I promise you, the truth will prove my innocence."

We ate and drank our tea in silence. I knew he was forcing down his food, and mine no longer excited me.

Ten minutes later, Alberto stood. "I still haven't made those calls to Andre and Emilio. I hope I can reach them, since they are supposed to be here to talk to the captain tomorrow afternoon."

"If they can't make it by tomorrow afternoon, it won't be the end of the world, Alberto. I'm sure they'll make it sooner or later." I put the empty cups and plates on one tray and stacked it on top of the second one. It seemed I was always leaving the room while Alberto was talking on the phone. I hoped it didn't matter.

A few minutes later, I placed the dishes in the dishwasher then pulled out my cell. Now would be a good time to check in with my honey.

"What's up?" Amberly asked, when she picked up.

I gave her a brief run-down of the developments. "Looks like I've been elected to go with Alberto to pick up Rosalia's parents at our airport." I glanced at my watch, "It's close to nine, and I think they'll be here around ten. So I suppose it will be after eleven before I can leave – that is, barring no new developments! I hope you've eaten."

"Yes, I've just finished two slices of pizza."

"If you get sleepy, go on to bed. You can put your key under the second flower pot on the steps."

She chuckled. "Oh, sure I will. That's the first place a burglar looks!"

"I see what you mean. So I guess I'll wake you by ringing the doorbell."

"I'm planning on staying awake until you get here. Tomorrow is Saturday, and we can sleep in."

"Yeah, it's one of the rewards of teaching. Oh, I almost forgot, you don't need to keep the pizza out. I was so starved I made a few sandwiches for Alberto and me."

"Good! I know how grouchy you can get when you're hungry. Brandon, from what you've told me, I get the feeling that some kind of bond is developing between you and Alberto."

"You're quite perceptive, sweetheart. For reasons I don't understand, I feel protective of him. And yet I know he's actually the prime suspect."

"Some people have great persuasive powers. They can easily con people and especially sympathetic people like you, Brandon."

"You're absolutely right, Amberly, and I've taken that into consideration. I'm not naïve, but I must say, I really don't want him to be the murderer. Also my gut tells me he couldn't have killed Rosalia."

"Don't forget, many women have been killed by their husbands or lovers because they didn't want to believe their loved ones could be capable of murder. It happens all the time."

I pulled in a deep breath and let it out slowly. "I know where you're coming from, honey, and I promise you I won't let my guard down."

"Okay, big guy; see that you don't!"

"I'd better get back and see if Alberto has contacted Emilio or Andre. Perhaps when I meet those two, I won't want them to be the culprit either!" I could visualize my girl shaking her head.

"I wouldn't be a bit surprised, Brandon! I hope your guardian angel is looking after you. You're such a softie, but then that's one of the reasons I love you. Just you take care, okay?"

"I promise you, I will. I'll call you later."

"I'll be waiting."

I walked down the hall hoping my guardian angel would be hovering around me all evening. I had a feeling I'd need him or her before this night was over.

I entered the living room just as Alberto hung up the phone. "Were you able to get in touch with Emilio and Andre?"

His expression was somber. "I had a brief conversation with Emilio." He wandered over to the bar and picked up the brandy bottle. "Don't scold me, Brandon. I ate, and I'm stone cold sober. That's the trouble; I'm not numb anymore. Since you're driving, it shouldn't be a problem."

"But I'm sure you don't want to appear incoherent when we pick up Eduardo and Estrella. That would be disrespectful, especially under the circumstances."

"Don't worry, Brandon. I won't embarrass anyone." He brought over his filled snifter and sat down next to me.

"So did you find out where Emilio's isolated cabin is located?"

He took a sip of brandy and said, "Emilio said he had rented a cabin at a fishing camp somewhere around Kissimmee, Florida, and that surprised me. He was in his car at the time I called and said he was on his way to a store to pick up groceries. He must have rented a lemon because I could hear loud engine noises."

Kissimmee? That's interesting. Kissimmee is not that far away.
"Oh? So what did he say about coming to the police station

tomorrow afternoon?"

"He said it wouldn't be a problem. He'd stop by here first around one-thirty, and we could go together. Understandably, he is most upset over...over the situation."

I leaned back on the sofa. Weariness was about to take over, and my eyes threatened to close. I should have made strong coffee instead of tea. "I'm glad to hear that, Brandon. We wouldn't want to get on the wrong side of the captain."

"No, indeed not. I don't think the captain is a very patient man."

I stifled a yawn. "No, patience does not seem to be one of his virtues. How about Andre? How did he react when you told him about Rosalia?"

"Andre didn't answer his home phone, and his cell was turned off. For some reason he doesn't have an answering service at home. I'll try later. Since it's Friday, I suppose he's out with his pals.

"But personally, I always felt that Andre was in love with Rosalia. I'd catch him looking at her sometimes, and I thought it was a look of love – you know, like sending love messages with his eyes. If you remember, they are not kin."

I suddenly became fully awake and sat up straight. "If he was in love with her that could possibly give him a motive."

Alberto appeared perplexed. "What do you mean, Brandon?"

"Remember when we were talking earlier about how a secret lover may have shoved Rosalia in a jealous rage? Perhaps it wasn't a secret lover, but Andre who had been in love with Rosalia for years. Knowing she was planning to marry you in a few months, he could have made one last plea; when he was rejected once again, he flew into a rage and pushed her from the cupola."

Alberto shook his head. "That sounds like another far-fetched theory to me. I can't imagine Andre doing such a thing."

"I remember you saying Andre has a chip on his shoulder. If so, it could have come from being in love with a beautiful young woman who continually rejected him."

Alberto paused for a few moments. "I think you're reaching, Brandon. If Andre loved Rosalia so much, he couldn't have killed her. And the same goes for me."

"Many murders are crimes of passion, Alberto, and those

crimes aren't usually premeditated, from my understanding."

"If Andre had confessed to Rosalia that he was in love with her, I really believe she would have told me."

I rebutted. "Maybe he never told her he loved her until the day he killed her."

He gave me an appraising look. "That's possible, but not probable."

"I guess I *am* reaching. But you keep forgetting that I witnessed the attempted murder and saw the murderer even if it was only briefly. As I've mentioned more than once, the killer looks like you, and you say that Emilio looks like you, and Andre appears from his photo to also be tall and blond; so it would seem that Rosalia was murdered by one of you three. I have to admit I don't want it to be you, Alberto. So I suppose that's why I'm reaching."

He smiled. "I appreciate your loyalty more than you could know, Brandon. But I can't believe Andre or Emilio would be capable of harming anyone."

I watched his eyes take on a wounded look. "I'm sorry, Alberto. I'll try not to bring up the subject again. Look, I think I'll put my head back and take a little rest. If I fall asleep, wake me up if something important comes up."

I closed my eyes, but I doubted I'd sleep. My thoughts were tumbling like a circus acrobatic act. It was enough of a coincidence that there were three family members fitting the description of the man who pushed Rosalia from the cupola, so it would be a mind-blowing coincidence if an unknown kidnapper would just happen to be tall and blond and resemble the guy I saw rushing down the steps. But I suppose stranger things have happened. I looked forward to meeting Emilio and Andre. It would be interesting to feel my gut reactions when I met those two.

Chapter 4

I was driving the silver BMW towards the airport and trying to overcome the overwhelming desire to find out how fast the dream car could go! I knew I'd have to come back down to earth when I climbed back into my three-year-old Ford, but at this moment I was enjoying every minute behind the wheel. Perhaps I could talk Eduardo into letting me take it for a spin now and then just to keep the engine in shape. It was bad for a car to sit idle for months at a time. My companion, Alberto, had been sitting quietly since we started our trip. I didn't envy his meeting with Rosalia's parents. He could very well be praying.

In a few minutes, we pulled up to our small, local airport. I parked in a space close to the door and turned off the ignition.

"Would you like me to come with you, Alberto?" I asked.

"Thanks, but I guess I'd better do this myself. I'd appreciate it if you'd not mention that Emilio, Andre, and I are suspects. It might be too much at this time. Somehow I'll break it to them later."

"Of course, but the captain may not be as considerate."

Alberto opened the door. "As someone once said, 'I'll cross that bridge when I get to it.' "

As I watched him moving slowly towards the airport door, the phrase 'dead man walking' ran through my mind. I also dreaded meeting Eduardo and Estrella.

Not knowing who would be doing the driving back to the beach, I got out of the car and leaned against the hood. It didn't take long for Alberto to return with the grieving parents. Though it was semi-dark, I could see that Estrella and Eduardo were even more striking than they had appeared in the photograph. Both tall and slim with dark hair, they were wearing expensive, casual clothes and each carried a small bag. Alberto was pulling two larger ones. I assumed Eduardo piloted the plane since I saw no one else with them.

"Alberto has told us of your kindness and consideration, Brandon," Eduardo said, holding out his hand, "and we both want to thank you. This is my wife, Estrella."

"I'm glad I could be of some help," I answered, shaking the couple's hands. "Would you like me to drive, Eduardo?"

"Yes, that would be fine. Estrella and I will sit in the back seat."

We walked to the back of the car, and I pressed the electronic key to open the trunk. Nothing happened. "I wonder why the lid won't open," I said, surprised that a BMW would dare have any defect. I pressed a few more times with no results.

"I suppose computerized cars do have problems on occasion. We'll have to pile everything in the back," Eduardo said. "Estrella, you sit in the front, and Alberto can sit in the back seat with me."

I was impressed with Eduardo's calm demeanor. Some men would have been screaming oaths under the circumstances. But I was sorry that one more problem had cropped up to add to their stress.

I placed the baggage on the floor and seat. Eduardo and Alberto would need to sit close together.

I opened the door for Estrella and noticed her eye make-up had smeared. I presumed it was from crying. She still looked beautiful.

When we and the baggage were finally ensconced in the car, I turned on the ignition and was relieved to hear the motor start. If something had happened to keep the trunk from opening, it might have also prevented the ignition from turning on. Someone would need to take the car to a garage tomorrow to check out the problem. But in the scheme of things, maybe that particular problem didn't seem so important. I backed out of the parking space and headed back to the beach house.

Eduardo leaned forward and said, "Since we only talked briefly on the phone, Brandon, and you were the last person to see Rosalia, would you please try to tell me exactly what happened?"

I glanced at Estrella.

She nodded. "I know you don't want to describe the scene in front of me, Brandon, but you must. I have to hear the gory details sooner or later."

I could tell she was holding back tears. I pulled in a deep breath and told them what I'd witnessed but leaving out the more horrible details like my thinking her neck was broken.

"Do you think our daughter could possibly be alive?" Estrella asked softly.

"It's possible, I think. At this point, the police don't know why the assailant would abscond with...with....(I didn't want to say with the body) Rosalia. There are several theories – one being that it was a planned kidnapping that went wrong, though it appeared to me from my view from the beach she was deliberately shoved from the cupola."

"And what are the other theories, Brandon?" Eduardo asked.

Stalling for time, I cleared my throat. "Well, one theory is the assailant knew Rosalia, and if he left her where she was and she survived, then she could identify him."

"And if kidnapping is not the motive for the...the...attempted murder, then what do the police believe the motive is?" Eduardo asked, his voice catching in his throat.

I let out a sigh. "At this point, no one has come up with a definite motive."

Alberto spoke for the first time. "I was hoping I could spare you this for a while, but I might as well tell you now. As you may or may not know, family members, or close friends are always the first suspects in situations like this. Although Brandon only got a glimpse of the man, as you heard him say a few minutes ago, he described him as blond, slim, and around six feet tall wearing sunglasses, a white shirt and shorts. That description fits me, except I was wearing blue shorts when I arrived from Orlando. After looking at the family portrait, Brandon says that Andre also resembles the assailant. And since Emilio and I closely resemble each other, he could also be a suspect. We all need to have air-tight alibis."

Estrella placed her hand over her mouth to stifle her cry, but it didn't work.

"This is almost too much to take in," Eduardo said. "Alberto, even if you, Emilio, and Andre don't have air-tight alibis, I could never believe you or anyone in our family could be guilty of such a despicable deed."

"Thank you, Eduardo," Alberto said. "I love Rosalia with all my heart, and I could never have harmed her in any way. I'm sure Emilio and Andre could never have harmed her either." His emotions took over, and he sobbed uncontrollably.

I'm sure Alberto was relieved to hear Eduardo's vote of confidence, but I wondered what his reaction would be when he heard that Alberto had not been honest with his alibi. My heart ached for them all.

Having pulled himself together, Alberto said. "I forgot to mention that I was not able to get in touch with Andre, Estrella. Since it's Friday, he's probably out with some friends. Please remind me to try again when we get home."

"I will, Alberto. Perhaps I'd better speak with him. It's going to be a terrible shock. Though he loves both of his sisters, he's always been particularly close to Rosalia."

"Yes, I know," Alberto answered, with a catch in his voice. "Were you able to get in touch with Fernando?"

"Yes," Eduardo sighed, "though it took a while. He was at a movie with a friend. As you would expect, he's all broken up. He called back and said he'd be arriving in Orlando by midafternoon tomorrow. He'll rent a car, so we won't need to pick him up."

Suddenly, the car was filled with the sounds of quiet sobbing. Would this night ever end?

Chapter 5

After I pulled the BMW into the garage, and everyone got out, I quickly made the introductions to the captain who was waiting for us in his usual rocking stance. I helped Alberto carry the luggage into the house, and then I said my goodnights. I hurried past the captain before he could waylay me, and I sprinted to my Ford.

As much as I enjoyed driving the magnificent BMW, I was delighted to slide into the seat of my humble, but reliant car. I glanced once more at the pink beach house that had once intrigued me, but because of the events of the past hours, it now seemed to be surrounded by an aura of sadness and despair. I hoped the depression of the occupants hadn't seeped into my psyche.

I pulled out my cell phone and punched in Amberly's number. After ringing for what seemed like an eon, her answering machine came on. Puzzled, I turned off the phone, turned on my ignition, and backed onto the road.

The anxious state I'd been in since five-thirty this afternoon turned up a notch as terrible imaginings bombarded my senses. Had the murderer somehow found out that Amberly was my girlfriend, and he was now holding her captive until I promised not to reveal who he was to the family or police? I knew that thinking was absurd, but in my past experience, I'd found that it's difficult to argue with fear. "Stay calm, you crazy fool," I admonished myself. "She's probably in the bathroom or standing outside looking at the stars and couldn't get to the phone in time." I finally pulled into her apartment complex.

Still stressed out, I was breathing heavily when I rang the doorbell. When Amberly opened the door apparently unharmed, relief surged through me like I'd been sitting on a hill of piss ants and had just gotten up.

"Brandon," she said, "what's the matter? I've never seen such an anxious expression on your face."

I walked into the living room, grabbed her, and held her tightly. "When you didn't answer your phone, I imagined all kinds of scary things. Don't ask me what I was thinking. You'd probably laugh at me."

She rubbed my back in little circles. "I wouldn't laugh at you, Brandon. I'm not insensitive. I know you've been through a rough time."

"By the way," I said, in a muffled voice as I buried my face into her damp hair that smelled like exotic flowers. "Where were you when I called?"

"I must have been in the shower. I barely had time to put on my nightshirt when you rang the bell. No comments, please."

I pulled back and kissed her. She looked so precious in her white v-necked nightshirt that stopped just below her knees. Suddenly, my world was okay again.

"Would you like some pizza, Brandon? While you're eating, you can catch me up on what has been going on."

"That sounds good, sweetheart. (I often called her sweetheart after watching an old Humphry Bogart movie). My appetite has made a swift return. Are you going to eat with me?"

"No, but I'll have a beer with you."

"Good," I said, walking to the refrigerator.

A few minutes later, Amberly and I were sitting at her round, glass-topped wicker table in her cozy dining room. I felt warm and contented munching on my pizza in the yellow-painted room that matched the yellow-and-white striped cushions in the wicker chairs. Not too long ago, I'd been admiring the most beautiful furniture I'd ever seen in a huge, gorgeous house, and I'd felt a bit envious, but my envy had made a quick exodus after a few hours. I filled her in on what had taken place, and I'm sure it sounded like a fictitious TV movie.

Amberly placed her glass of beer on the table and folded her arms. "As I mentioned in our phone conversation, it looks like you've developed a strong bond with the charismatic Alberto Cardoza."

I nodded. "Alberto is easy to like, even though he lied or simply forgot that the personnel in Orlando had left around four-thirty leaving him without his alibi of leaving at five. If he did leave at four-thirty, he still had to find a way to get rid of the body and change clothes before driving up to the beach house at six-fifteen. And as I told you, the police could find no trace of blood in his rented car."

For a few seconds, Amberly appeared pensive. "If Alberto is the perpetrator, it stands to reason the body could still be somewhere in the house. Of course, he could have changed from white shorts to blue in no time and put them into his suitcase or dresser drawer, so that would be no problem. But if he did hide the body, perhaps he could have placed her in a garment bag – you know, the luggage you hang your clothes in and fold up. You said she was small." She shook her head, her expression grim. "This is a grizzly conversation."

"Uh huh. And before the mystery is solved, things might get even grizzlier."

I almost yelled eureka. "Amberly, as I know of, no one bothered to check out the BMW because it was in the garage when Alberto drove up. If he is the perpetrator, he could have placed her in a garment bag, as you suggested, then put her in the trunk, hoping he'd have a chance to get rid of the body at a later time. He would have time to change shorts, run back to his rental, and drive away, giving the police time to get to the house. Remember, when I was giving you the run-down, I mentioned that something was wrong with the trunk in the BMW because it wouldn't pop up. Maybe Alberto fixed it so it wouldn't come up!"

Amberly pursed her lips. "Certainly it's all possible, but Alberto would have to be an expert on vehicle computers to keep the trunk lid from opening. And he'd need to be a near genius to figure it all out so quickly to pull everything off, don't you think?"

I sighed. "You're right. And as I thought so many times this evening, he'd have to be an academy-award-winning actor as well."

"But to be on the safe side, do you think you should call the captain and have him bring in a mechanic to force open the trunk?"

"It's a good idea, but not tonight. I don't think Alberto will have a chance to go for a joy ride with everyone in the house. It would be too risky. I'll call the captain in the morning and talk over the situation with him."

"Brandon, why do you think the murderer didn't come after you since he knew you'd seen him?"

"Yeah, I've thought about that, too. But he would not have been aware that I did not have my cell phone available. For all he knew, I could have been calling the police as I ran down the beach, so he would need to get the hell out of there instead of chasing me. And though that area of the beach is sparsely populated, there would always be a chance of another jogger passing by or a couple taking a walk."

"That makes a lot of sense. But what a cold, calculating person Alberto would need to be if he wrapped Rosalia up, changed his shorts, fiddled with the trunk, and left in his rental and waited until the police arrived to make his appearance."

I leaned back in my chair. "I totally agree, sweetheart. After being in the company of Alberto for more than a few hours, I simply can't imagine him doing all that."

"From what you've told me, they sound like an intriguing group. I'm hoping for a miracle that Rosalia was kidnapped by someone other than her family, and she'll be found alive."

I stood behind her chair, placed my hands around her shoulders, and kissed her cheek. "I'm lucky to have you, Amberly. Let's go to bed. I want to make mad, passionate love to you."

She turned her head and kissed my hand. "I'm lucky to have you, too, Brandon."

I laughed, pulling out her chair. "But I think I'd better take a shower. I've done a lot of jogging, running, sweating, and freezing this evening. I'm afraid to think of the havoc wrought to my skin cells."

She took my arm and sniffed it. "Now that you mention it, you do have an interesting fragrance!"

I kissed her passionately then whispered, "Can you imagine what the cave men and women must have smelled like? Obviously, it didn't keep them from having sex! I guess they must have gotten used to not smelling good. And remember, they didn't have deodorant. Now that I think about it, I read that B.O. was considered a natural attraction to a female in the cave-man days."

"And I've read that several hundred years ago people took a bath only once a year, and often it was for a special occasion like getting married. I'm glad we didn't live back in those times. So get

52

going, Brandon. I'll clear the table and put away the food." Her eyes were teasing. "I'll be waiting for you in bed."

I gave her a quick hug. "I won't be long."

As I showered, I was thinking about the arrangement Amberly and I had fallen into. During the week, most often we only talked on the phone and generally met for dinner in a restaurant around mid week, as we both usually had to work on lesson plans and grade papers. But on Friday evenings, we'd go to a nice restaurant, and I'd spend the night at her place. Saturdays we were with each other all day either playing tennis, walking on the beach, swimming in her pool, bike riding, fishing, or going to a movie. During bad weather, we'd often curl up with a good murder mystery. Saturday evenings I usually bought something for the grill, and we ate by candlelight. Not a bad existence at all. We discussed that we'd marry one day when the time seemed right, but at this point, we both liked our arrangement the way it was.

Tonight I was grateful that I always kept a change of clothing in case of emergencies. A clean pair of shorts, underwear, and a tee shirt was what I'd need for tomorrow, since I hadn't had a chance to go home after jogging. I also kept shaving gear in her bathroom cabinet. I turned off the shower, grabbed a towel, and wrapped it around my waist. I reached for my aftershave and slapped it on my face and neck. Amberly only had to tell me once that aftershave turned her on!

I turned off the bathroom light and with great anticipation, I padded into the bedroom. This lovely room, painted white, was furnished in white wicker and white pine, with pink-and-white curtains and bedspread. It was certainly a feminine bedroom, but it didn't make the sex any less fun! The only light was a night-light on the wall under a double window.

I dropped my towel and slipped into bed saying, "Here I come, ready or not."

Amberly giggled. "Well, I for one, am ready!"

Later, with our arms and legs intertwined, I closed my eyes and was sure I'd be drifting off to sleep as always. But tonight would be different, I was soon to find out. Sleep did not come until much later, for I kept seeing a beautiful young woman falling from a cupola, a man running down the beach to his car, and on and on...

Chapter 6

At nine o'clock the next morning, Amberly and I were eating waffles, eggs, and bacon and drinking the best coffee in the world, or at least in Lo Verde Beach. She told me that she did nothing to make it special. She thought it had to do with my weekend testosterone level. I believe she's right, because everything tastes better at her place.

"So, what would you like to do this morning?" I asked, wolfing down the last bite of waffle. "I don't have to be at the police station until two."

Amberly leaned back in her chair and stretched. "It's a lovely morning, so how about a tennis game? If you'd prefer to play doubles, I'll call Jan and Tom."

"Sounds good to me, luv. You make the call – doubles or singles."

Our discussion of tennis was interrupted by my cell phone's rendition of *The Entertainer* from the direction of the bedroom. I jumped up. "I've got a feeling this call means trouble." I hurried towards the bedroom. "I bet it's the good captain."

"Hello," I said. My prediction was correct.

"I have just received some news that I think you'll be interested in, Sterling. I've just got a call from Eduardo Vargas. He said he received an anonymous call from a person demanding one million dollars for the return of his daughter, Rosalia. The caller gave instructions of how to send the money to a Cayman bank account. The kidnapper also said not to get in touch with the police or Feds, but the idiot must know it would be too late for that. The sergeant and I are on our way over there now."

Once again, I felt the spill of adrenaline rushing through my arteries. "Did Eduardo actually speak to Rosalia?"

"No, the kidnapper told him that his daughter was too weak to talk."

"Then I would say there's a good chance she's not alive."

"Yeah, that's my theory also, Sterling. Hey, we're pulling up to the house. Since you seem to have developed some type of bond with the family, it might be a good idea for you to come on over."

"Give me ten minutes."

I rushed into the dining room. "Eduardo just received a call from the kidnapper demanding one million dollars."

Amberly's expression was one of surprise and hope. "Do you believe we got our miracle? Does that mean Rosalia could still be alive?"

"Not necessarily. Evidently, Eduardo didn't speak to Rosalia. The kidnapper told him she was too weak to talk. I wanted to tell the captain to put a tracer on the house phone last night, but at that time, he was treating me like he thought I was a smart ass, so I didn't mention it."

Amberly pushed back her chair and stood. "It probably wouldn't have made any difference. From what we've seen on television, abductors use throwaway cell phones now, so they can't be traced."

"I kissed her nose. "Hey, you're right. Anyway, the captain has asked me to come over. I can't figure that man out; this morning he's treating me like one of his buddies."

"Perhaps the captain doesn't handle emotional situations well and needs your calming assistance, Brandon."

"Huh, you think so? Yesterday, my emotions were on a seemingly endless rollercoaster ride, and when I pull up to the pink beach house, the ride will most likely start again. I'm sorry we won't get in our tennis game. Maybe Jan and Tom might play a few sets of Australian tennis with you."

"Don't worry about me. I need to catch up with many little projects. I'll probably take a walk on the beach later in the afternoon. You just do what you have to do."

I reached out and gave her a squeeze. "Okay, sweetheart; I'd better run."

I headed back to the bedroom and picked up my keys, wallet, cell phone, and sunglasses. "See you later," I yelled, heading out the door.

Once again, my thoughts were churning like butter in an old-fashioned butter churn. I found it difficult to believe that Rosalia could still be alive, unless the abductor got her immediate medical attention, and even then it would be doubtful. The Vargas family was in a vulnerable spot. If they didn't comply with the kidnapper's demands, they would always wonder if they could have saved their daughter's life. If she were alive, the perpetrator would need to kill her to keep her from identifying him, unless he planned to leave the country quickly. With the million dollars he could live very well in many places on the planet.

I pulled up one the side of the road so I wouldn't block the driveway. I didn't look forward to this experience one little bit. The garage door was pulled up, so I walked in. "My God, the BMW is gone," I mumbled. "I should have called the captain last evening and voiced my concerns that Rosalia's body could have been placed in the trunk. If Alberto is the one who took the BMW out this morning, it's a strange coincidence that the kidnapper's call may have come while he was out." I stopped my audible ramblings and knocked on the kitchen door, but no one answered. I presumed everyone was in the living room, so I walked into the kitchen. I saw a coffee pot on the table with cups and saucers, but no plates. I continued on down the hall. The house had become quite familiar. I was no longer intrigued. I met the captain in the hall.

"Hey, Brandon," the captain greeted. "The boys are on the way from Orlando with phone tracing equipment, though the ransom call was probably made with a throwaway cell phone that can't be traced. But just in case, we need to put the tracer on. I also contacted the Feds, since we now know we have an actual kidnapping."

I nodded as we continued down the hall. Now I understood the captain's change of attitude towards me. He finally believed me since the abductor made the call.

Entering the living room, I addressed the somber couple sitting on the sofa. "Good morning," I said, holding out my hand to Eduardo and then to Estrella.

"Good morning," Eduardo and Estrella said in unison, standing and shaking my hand. Estrella sat down. I noticed her swollen eyes and would have liked to hug her, but I felt it might seem forward.

Not surprised, I noticed the absence of Alberto. "Where is Alberto?" I asked.

"When we got up this morning and went into the kitchen, we saw that Alberto had made coffee. There was a note on the table that said he had gone to town to pick up some bakery goods for breakfast," Estrella said. "That must have been maybe thirty minutes ago, but I'm not sure what time he left. I'm surprised he hasn't returned by now. Then we received the kidnapper's call about fifteen minutes ago, wouldn't you say, Eduardo?"

Eduardo nodded. "I'm sure the captain informed you about the call. We're trying to remain hopeful even though we didn't get a chance to talk to Rosalia. I've already notified my banker, and he's making arrangements to send one million dollars to the requested location in the Cayman Islands."

Estrella placed her hands over face and sobbed.

Eduardo leaned over and pulled her into his arms. "There, there, Estrella; we must be brave and remain hopeful."

I moved over to the captain. "Would you come out into the hall with me for a minute?"

"What's on your mind, Sterling?" The captain asked when we were out of earshot.

"When we picked up Eduardo and Estrella from the airport last night, the trunk of the BMW wouldn't open. I know this may sound far-fetched, and I pray that I'm wrong, but if the murderer is Alberto, he could have placed the body in the trunk and jammed the lock somehow, then fled in his rental, and driven up after you arrived. If that was the case, then this morning may have been the only time he had to get rid of the body. And the kidnapper's call just happened to come in while he was not in the house."

The captain wore a look of concern. "Well now, that is a bit far-fetched, but within the realm of possibility, I'd say. But once again we're posed with the question of where he'd dump the body. It's daylight, you know."

"Yes, that's true. Since you are a policeman in this area, I would think you'd be familiar with this road. How far does it go?"

The captain took on his rocking stance. "It ends in about five miles south of here. There are just a few houses here and there but mostly empty lots."

"Estrella said he'd been gone for at least thirty minutes and perhaps more, since she didn't know exactly when he left. There's a grocery store less than a mile from here that has a bakery. He should have been back by now."

"Okay, you've convinced me. I'll go out in the garage and call one of my men who patrols this area. I'll tell him to check out the end of this road for a BMW. You go back and wait with the parents. There may be another call from the kidnapper."

I nodded in agreement and returned to the living room thinking that I wanted to ask the captain if, when Emilio and Andre arrived, he would permit a re-enactment of the assailant coming down the stairs. Those two, along with Alberto, would need to don white shorts and a white shirt and wear sunglasses. I would stand at the gate and turn my head for a quick glance just as I had done yesterday. It would be a type of line-up. I felt the captain would agree to the experiment, since I was now in his good graces.

Estrella had stopped sobbing for the moment. She gave me a furtive smile and said, "I can't imagine what has happened to Alberto."

I wanted to assure her that everything was okay. With all the stress she'd endured, she didn't need to think Alberto was up to no good. "Perhaps Alberto had to wait in line. I think everyone in town goes down on Saturday mornings for fresh bakery goods. I'm sure he'll be here soon. If you're hungry, I'll make some toast. I know there is bread in the cabinet, because I made sandwiches for Alberto and me last evening."

"You're most kind, Brandon," Estrella said. "I'm really not that hungry. I'm just concerned that it's taking Alberto so long. I suppose I'm worried that something bad might happen to him or to any of us. Who would have ever thought that Rosalia would have gone through such a terrible ordeal?" She dabbed at her eyes. "I feel so helpless."

"I'm sure you do, Estrella. I'm so sorry," I answered. "By the way, did you ever get in touch with Andre last evening?"

"No, we were unable to reach him, but I called again this morning and finally got him. He said he'd fallen asleep on the sofa and didn't hear the phone. He's always been a sound sleeper. He'll be here this afternoon. Of course, he's devastated."

Before I could answer, the phone rang.

Eduardo jumped up and moved quickly towards the phone.

"This is Eduardo Vargas. Who is this? Maria? We want to keep this line open. Call me on my cell, please." He hung up the phone. "I'm going into the hall to talk with Maria. I suppose I'll have to tell her about the kidnapper's call."

As Eduardo walked towards the hall, Estrella's eyes filled. "I know Maria is in shock. She and Rosalia are so close. Sometimes they pick up each other's feelings if one of them is sick or is in emotional turmoil. I feel sure Maria felt Rosalia's pain when she was pushed."

I tried to get her mind off of her terrible visual. "I've always been interested in twins, because my best friend, whom I've known all my life, is a twin. He and his brother used to pick up on each other when they were growing up. I guess they still do. Not having any siblings, I was often jealous of their close bond."

Eduardo returned, closing his cell phone. "As you would expect, Maria is beside herself with grief. She'll land in Orlando this evening and said she'll rent a car. She also said she'd heard from my parents and they would be calling us soon. As much as I love my mother and father, I hope they won't feel it's necessary to fly down just yet. Estrella, you know how emotional Delores is. There will be quite enough emotion when Maria, Fernando, and Andre arrive."

Estrella clasped and unclasped her hands. "And don't forget Emilio. Though he doesn't show his emotion like Alberto, I know he cares deeply about Rosalia."

Eduardo sat down next to his wife and folded her hand in his. "Speaking of Alberto, I'm getting quite worried that he hasn't returned. I pray nothing has happened to the boy."

And I'm praying he's not burying your daughter's body in the sand or dumping her out to sea.

The phone rang, startling us once again. Eduardo ran quickly to the desk.

"Hello. Who is this? I'm sorry, Mother. I need to keep this line open. I'll call you when I get a chance. Try to stay calm." He hung up and returned to his place on the sofa. "I'm not ready to deal with my mother just yet."

When I heard the door to the kitchen slam shut, I was hoping it was Alberto. I was not disappointed. I noticed his eyes were swollen and red when he walked into the room carrying a large paper bag.

"I thought that since you were so worn out, you would sleep in," he told Estrella and Eduardo. "I hope you weren't worried about me. After I bought the bakery goods, I felt so distraught when I drove back here, I didn't feel like coming in. So I kept driving until I came to the end of the road. I sat in my car looking at the ocean for ten or so minutes then went for a walk on the beach trying to clear my head. I'm afraid it didn't help much. You must be really hungry. Would you like me to bring in a tray with coffee? How about you, Brandon?"

Alberto went into a lot of detail to explain where he'd been. "Thanks, but I've already eaten."

"Don't worry about it, Alberto," Eduardo told him. "No one has much of an appetite anyway. While you were gone, we were finally able to get in touch with Andre. He'll be here this afternoon. Then we received a call from the kidnapper."

"What? Oh my God! What did he say? Does that mean Rosalia is alive?"

I walked over and took the white bag from Alberto's hand. "I'll fix the tray. You stay here. Eduardo will fill you in."

There was another reason for taking the bakery goods. I needed to get away to talk to the captain. I entered the kitchen and opened the door to the garage. I approached the captain who was having a conversation with a policeman I'd seen before. "What's happening?" I asked.

"This is patrolman Mark Sanders, Brandon. He followed Alberto as he was returning back here. You were right. He was coming back from the five mile drive to the end of this road. We tried the trunk, but it's still locked. A BMW mechanic is on his way from Melbourne. When he opens it, and if the body is not there, we'll have forensics go over every inch. If we find something, we'll know Alberto probably buried her body somewhere along the side of the road or perhaps dumped her in the ocean."

I nodded. "I do hope that is not the case. It's difficult to imagine that Alberto could be so cold and calculating."

"If Alberto is a sociopath, then he *is* a cold, calculating manipulator and a con artist to boot. Believe me; I'm no longer surprised at human behavior."

I felt a deep shudder. "But we'd have to wonder how he could open the trunk and then relock it, since he's not a mechanic."

"Yes, that's true enough."

I changed the subject. "Captain, this afternoon after Andre and Emilio arrive, I'd like to do a re-enactment of the assailant running down the porch steps. Alberto, Andre, and Emilio should wear white shorts, a white shirt, and sunglasses. I'll stand at the gate and glance towards the steps just as I did yesterday. I'd like to do it at the same time: five-thirty. That way the light will be the same. To make it an even better line-up, I could call one of my blond students who is about the same size as the other three. Of course, if you find Rosalia's remains in the trunk, a re-enactment won't be necessary."

"Yeah, you got that right! Sure, an enactment is a good idea. Just in case the kidnapper makes another call, I've already decided I'll do my questioning of the other members of the family here instead of at the police station."

"Okay. I'll get in touch with my student. Please do let me know how the trunk scenario turns out." I pointed to the white bag I was holding. "I'm getting ready to fix a tray for the family and take it to the living room. That way they can stay close to the phone."

I opened the kitchen door relieved that the captain's attitude had totally turned around since yesterday. Besides trusting me now, perhaps he was in a better mood because his wife had been nice to him in bed last night, or his son brought home a good report card or whatever.

I poured the rest of the coffee from the coffee maker into the silver urn on the breakfast table and started another fresh pot. I reached for the large tray on the baker's rack and prepared a tray with dishes, flatware, napkins, and pastries and carried it to the living room.

"These pastries look delicious," I said, placing the tray on the coffee table. "Perhaps the sugar and caffeine will make everyone feel a bit better."

Estrella managed a smile. "Everything does look delicious, Brandon. I think I'm going to have to adopt you."

"Thank you, Estrella. Anymore calls?"

Eduardo reached for a plate. "I'm afraid not, Brandon. I'm not sure the bank has made all the arrangements. I'm thinking that the abductor is in contact with his banker in the Cayman Islands, and he'll know when the transaction has gone through. When everything clears, then maybe he'll call and let us know where we can find Rosalia." His eyes brimmed. "I doubt seriously we'll find her alive, but at least we'll have her back with us where she belongs."

My heart ached for them. "We can't give up hope, Eduardo."

Estrella poured coffee into the mugs. "I know I can't. It's the only thing that's keeping me from a breakdown. If we find out later she's not alive, I'll deal with it then."

"That's exactly the way I'm dealing with it, Estrella," Alberto answered, reaching for a cup of coffee.

This is going to be a very long day, I thought as I picked up a plate with a blueberry pastry – *a very long day indeed.*

Chapter 7

It was one-thirty in the afternoon. As I had expected, the day had dragged by with no call from the abductor. Alberto and I had volunteered to pick up a carryout from a Chinese restaurant. Once again, we all ate in the living room. I finished my sweet and sour chicken and excused myself to go to the garage to check on the BMW trunk situation.

When I entered the garage, I noticed that the trunk was now open. My heartbeat accelerated as I approached the captain and another man who were standing by the car. I peered into the trunk and was very relieved to see that they were not looking at Rosalia's dead body. I had continued to hope that Alberto was not the perpetrator.

"What was wrong with the trunk?" I asked.

"Hey, Brandon Sterling," the captain said. "This is Joe Jamison from the BMW dealership in Melbourne."

"Glad to know you," I said, holding out my hand.

Joe shook my hand. "I found the computer glitch. Cars have gotten so complicated, it's a wonder that more problems don't occur."

"So Alberto couldn't have hidden the body in the trunk after all," I commented.

"Yeah, it looks that way," the captain answered. "But it doesn't hurt to cover all bases. If he did kill her, he still could have used the rental to dump the body down the road, though he would have had to wrap her in something that wouldn't leave any blood or any trace of DNA."

I hated to bring up the subject of the luggage garment bag, but I knew I had to. "My girlfriend and I were thinking that a full-length garment bag would make a good body bag. If Alberto left Orlando at 4:30 and did the deed, he would have had time to pull a bag from the closet, change his shorts, place Rosalia into the bag and into his rental, then hide the body in the palmettos or dump it into the ocean on that five-mile deserted road south of here. He could have done all that in the forty-five minutes before he showed up here."

The captain folded his arms and rocked. "Right. And he just happened to be gone this morning when the kidnapper's call came in, so he could have made that call from his cell phone. I'm sure he'd be smart enough to use a throwaway cell so the call couldn't be traced. But we don't have a motive. He seems to have plenty of money, so why ask for that million-dollar ransom?"

"Yeah, that's the million-dollar question. And I still feel in my gut that Alberto wouldn't be capable of something like that."

The captain pursed his lips. "Well, as I said, you need to explore every possibility. Maybe we'll get a better handle on things when Emilio and Andre show up."

As if on cue, a red convertible sports car pulled in. I would soon find out if it was Emilio or Andre. I watched a blond male wearing sunglasses, who had an uncanny resemblance to Alberto, step out of the spiffy sports car I knew it had to be Emilio.

He walked up to the captain and held out his hand. "Hi, my name is Emilio Cardoza. I'm Alberto's brother and am also employed by Eduardo Vargas."

The captain shook his hand. "I'm Captain Delaney," he said then nodded to me, "and this is Brandon Sterling."

"Glad to meet you, Emilio," I told him with a handshake. "Alberto and Rosalia's mother and father are in the living room." If Emilio was the assailant, he did a good job of acting like he didn't recognize me.

Frowning, Emilio shook his head. "I'm still having difficulty understanding any of this tragic situation. Why would anyone want to shove Rosalia from the cupola and then kidnap her?"

"The kidnapping was for a ransom obviously, but we haven't come up with a motive for the shoving incident," I answered, "but we're working on it. Perhaps you or someone else in the family might know something you haven't thought of that may help solve the mystery."

"I've been thinking of nothing else since my brother called me, and I can't think of any reason why anyone would want to hurt

Rosalia. I don't believe she's ever harmed anyone in her life—unless it could be a business rival who hated Eduardo and wanted to get even."

"Certainly that's a possibility," the captain said, folding his arms and leaning against the BMW. "But as you may know from watching TV, the family or close friends are always the first group on the suspect list. So after you visit with the family for a few minutes, I'll need to talk to you. Meet me in the kitchen, and you can establish your alibi. I hope Andre will arrive shortly, because at five-thirty we're setting up a re-enactment of the incident." He nodded in my direction. "I suppose Alberto told you over the phone that Brandon is the witness who saw the perp shove Rosalia from the cupola."

I'd been carefully observing Emilio's facial expressions while the captain had been talking. I thought I noticed his eyes widen at the captain's last sentence.

Emilio pursed his lips. "Yes, Alberto told me there is a witness."

"I'm not sure exactly what Alberto told you," I added, "but the assailant was blond and your brother's size. I was at the gate when I turned and saw him, and though he was wearing sunglasses and I only got a glimpse of him, he looked a lot like Alberto."

The captain smiled coyly. "And since you look so much like your brother–"

"Then the assailant looked like me also," Emilio finished.

"It's indeed amazing how much you two do look alike," I added. "You could almost pass for twins!"

"So we've been told," he answered. "However, I am a few years older. I'd better go on in, though I don't look forward to it. I know Rosalia's family and Alberto are devastated."

"Yeah, pretty much, as I'm sure you are," I said.

A look of consternation quickly passed over his face. "Yes, yes, of course I'm devastated. As I said, everyone loved Rosalia." He turned to leave.

As soon as Emilio closed the kitchen door behind him, the captain said, "Well now, we'll need to check out that pretty little sports car. I'll call the DNA lab boys, and while they're checking out the car, one of them can swab Emilio's mouth."

I glanced at my watch. "I hope Andre will soon arrive. I'd

better call my student and see if I can grab him for the line-up. I'll tell him to wear a white shirt and shorts. I'm not sure if Emilio brought those items with him, and Alberto may not have white shorts either. When I saw him last night, he was wearing blue shorts."

The captain grinned. "If all else fails, I'm sure someone can pick up a white shirt and shorts at Walmart."

I chuckled. "Uh-huh. I can just see those rich guys picking up clothes from Walmart. I doubt if any one of them have ever darkened the doors of that establishment."

"You're probably right."

I pulled out my cell. "I hope I can catch up with my student." I punched in my address book and found the number. A minute later I heard Jimmy's voice.

"What's up, Mr. Sterling?" Jimmy asked.

I explained the situation, and he seemed quite excited to be asked to take part in a line-up. Then I told him to bring something to change into in case the other line-up suspects might need to borrow his white shirt and shorts. Since the captain was on his cell calling back the DNA boys, I punched in Amberly's number.

I immediately felt better when I heard her voice. "Hey, sweetheart, what's happening?" I asked.

"Not much. I took a walk on the beach this morning and spotted some dolphins, which thrilled me of course. I caught up with some ironing and did a bit of cleaning. Then the library called and told me a mystery novel I'd ordered had come in. I picked it up and have been reading ever since. It's a good read, but I wish you were here. What's going on over there?"

"No more calls from the kidnapper, and of course the family is distraught. I'll catch you up with the morning activities when I see you. I just met Emilio, and he's a clone of Alberto. The captain, who by the way, has been treating me like a long-lost buddy, is going to question Emilio and check on his alibi shortly. Haven't seen anything of Andre yet, but he should be arriving at any time."

"Sounds like you've had a busy morning."

"Uh-huh. And I just called Jimmy Taylor, one of my students as you may recall, and he's going to join the line-up. He's blond and about the size of the three suspects."

"Hey, that's a good idea. But won't it be embarrassing if you pick out Jimmy?"

I laughed. "No, not really. If we find out later that the bad guy turns out to be Alberto, and I pick out Emilio, or even Andre from the line-up today, a prosecutor could still say the assailant was blond and the correct size as the witness pointed out. However, during the line-up, there may be just that little difference between the guys that will indicate to me which one of them is the culprit. I'm looking forward to the experience."

"I'm sure you are, Brandon. Perhaps you'd better go back to college and get a job in law enforcement."

"I think not. I'll most likely be happy to return to my classroom on Monday."

"I doubt that, but I won't argue. I'm sure you have no idea what time you'll get away, do you?"

"No, I don't. The line-up should be over by six. Maria is supposed to arrive this evening in Orlando, but I don't know the exact time. She said she'd pick up a rental, so I don't think my services will be needed there. Strangely enough, I've been pinch-hitting as chauffer, waiter, and all-around supporter of the family that may include a murderer! But if nothing unforeseen pops up, I should be able to leave sometime after six. I'll call and let you know. If I can get away, I'll stop by my place and pick up some decent clothes. We can go to a nice restaurant. You be thinking of a place."

"Okay, but if you feel you're needed there, don't try to rush back to take me to dinner. I can fix something for myself. We have many more weekends to look forward to."

"That's true enough. Thanks, Amberly. Understanding is only one of your sterling qualities. I'll talk to you later."

I folded my phone just in time to see another expensive sports car pull up. Once again, a handsome blond young man wearing sunglasses got out of the car. I could see a resemblance to the person I saw running down the porch stairs. I was sure he was Andre.

The captain ambled over next to me and leaned against the car. We were both observing our third possible suspect as he approached us.

"I'm Andre Vargas," he said, holding out his hand to the captain. "I'm Eduardo's and Estrella's adopted son."

"Nice to meet you," the captain replied. "And this is Brandon Sterling who witnessed the incident."

I held out my hand. "Glad to meet you, Andre," I said.

"Has there been any more contact with the kidnapper?" Andre asked, his expression solemn.

"No," the captain answered, "I'm afraid not. If Eduardo's money transference has gone through, there would not be much need to hear from the abductor again. I'm sorry to say that there's not much hope that the victim is even alive. I hope, for the sake of the family, that the son of a bitch would at least tell Eduardo where the body is. I think it's all that you can hope for."

Andre's eyes filled and tears ran rampant down his cheeks. He reached into his white shorts pocket and grabbed a handkerchief. He removed his sunglasses then covered his face and sobbed for a few minutes before wiping his eyes and blowing his nose. "I'm sorry. I am very close to my sister. I keep hoping I'm in the middle of a nightmare."

"I'm sorry I was so brutally frank, Andre. Sometimes policemen say things without thinking."

"I understand, Captain. I suppose it's better to know the truth instead of holding on to false hope."

"Well, anyway your family is in the living room. As I told Emilio, I'll need to question you in the kitchen later, so go on in. I'll call you when I'm ready."

"And there will be a re-enactment of the incident at five-thirty," I told him. "We're asking you, Alberto, Emilio, and another young man to wear white shirts, shorts, and sunglasses and run down the cupola steps, so I can see which person looks more like the assailant."

A look of incredulity swept across Andre's face. "You mean we're all suspects?"

I nodded. "Though I only got a glimpse of the perpetrator, I saw that he was blond, wearing sunglasses, and about your size. Perhaps you've never recognized the fact that you, Alberto, and Emilio are all blond and about the same size."

Andre drew his shoulders back and answered rather curtly. "No, I suppose not. It's difficult to believe that you'd think anyone in the family could have possibly had any reason to kill and then kidnap Rosalia."

"I can understand how you feel, Andre," the captain answered, "but perhaps you aren't aware that most murders are committed by family members or close friends. They have to be excluded from the suspect list first."

Andre was visibly angry. "I'll expect an apology when you find out we're all innocent!"

"I'll be happy to apologize," the captain said, "but then you may need to apologize to me if we find that you or one of your family members is the guilty person."

Without another word, Andre brushed past the captain and me. He entered the kitchen door and slammed it behind him.

"Alberto told me last night that Andre has a chip on his shoulder, and he wondered why, since the family had always treated him so well," I told the captain. "Alberto also said he thought maybe Andre had been in love with Rosalia for years. You know they are not kin to each other."

"Hey now, that's certainly an interesting bit of news. Perhaps he was angry and jealous enough to do the deed because Rosalia was soon going to marry Alberto. The kidnapping could be a cover-up to make it appear like it was someone outside of the family."

"As you're fond of saying, Captain, 'it's certainly a possibility.' "

The captain hit me on the shoulder and said, "Speaking of apologies, I owe one to you, Sterling. We got off on the wrong foot yesterday. That sarcastic comment about your deceased grandfather was inexcusable. Personally, I thought you might be making stuff up since there was no sign of a body. You can't believe how many kooks I've been involved with since working on the police force. Not only was I wrong, but you've actually been a help. You seem to have good deductive reasoning, and you're able to communicate well with the family. I'd like you to sit in while I'm questioning Alberto, Emilio, and Andre."

For the second time this weekend I found myself rendered speechless! After a few seconds, I found my voice. "I accept your apology, Captain, and I'd be happy to sit in while you're questioning the three guys. By the way, where is your sergeant today?"

"Sergeant O'Grady asked to have the weekend off a few weeks

ago to take his son to his team's soccer playoff."

The lab truck pulled up and the captain said with a sly smile, "Since you're on good terms with the family, I think it would be nice if you went in and got Emilio's and Andre's car keys, so the lab boys can check out the trunks."

I rolled my eyes. "Gee, thanks."

"Oh, and while you're in there, you can tell Emilio I want to see him in the kitchen in ten minutes. Okay?"

"Okay." I entered the kitchen, thinking that the good captain had elected me to be a substitute for Sergeant O'Grady, and then my thoughts switched to Andre. Not only did he have a chip on his shoulder, but he seemed to have a hair-trigger temper as well. Of course, he was young and probably immature. It was going to be interesting to observe his reactions during the questioning.

When I entered the living room, I noticed that Andre was sitting close to Estrella on the sofa and holding her hand. It was obvious that the two had been crying. They all turned and looked at me.

Estrella gave me a furtive smile. "Andre and Emilio are upset that they are considered suspects."

It was good to see Alberto actually grin when he said, "I told Emilio and Andre that I'd been the object of scrutiny for the last twenty-four hours. Now it was their turn and they might as well get used to it."

Andre's glare indicated that he did not find Alberto's remarks amusing. "I think we should call Dad's lawyer. I don't like being treated like a common criminal."

"I'm sure you're welcome to call anyone you like, Andre," I answered. "But I think any lawyer would tell you that the captain has every right to question you, ask for an alibi, and expect you to cooperate in a line-up. If you're innocent, you have nothing to worry about. It's just normal procedure. You do want the perpetrator to be caught, don't you?"

His face turned red and contorted in anger. "Of course, I want you to catch the perpetrator. So why aren't you trying to find him? How could it be one of us? Don't you understand? We're here, and he's out there somewhere!"

"Not necessarily so, Andre," I answered, forcing myself to speak calmly. "The kidnapper's call came this morning. You and

Emilio were not here at that time and neither was Alberto."

"What?" Andre shot up from the sofa and wagged his finger at me. "What possible motive could we have?"

"There are a number of motives in every murder – jealousy, you know, like a spurned suitor; money, perhaps someone had a huge gambling debt, or maybe Rosalia found out a secret and threatened to tell, and it would ruin the guilty man's life." I noticed a change of expression in Andre's eyes when I mentioned 'a spurned suitor.'"

"Sit down, Andre, and control yourself," Eduardo commanded. "I know you're upset, as we all are, but don't take it out on Brandon. He's been considerate and kind, and I believe he only wants justice done. And you're forgetting one crucial fact: Brandon witnessed the incident and got a glimpse of the man as he ran down the steps. He told the police the man was blond and about the same size as you three men! So under those circumstances, you must understand why you are under such scrutiny. I might add that if any one of you committed this terrible deed, I may save the state the job of execution and kill you myself!"

Andre sat down and stared at the floor.

I hated to make my request. I didn't want a black eye. "The captain has asked me to take your keys, Andre and Emilio, so the DNA lab boys can check out your trunks." I was tempted to duck behind Eduardo's chair.

Once again the charming Alberto came to my rescue. "Hey, they've already checked out my rental and probably called a BMW computer expert to open the trunk. Right, Brandon?"

I nodded. "Right."

"I don't know how you can take all this harassment so calmly, Alberto," Emilio said curtly.

"It's not harassment, Emilio. As I said before, it's normal police procedure. Don't you ever watch any true-crime TV shows?"

"Of course, I do. But it's different–"

"Yes, it's different when you're in the hot seat," Alberto answered. "But the more you object, the more guilty you'll appear. So if I were you, I'd stop complaining and hand over your keys. Oh, you can also count on the lab DNA boys coming in and swiping out your mouth."

"That's the last straw!" Emilio shouted, coming out of his chair.

"Oh, for God's sake, Emilio," Eduardo said. "Sit down. I expected more of you. You're both acting like rich, spoiled brats. Alberto is right. If you don't cooperate, it will make you look like you have something to hide."

I held out my hand to Emilio and Andre, and they reluctantly handed over their keys. I wanted to be close to the door when I gave them another instruction from the captain. "Emilio, the captain wants to meet with you in the kitchen," I glanced at my watch, "right about now, I'd say."

Emilio stood. "Oh, all right," he shouted and stomped towards me. To say the captain would be questioning a reluctant suspect, would be an understatement.

We walked down the hall in deafening silence. In the kitchen, Emilio sat down and folded his arms. He was the picture of a petulant child.

"I'll give these keys to the captain," I told him. "I'm sure he'll be here in a few minutes."

I didn't expect an answer, and I didn't get one. When I entered the garage, I handed over the keys to the captain. "Not surprisingly, there was a ruckus in the living room when I asked for these," I told him. "Emilio and Andre think they're being harassed. Andre said he thought we should call his dad's lawyer. However, Eduardo put them in their place by telling them they were behaving like rich, spoiled brats. Alberto continues to be cooperative."

The captain took the keys saying, "I'm not surprised. Of course, Alberto could be behaving so we will think he's a good guy."

"I've thought of that. I know sociopaths can fool most people and even beat a lie detector test."

"And that's why lie detector tests are not permissible in court," the captain responded. "So far as I'm concerned, all three of those guys in the living room are prime suspects."

"Oh, I forgot to mention that Emilio is, most likely impatiently, waiting for you in the kitchen."

The captain cocked his head. "Oh, then we'll get right in there as soon as I give the lab guys the keys to the trunk. We wouldn't want Emilio to spend his precious time waiting for us, now would we?"

I was happy that the captain's sarcasm was no longer directed at me.

A few minutes later, the captain, carrying a large manila envelope, and I sat down at the dinette table.

With his arms still folded, Emilio glared at me. "Why is this guy sitting in on the questioning?"

The captain pulled out a pen, a large note pad, and a small recorder from the envelope. "Because Mr. Sterling, here, is the only witness to this crime, so I decided to deputize him this morning. He may think of something important he saw at the scene of the crime and can question you about it. I hope you have no objections to his presence, because it would do you no good."

I hoped my total surprise at the captain's remarks didn't show on my face. Perhaps I'd been asleep on my feet when he deputized me! I chuckled silently and winked at the captain.

"Okay, just get on with it then," Emilio growled.

I was beginning to understand what Alberto meant when he stated that he and his brother looked alike but had totally different personalities.

"Exactly where are you staying in Kissimmee, Emilio?" the captain asked, switching on the recorder and picking up his pen.

He let out an audible sigh. "I'm staying at a rented cabin on a large lake. It's pretty deserted. Since I'm with clients most of the time, I like solitude so I can totally relax."

"Then I assume you like to fish?"

Emilio rolled his eyes upward to show his distain at the captain's question. "Actually, I don't care anything about fishing. I like to read and hike. On the Internet, I read about the cabin and its location; it seemed like a good spot."

"Do you usually come to Florida on your vacations?" I asked.

"No, I usually go out west to the mountains where there are good hiking trails."

"So why did you decide to come to Florida during this vacation?" I asked.

"I thought a change would be nice. I also knew Alberto and Rosalia were going to be in the vicinity, and we could get together and do something."

A red flag went up, and I said, "According to Alberto, he was not aware you were in the Kissimmee area. He found out that information after calling your mother to tell her about Rosalia's incident and kidnapping. And weren't you supposed to meet at your family home tomorrow?"

Emilio appeared even more annoyed. "Yes, I was supposed to meet Rosalia and Alberto at our home in New York tomorrow afternoon. So during the week, since I was enjoying my solitude and knew that we were all meeting on Sunday, I decided I wouldn't bother to call them. I also figured they might be having an early honeymoon here at the beach and would be just as happy to be left alone."

"Or perhaps you found out from the Orlando office that Alberto would be in their office yesterday afternoon. That gave you the opportunity you were hoping for, Emilio. Rosalia would be alone. We don't know what your motive is at this time, but if you did shove her from the cupola then kidnapped her, we'll find that motive," the captain retorted.

Emilio shot the captain a mean-eyed look that put the captain's mean-eyed look to shame. "That's pure fantasy. There is no reason in the world that would make me want to harm Rosalia. I still stick to my theory; someone who had a vendetta against Eduardo must have been following her and watching for an opportunity."

"That would be a possible theory, Emilio," I stated as much like a deputized officer as I could muster, "except she must have known and trusted her assailant. When I first noticed her in the cupola, she was looking out to sea with binoculars. Then I heard her scream and watched as she plunged to the ground. She wouldn't have been looking out to sea with binoculars while an unknown assailant stood behind her. No, someone she knew and trusted pushed her from the cupola."

Emilio's eyes narrowed speculatively, but he made no comment.

"Where were you at five-thirty yesterday afternoon?" the captain asked.

Emilio leaned back in his chair and glanced at the ceiling for a few seconds. "At five-thirty...let's see...I was probably returning to my cabin from my trip to the grocery store."

"Where did you do your shopping?" the captain asked.

"I went to a Publix grocery store which was...I don't know...maybe six miles from my cabin."

"Did a man or woman check you out?" I interjected.

"It was a woman who was probably in her forties or fifties."

"That will be easy enough to check," the captain commented. "And I suppose anyone who grocery shops would know that most of the employees who work at the check-out counters are often women in their forties or fifties."

"Well...you know...I wasn't totally focused on the woman who checked me out. She could have been younger."

"Okay, describe her to your best ability," I said.

Emilio puffed out his cheeks and blew out air. "Hey, I wasn't paying that much attention. I don't usually scrutinize people working behind counters in grocery stores. I had other things on my mind."

"Do you remember which counter it was? One, two, three–" I continued.

"I think it was two, but it could have been three. I told you I wasn't paying that much attention."

"So what kind of groceries did you buy?" the captain asked.

"Let's see...I bought a carton of beer, bread, peanut butter, strawberry preserves, and milk...oh, and a dozen eggs."

"Emilio, I was in the room with your brother, Alberto, when he called you. I'm not exactly sure of the time, but it had to have been between seven-thirty and eight. You told your brother you were coming back from the grocery store then. He also stated that you must have been driving an old clunker because he could hear engine noises."

The captain grinned. "Well, now, you must have been real hungry if you were on your way back from the grocery store for the second time."

Emilio pursed his lips and hesitated before he answered. "Obviously I was wrong about it being five-thirty. It's daylight saving time now, and it gets dark later. It was probably seven-thirty as you said, and I was just not paying much attention and thought it was around five-thirty."

The captain was busily writing on his notepad. "I've noticed you've used the phrase 'not paying attention' several times. I hope you concentrate more thoroughly when you're dealing with your clients, Emilio. So since you now agree you were coming back from the grocery store around seven-thirty, then can you remember where you might have been at five-thirty?" He stopped writing and glanced up, his eyebrows climbing toward his hairline.

I held my breath and hoped desperately Emilio would not say he was 'not paying attention,' because the captain might take a swing at him.

Emilio paused and pulled in a deep breath. "I'm usually on tight schedules meeting planes and clients and racing to work, so when I'm relaxing on vacation, I make it a habit not to look at my watch. I'd say I was relaxing on the couch reading one of the several books I brought with me."

"Then you don't have an alibi. Right?" The captain smirked.

Emilio shrugged. "I suppose not. But neither can you prove I wasn't on the sofa reading. Right?"

"No, I can't prove it at this time," the captain declared. "But I'm curious, Emilio; you have a fine-looking, expensive car. When you pulled up, I didn't notice any engine noises. Can you explain why Alberto heard engine noises while he was talking to you over the phone last evening?"

"Yes, I can explain that. When I landed at the airport, I rented the car I drove over today. The owner of the cabin keeps an old clunker at the cabin, so when he uses the cabin, a car, actually it's a truck, will be at his disposal. The road to the cabin is a dirt road, and if it's dry and dusty, your car will get dirty; if it's rainy, your car will get muddy. It's also a really bumpy road, so it could mess up your shocks if you drove on the road a lot, I suppose. Anyway, the owner told me to feel free to use the old truck. I picked up the keys to the truck when I picked up the keys to the cabin at the real estate office."

Somehow I couldn't picture Emilio behind the wheel of an old truck. From what Alberto told me, he likes nice and expensive things.

"So how close is the nearest cabin, or house, to you on that dusty, bumpy road?" I asked.

"I guess the road is around four or five miles long. The nearest cabin or cottage would be maybe two miles away."

I folded my arms and leaned back. "So you really are in a

deserted area. Do many vehicles pass by?"

"Actually, I'm in the last cabin on the road."

"How fortuitous, that is, since you really wanted solitude. But if you're a seasoned hiker, I'm surprised you'd enjoy hiking on a bumpy, dusty road," I told him.

His voice held a note of exasperation. "What does that comment have to do with anything? What exactly are you driving at?" His glare would have scared a rattlesnake.

"I think what he means is if you were looking for an isolated place where you could hide or bury a body, you couldn't have found a better place," the captain answered.

"That's utterly preposterous!" Emilio shouted. "You're insinuating that I planned to murder Rosalia, and I just happened to find a time that she'd be alone so I could shove her from the cupola and bring her back sight unseen, and I just happened to find a secluded spot to bury her."

"No, Emilio," the captain said, "I don't think anything just happened. I think you're a smart young man, and you could carefully plan everything."

"So, Captain, are you accusing me of murder and kidnapping?"

"Not yet, but let's say you're a person of interest. You can go now, but I caution you not to leave the area just yet." He handed over the notepad he'd been using. "Please write down your cell phone number and the directions to your cabin."

He turned to me. "Sterling, tell Andre I'd like to talk to him."

I could have sworn I saw puffs of smoke pouring from both of Emilio's ears. He was not a happy camper. As I walked down the hall (I believe I could have walked blindfolded), I had a feeling Andre would be just as ornery as Emilio.

Chapter 8

When I entered the living room, I noticed everyone was holding a brandy snifter. Since I'd developed a taste for the warm liquid yesterday and had learned to twirl so expertly, I longed to join the group. But since I was now a deputized law officer, I'd better not drink on the job. They all looked up with expectant expressions when I entered, though Andre was more or less glaring. He was sitting on the sofa next to Estrella.

"Would you care for some brandy, or perhaps something else alcoholic?" Eduardo offered.

"Thank you, but no, Eduardo. The captain wishes to speak with Andre in the kitchen." I braced for an outburst.

Andre pecked Estrella on the cheek then stood holding his snifter. "I don't suppose I have any choice, do I? Lead the way, Mr. Deputy Sheriff, or whatever title the good captain has bestowed upon you," he said sardonically.

I thought the reaction could have been worse, but then I might be getting used to sarcasm – first from the captain yesterday and now from Emilio and Andre. We left the group and, on the way to the kitchen, we ran into Emilio.

"So, Emilio, how did it go? Are you still a prime suspect?" Andre asked with a smirk.

Emilio's eyes were filled with dark portents. "Actually, I'm a person of great interest. No doubt, you'll be one also if you can't substantiate your alibi."

Andre appeared to be searching his mind. I had a good idea what he was searching for. He didn't make a comment but merely nodded.

We entered the kitchen, and I noticed the captain had vacated his place at the table. "If you'd like to take a seat, I'll go check on the captain's whereabouts."

Andre didn't bother with an answer and pulled his chair out with such force, I wondered if he left marks on the beautiful parquet floors. He appeared to be quite strong.

I left the kitchen and found the captain talking with some men. By listening, I discovered they were a group from Orlando who were there to put tracers on the phones.

"Just a minute, Sterling," the captain told me. "I'll be right there."

Reluctantly, I returned to the kitchen alone. I didn't look forward to making small talk with Andre. I sat down opposite him. He looked at a spot over my head. The silence hung heavy.

I cleared my throat. "Andre, I know you were very close to your sister. This entire experience must be unbearable for you."

He lowered his gaze. "Are you trying to soften me up for the kill, Deputy Sterling? Is that your job? Softening me up so when the captain returns I'll cooperate?"

"No, that's not my job. I'm merely trying to put myself in your place. And even if you did the terrible deed, I believe you'd be in even more pain, because I sense you really loved Rosalia."

Andre winced. "So now you're playing psychiatrist, huh? Listen, I don't want to talk to you or the captain. But I *have* to talk to the captain. I don't *have* to talk to you!" He took a long swig of brandy.

I thought his shoulder chip had probably melded into a five foot log. I was surprised his shoulders weren't sagging. He made me feel like I used to when my dad scolded me for a childish misdeed. I was saved from an immediate answer by the captain entering the kitchen followed by the phone-tracer group.

"I'll be back in a few minutes," the captain informed us.

For a lack of something better to do, I got up and opened the fridge. I spied a couple of cans of pop. I popped one open, took a swig, and pretended it was brandy. I heard the heavy-footed captain coming down the hall and was immensely relieved. I took my seat at the table.

The captain's notepad, pen, and recorder were still on the table. He sat down and smiled sweetly. "Sorry I was delayed." He switched on the recorder and picked up his pen. "How long have you attended Miami University, Andre?"

He let out a long sigh. "I'm a senior about to graduate, so I've lived in Miami for four years."

"Do you live in a dorm?" the captain asked.

Andre looked at the captain like he thought he was talking to a moron. "No, of course not! I live off campus in a house. You can't study in a dorm or do anything else for that matter."

"You mean like partying?" I asked, grinning and showing my pearly whites. I'd just had a cleaning job at the dentist.

"Yeah, I have a few parties once in a while. Is there anything wrong in that?"

I shook my head and the captain said, "No, of course not. Just how are your grades, by the way?"

Andre shot us both a scorching look. "I don't know why my grades have anything to do with this case, but if you must know, I'm a B student. My parents seem happy with that."

I was surprised. I thought he'd be a real party animal since he had his own pad.

The captain nodded. "Is your house located close to the university?"

His voice was a lifeless monotone. "Since I have a car, I can drive to classes. I live about five miles from campus."

"Is your house secluded?" I asked.

Andre shook his head and rolled his eyes, indicating he was now talking to two morons. "If you've ever been to Miami, you should know that there are no secluded houses anywhere in the city. So the answer to your question is absolutely not."

I wondered how much longer it was going to take before the captain lost his cool. I knew I was about to lose mine.

The captain pursed his lips. "Where were you yesterday around five-thirty, Andre?"

"Yesterday at five-thirty, I was in my house all by myself having a beer and watching ESPN. I'd planned to go out around eight and meet some guys at a sports bar a few miles from my house. After drinking a few beers, I fell asleep on the sofa. I didn't wake up until after twelve. I suppose I was unusually tired because I'd run three or four miles on the beach that morning before my morning classes. After I woke up, I nuked some leftovers, ate, took off my clothes, brushed my teeth, and went to bed. And no, there was no one around to corroborate what I've just told you." He spoke as if he'd been rehearsing.

"What was the reason you turned off your cell last evening?" I added.

The question seemed to throw him for a few seconds. "I don't remember turning it off. Oh, now I remember. I turned it off while I was running yesterday morning, and I guess I forgot to turn it back on."

"Didn't you think it was strange not to receive any calls all day yesterday?" I questioned.

He took a sip of brandy before he answered. "Hey, I cut my afternoon class and visited the Miami Aquarium most of the day. Since I'm going home soon and will be working for my dad, I thought I'd take a holiday. And besides, unlike some people, I don't walk around with a phone stuck to my ear. I'm not a chit-chat. I only use the phone when I have to."

"Uh-huh," I commented. "I think you're the only person I know who doesn't have an answering machine on his home phone."

He shrugged. "Like I said, I don't like to chit-chat. If someone has something important to tell me, they can call until they reach me."

"Alberto and your mom tried to reach you last evening," I told him. "Are you saying you were sleeping so soundly you couldn't hear the sharp ring of a phone?"

"If you remember, I said I fell asleep watching ESPN. That channel is pretty noisy. And I'm a sound sleeper. My mom will vouch for that."

The captain cut in. "It's quite possible you slept through two phone calls and turned off your cell while you were running on the beach. And it's also possible you cut your afternoon class and were at the Miami Aquarium most of the day. But there is another possibility: I propose that you found out that Alberto was going to be in Orlando for most of the afternoon, so you high-tailed it to Lo Verde Beach. You've been in love with Rosalia for years, and you couldn't stand the idea that she was going to marry Alberto. You declared your love for her and begged her to stop the marriage. She probably treated you in a condescending manner like: 'Andre, you're still so young. You'll find someone, and she'll be much better for you than I. Let's go up and watch the dolphins. It's time for them to feed.' If you couldn't have her, then no one would have

84

her. In a fit of rage, you shoved her from the cupola, wrapped her body in a garment luggage bag, placed the bag in the trunk of your car, and fled the scene. We'll check the trunk of your car of course. You made a call with a throw-away cell phone pretending to be a kidnapper, thinking the police would assume the murder was done by a stranger who wanted money. But the money would also come in handy in case the police found enough evidence to convict you, and you'd need to run away to another country."

From Andre's facial expression, I knew the captain had hit a nerve. Though he may not have killed Rosalia, at some time recently he'd probably declared his love and had been rejected.

His face twisted in anguish. "So you two think you have it all figured out, huh? I don't care if you check out my trunk or swab my mouth for DNA. There's no way in hell I could have ever hurt Rosalia. As I said before, I'll expect an apology when you find the real killer. Are you through with me?"

The captain pushed the notepad over. "Yes, but I'll need you to give me your cell number and home phone number. Also write down your address."

While Andre was writing, I rolled my eyes at the captain. "Would you like for me to get Alberto?"

He nodded. "Yeah, we've interviewed him already, but it wasn't recorded or written down."

Once again I headed down the very familiar hall and into the very familiar living room. I heard Emilio's voice, which stopped when he saw me approaching. No doubt he was bad-mouthing the captain and me. The phone guys must have finished their job and were probably upstairs.

"Where's Andre?" Emilio snapped.

"He's writing down his address and phone numbers. He'll be here shortly." I turned towards Alberto and smiled. "It's your turn again. The captain wants to record your statements this time."

Alberto picked up his snifter with one hand and waved with the other. "Come and get me if you get another call from the kidnapper," he said to Emilio.

We passed Andre who was walking with his hands in his pockets. No one spoke.

The captain was waiting for us. "We'll just briefly go over some of the questions we asked you before, Alberto," he said, pointing to the chair in front of him.

So far, Alberto had been the only suspect who had not been surly. I hoped he'd continue to be cooperative, because my nerves were frayed from the last two interviews. I would have accepted Alberto's offer for a brandy, but I wanted to stay sharp for the line-up scenario – accepting a brandy really should not have hurt my faux-deputy status.

The captain switched on the recorder. "Okay, Alberto, tell us where you were yesterday afternoon."

With a faraway expression, he began. "Yesterday afternoon, I was in the Orlando office doing some work. Rosalia and I had reservations at the Chart House for seven. I was so engrossed in my work, I vaguely remember the other employees leaving somewhere around four-thirty. I finished my work around five and left. I did not see anyone in the elevator or in the parking lot when I left. There was heavy afternoon traffic, and I arrived here at the beach house around six-fifteen."

"So you'd agree that since you were left in the office alone, you could have left shortly after four-thirty instead of five o'clock," the captain stated.

"That's correct. I could have. But I didn't leave until five."

"And if you did leave the office at four-thirty-five, you could have had time to get back here, push the victim from the cupola, place her in a garment bag, bury her at the end of this sparsely populated road, or dump her in the ocean, and arrive here around six-fifteen."

Alberto nodded. "If you say so, Captain."

"For the record, you are admitting that you do not have an airtight alibi. Right?" the captain asked.

"It appears that I don't. But also for the record, I did not murder the woman I love."

"Okay, Alberto, write down your address in New York and all your phone numbers." The captain pushed the pad and pencil over.

After Alberto wrote down the information, he stood. "I assume I can go now. And you don't need to tell me not to leave the area. I'm not going anywhere until we find Rosalia."

"And I hope that will be soon," I added, wishing I could say something more encouraging.

He picked up his snifter. "Anyone else you wish to speak to

again?"

The captain shook his head. "Not at this time."

I noticed the dark circles under the Alberto's eyes and how his shoulders seemed to slump as he exited. He wore the look of defeat and despair. Once again, I fervently hoped he was not the perpetrator.

The captain placed his pen on the table and folded his arms. "Well now, Sterling. We have three suspects without alibis. Who do you think is our most qualified murderer?"

"That's hard to say, Captain. I think Emilio was for sure lying about the grocery store business and reading a book on the sofa at five-thirty. My bet is if he did the deed, he drove the beat-up truck and stashed Rosalie in the back in a garment bag. When he answered Alberto's call around seven-thirty, he was driving the truck and maybe returning to his cabin with the body. The time would fit. He could have cleaned out the truck later with no problem. He has an entire four or five almost-deserted miles to choose from as to where he'd bury her. He's also close to a big lake, probably full of alligators, which almost gags me to say the words, and he had plenty of time to dispose of the body last evening. The fact that he chose this vicinity for his hiking and reading vacation is questionable as he doesn't enjoy fishing. And the fact that he didn't call Rosalia and Alberto, being only forty or so miles from here, is also questionable. So we have opportunity but no motive yet."

"That's pretty much how I see it as well. So give me a summation of Andre's situation."

"Ah, Andre. My character analogy is probably the same as yours. He's a rich, immature kid who is used to having what he wants when he wants it. Alberto said that when he was adopted, the twins spoiled him terribly and probably his parents had also. As we discussed earlier, he most likely was in love with Rosalia. He, too, could have found out that Alberto was in Orlando and driven the approximately one hundred eighty miles here, been rejected by Rosalia one more time and, in a fit of passion, pushed her from the cupola, wrapped her body in a sheet or garment bag, hauled her back to Miami, and disposed of her body – Lord only knows where! It was dark by the time he arrived in Miami. He certainly had the opportunity, because his story of turning off his cell, visiting the Miami Aquarium, and falling asleep on the sofa was just plain ridiculous. A jury would actually laugh at that lame alibi. If he did the deed, I don't think it was premeditated. It's difficult to think he'd be so full of rage he'd harm her."

"I understand and agree up to a point. But remember the O. J. trial? A narcissist can't stand rejection. From what we've observed, Andre is something of a narcissist wouldn't you say?"

"Yes, I'd say so. But somehow killing the person you love is difficult for me to grasp."

"That's because you not a narcissist, Sterling."

"Yeah, it's difficult to put yourself inside the mind of a murderer."

"Uh-huh. And ain't we glad! I wouldn't want to venture into that dark, ominous place. Now how about your friend Alberto? Give me your thoughts about him."

I grinned. "Yes, I do think of Alberto as my friend. From what I've observed, he's a thoroughly nice guy. He's kind and considerate, and I can't imagine him killing anyone, much less the woman he loved. But as you so carefully pointed out to me, and I know you've had much more experience than I, we're aware of the Dr. Jekyll, Mr. Hyde personality like that of Ted Bundy. We know that at first Alberto lied about when he left Orlando, so he also had opportunity, but like Emilio, we don't have a motive as yet."

The captain locked his hands behind his neck and leaned back in his chair. "Yep, I think the motive for Andre would be rejection. Perhaps Rosalia found out something about Emilio or Alberto that would hurt or even ruin their lives. It will take a lot of probing to find what it could be."

"Maybe when Maria arrives, we can question her and see if she has a clue. Rosalia might have dropped some kind of hint to her."

"I think you're onto something, Sterling. If she arrives too late this evening, we'll talk with her in the morning."

"Okay. It appears that this beach house has substituted for the police station, huh?"

"Strangely enough, it has. We've had so much going on here with the DNA lab guys, the BMW mechanic, the searching and examining of the car trunks, and the phone tracer boys. And I'm sure the Feds will be arriving soon to question the family. I also believe the anxious parents are more comfortable here, and if another call comes in from the kidnapper, it will be good to be on the premises."

I nodded then looked towards the door when I heard someone running down the hall.

Alberto's face appeared red from excitement. "Come quick! We think the kidnapper is on the phone."

The captain and I jumped up from our chairs and raced down the hall behind Alberto. We entered the living room just as Eduardo was hanging up the phone. Everyone in the room was standing around him with rapt attention.

Eduardo's face was a study in disappointment. "When I picked up the phone and said hello, the kidnapper said, "You'll be sorry if you call in the police or the FBI." Then he hung up. That's the same warning he gave me this morning when he asked for the ransom, but of course the police already knew about the abduction, and he must know that when there's a kidnapping, the FBI do get involved. And something else I just thought about; this is an unlisted number. How did he get it?"

My memory banks fired up full speed. The captain and I had not thought about the number here being unlisted. That meant that when the kidnapper made the first call, he had to have known the number, making it far more likely that the kidnapper was indeed a family member.

"Eduardo," I said, "Do you know how many of your business acquaintances have this unlisted number?"

Eduardo sat down in a high-backed chair close to the desk. "Oh, I'd need to think about that. I'd say...maybe ten people. I gave out the number before I became more dependent on my cell phone. Do you want the names?"

I glanced at the captain. "I think it would be a good idea. I'm sure the Feds would want the names also."

Eduardo stood. "Okay, I'll go upstairs and get them from my computer. If the phone rings again, should I answer it from the extension in the bedroom?"

"Yes, I think it's better if you answer, just in case the kidnapper makes another call," the captain instructed.

"Just a minute, Eduardo," I said. "Did this person sound exactly like the man who asked for a ransom this morning?"

"I guess so. It sounded like his voice was muffled this morning and also a few minutes ago; you know, like he was holding something over his mouth to disguise his voice."

Andre's eyes narrowed with contempt. "Well, pray tell us how we can be considered suspects when a call is made from the kidnapper, and we're all here in the room?"

The captain was clearly irritated. "If one of you here is the guilty party, you'd obviously need an accomplice to do the calling. But it's at least possible that the culprit could be some business associate with a grudge against Eduardo and has acquired this number through business. That's why he is going to look for the numbers of those people. Does that answer your question, Andre?"

His expression sullen, Andre mumbled, "I suppose so."

"That second call from the kidnapper could have been made to throw the authorities off, since all the family members are present. The caller didn't really say anything new. It's a good ruse, but it only fooled Andre," the captain said with amused contempt.

"And as I've mentioned before," I interjected, "Rosalia must have known and trusted her assailant, since she was looking at the ocean with her back turned towards the person who pushed her."

Estrella spoke up. "Rosalia knows a lot of people, and that includes Eduardo's business associates and also the people she works with personally. Someone may have known she was alone and pretended to stop by for a visit. There are many tall, blond young men in the world. Sunglasses, white shirts, and shorts are pretty much the mode of dress for people visiting the beach, don't you think?"

"That's certainly true, Estrella," I answered, "and if you or anyone else can give us a name of someone Rosalia knew that fits the description of the person I saw, I'm sure the FBI will look into it. Of course, that includes Eduardo's business acquaintances who have your unlisted number."

Eduardo opened his mouth as if to speak, but remained silent and exited the room.

Suddenly, all attention was suddenly focused on an object behind the captain and me. When I swung around, I looked squarely into the face of a tall, dark-haired, handsome, young man who resembled Eduardo. I presumed he must be Fernando, Rosalia's brother.

He gave the captain and me a nod and headed straight to

Estrella. "Mom," he said, holding out his arms, "how are you holding up?"

As he was too tall for her to reach his shoulders, Estrella laid her head on her son's chest. "I can't understand how this could possibly be happening," she sobbed.

Fernando patted her back. "Just hang in there, Mom. We have to think positive. I'm sure the police are doing all they can."

Estrella pulled back and nodded to the captain and me. "Fernando, this is Captain Delaney and Brandon Sterling. Brandon actually witnessed the...the...incident."

I held out my hand. "Sorry to meet you under these circumstances, Fernando."

Fernando shook my hand and then the captain's. He turned to me. "Brandon, do you mean you actually saw the man who pushed my sister from the cupola?"

"Oh, yes," Emilio said with a sly smile. Deputy Sterling told us the perpetrator was tall, blond, and wearing sunglasses."

Fernando's voice raised an octave. "What? Do you mean to say a deputy witnessed the incident?"

"Look here, Emilio," I growled in my scariest, school-teacher voice. "How about dropping this deputy business? I'm not a deputy. The captain said that as a kind of joke."

Emilio's voice sounded robotic. "You're a joke all right, Brandon. Fernando, we were informed by the captain that members of the family, close friends, or perhaps a fiancé are always the first people on the suspect list. And *Mr. Sterling* here said the perpetrator was tall, blond, and wore sunglasses. As you can plainly see, there are three men here that fit that description. We are all going to don white shorts, shirts, and sunglasses then run down the outside steps in a line-up of sorts. You're lucky that you're not blond, and you were in New York. I assume you were in New York, for even though you're not blond, you'd probably be joining us in the line-up."

"Why...why that's the most absurd thing I've ever heard! You all have alibis don't you?" Fernando appeared astonished.

"Yes, we do have alibis, but I'm not sure that the captain and Brandon believe them," Alberto said quietly.

"Alberto, please explain that statement to Fernando while Brandon and I attend some business," the captain said.

"Yeah, I'm sure Alberto, Andre, and Emilio would be happy to explain their alibis to Fernando," I added. "Oh, and let us know if you get another call from the supposed kidnapper," I said over my shoulder. I was happy to get away from Emilio before I was forced to put my boxing skills to the test.

By the time we reached the kitchen, I'd cooled off a bit. I sat down at the table, shaking my head. "Emilio has really been pushing my buttons." I almost added, "The way you pushed mine yesterday."

The captain grinned. "Yep, that guy can really get under your skin, can't he? That's one of the hardest things about being a policeman. You have to keep your cool when you run into difficult people. At times, I've clenched my fists so hard my fingernails have cut into my skin. But if you can't control yourself, you can be sued for harassment."

The phone tracer guys appeared and stopped at the table. "It's all finished, Captain," a short, stout man stated.

"Thanks," the captain said. "Were you able to trace that last call?"

The same man answered, "No, I'm sure most of the bastards use throwaway cell phones these days."

"I'm sure you're right, but as you know, we have to set things up anyway," the captain commented.

The men nodded and left through the kitchen door.

I glanced at my watch. "It's three-thirty. I think I'll go outside for a breath of air and call my girlfriend."

"Sure. And I think I'll check and see if Eduardo has the list of business acquaintances who have his unlisted number. I know the Feds will want to investigate those people as well as Emilio, Andre, and Alberto."

"By the way, Captain, how long does it take for the DNA lab people to finish their testing?"

"It depends on a lot of things, but generally it takes at least a week and sometimes longer."

"I see."

I leaned against the garage and punched in Amberly's number. The sun felt good on my skin. The pink beach house had become more oppressive by the hour.

"Hey, what's happening?" I asked when I heard her voice.

"Not much and probably nothing nearly as exciting as you're experiencing."

"Yep, there is quite a bit going on here; and one of the things going on is me trying to control my temper. Andre and Emilio have been pushing my buttons big time!"

Amberly chuckled. "Don't punch anyone out. Your fists would probably be considered lethal weapons since you're an amateur boxer!"

"Yeah...that's funny. Don't worry. I've had plenty of practice of keeping my cool dealing with high-school smart asses.

"Fernando, the oldest son in the family just showed up. He's got black hair and was in New York at the time of the murder. At least I presume he was. Maria will be arriving this evening, as I probably mentioned, but I'll be with you when she arrives. By the way, where did you decide we'd go for dinner?"

"We're going to the Chart House. I made reservations for eight, in case you might have problems getting away."

"Good girl. I hope we won't need to cancel like Alberto did last evening, though he probably forgot to cancel under the circumstances."

"Brandon, a few minutes ago you mentioned that you presumed Fernando was in New York at the time of the murder, and he had dark hair."

"Uh-huh. That's right."

"It's probably off the wall, but there are such things as wigs, you know. How does his size differ from the suspects?"

"Well...now...let me think. I suppose he is about the right height though he may be a bit slimmer than the other guys...I really wasn't noticing. So if he donned a blond wig and wore sunglasses, he might pass for the abductor. But why on earth would he be wearing a blond wig while he talked to his sister in the cupola? And how could any human being kill his sister?"

"I agree, Brandon. But remember, sociopaths usually act completely normal and are the last people anyone would suspect to be a murderer."

"That's true, sweetheart. I'll mention it to the captain. It will be easy enough to check on Fernando's whereabouts in New York. I must go. My student Jimmy Taylor should be showing up for the re-enactment at any time now. I'll call as soon as I can take off."

"You take care now, Brandon."

"Don't worry; I'm sure no one wants to harm me."

"I wouldn't be so sure. You're the only witness, and if you're dead, there won't be a witness."

"I never thought about that." *And I wish you hadn't either!* "I'll ask the captain to look out for me!"

After I switched off my cell, I discovered that a tiny, niggling had started on the worry side of my brain. I suppose if someone kills for the first time, there would be no hesitation to kill the second time. Ah well, *Que Sera, Sera.*

I jumped when I heard footsteps in the garage. Was someone watching and waiting for a chance to "do me in?" I was relieved when I saw it was the captain. He was holding a typewritten page.

"I'm leaving you in charge, Sterling. I need to get to the station to fax these names that Eduardo gave me of his business acquaintances. I'll be back in time for the re-enactment."

Damn, now who is going to protect me? "Okay, perhaps I'll just wait out here. The environment in the house seems awful hostile towards me at the moment. And also my student, Jimmy Taylor, should be arriving soon."

"It doesn't matter to me, but you might want to be in the living room in case the kidnapper calls again. You also might pick up something from the actions and attitudes of our three suspects."

"Okay, but hurry back. You don't want to miss any of the action, do you?"

The captain cocked his head. "Hey, I sense you've got something on your mind, Sterling. What is it?"

His statements surprised me. No way was this amateur-boxing champion going to admit he was a bit frightened for his life! Before I could answer, he interrupted my thoughts.

His smile was coy. "Don't worry, Sterling, no one is going to do you in with all the people in the house. I'm sure that thought has passed through your mind. Right?"

My smile was tentative. "I really hadn't thought about it until my girlfriend mentioned that my life might be in danger, since I was the only witness."

He patted my back. "Then I suggest you not talk to your girlfriend for a while. Hey, if I thought your life was in danger, I'd put you into the witness protection program. You'll be fine. I won't be long." Waving, he jumped into his police car.

I waved back, while watching a red neon light flashing "Watch out, watch out, watch out" flitting across my vision. "Okay, Brandon, you're letting your imagination run wild," I lectured myself as if I were speaking to one of my students. "Get on inside. It's still an hour before the re-enactment. Hell, you might as well have a brandy, if someone offers. One brandy isn't going to make you drunk. You'll probably make a better identification if you're more relaxed. When Jimmy Taylor arrives, he can ring the doorbell. No use waiting out here any longer." Happy with my rationalizations, I entered the kitchen with a buoyant step.

I was not deliberately trying to walk quietly, but I guess the heavy carpet muffled any noise my tennis shoes made. I stopped just short of the living-room entrance when I heard loud-mouth Emilio talking about the captain and me.

"Those two morons remind me of Andy Griffith and Barney Fife on *The Andy Griffith Show,*" Emilio was saying. "Imagine a re-enactment of a presumed murder – sounds pretty dumb to me."

"It doesn't sound dumb to me," Alberto commented. "But personally, I don't think Brandon is going to be able to tell the difference among us three. I've never noticed how much we are alike in size as well as being blond, so I think we'll all remain suspects."

"I agree with Emilio," Fernando said. "It's dumb to think that anyone in this family could have anything to do with harming Rosalia." He put his hand over his mouth as if to stop threatened sobs.

"When is the FBI supposed to get here?" Andre asked curtly. "They are the ones who should be looking at the names of the people Dad gave this unlisted number to and not those fumbling, bumbling bozos who don't know which end is up!"

Deciding that this would be a good time to make my appearance, I stepped into the living room and watched with interest the surprised, then concerned, expressions on the occupant's faces.

Glancing around, I said, "I didn't mean to sneak up on anyone, but as the saying goes: 'an eavesdropper never hears anything good about himself!' And just to clear up a few things, the captain is at the police station faxing those names on the list to the FBI. My understanding is the Feds will be here in the morning. The captain has been working with them all along. I'm sure they are doing a complete investigation on the backgrounds of everyone in the living room except Eduardo and Estrella. I might add they're checking on where everyone says he was yesterday." I wished I had a camera to take a picture of the astonished expressions on Emilio's, Andre's and Fernando's faces. Evidently they had not thought about the FBI checking up on their whereabouts. Alberto seemed as calm as usual.

"Don't pay any attention to Emilio and Andre," Alberto told me. "They've always held an exalted opinion of themselves. Perhaps they think they're above the law and shouldn't be investigated. Won't you change your mind and have a brandy?"

I didn't think he'd ever ask! "Sure, why not. Thanks, Alberto." I followed him over to the liquor cabinet.

Eduardo, holding his snifter, came over to where we were standing. "You can freshen up my glass also, Alberto. Please accept my apology for Andre's and Emilio's bad manners, Brandon. I believe Alberto is correct in his summation of their characters. Thank God my girls didn't turn out to be snobs." His eyes glistened at the mention of his girls.

I held back the urge to reach out and hug the sad man. I patted his shoulder instead. "Don't let it bother you, Eduardo. I'm sure they're just upset." I was so thrilled to be offered a brandy, I could have forgiven anyone for almost anything.

Alberto poured brandy into Eduardo's glass then poured one for me. "Thanks, Alberto," I said and tried not to gulp the contents all at once.

Eduardo returned to his chair.

"Come and sit by me, Brandon," Estrella said.

Fernando shot a few daggers my way and moved away from Estrella, leaving me a place on the sofa.

"I'm sure none of this…this…situation has been pleasant for you, either, Brandon," Estrella said, with a catch in her voice. "I'm afraid anxiety brings out the worst in people sometimes. I think if you'd met Andre and Emilio in different circumstances, you'd have seen a different attitude."

I don't think so, dear Estrella, I was thinking but said, "You have enough on your mind without being concerned about my feelings. How are you holding up? Do you have a doctor here in the area? Do you need something to keep you calm?"

The corners of her mouth crinkled up ever so slightly. "I've never been much of a drinker, but this brandy seems to be keeping me relatively calm. Thank you for your concern."

The sharp ring of the phone caused Eduardo to jump up, almost spilling his drink. He ran to the desk and lifted the phone quickly. "Hello," he said, breathlessly. After a few seconds he said, "Who is this please?" A few more seconds passed. "Who do you wish to speak to? Please tell me who you are and who you want to speak with? Hello, hello, who is this?" He held the phone for a few more seconds then hung up shaking his head. "Do you think the tracer had time to kick in?"

"From what I understand, the tracer is now instantaneous, but the captain is quite sure a throwaway cell would be used by anyone connected to a kidnapping."

"I think the kidnapper is deliberately tormenting us," Andre snapped.

"What would be the point, Andre?" Eduardo asked. "My bank has already placed the million dollars into the Cayman bank. If the kidnapper is someone not in this room, then I would expect he's left the states. It would make no sense for him to be making calls just to torment us."

Andre's face paled. "Dad, what do you mean by if the kidnapper is someone not in this room? You don't really believe that one of us could have harmed Rosalia, do you?"

Eduardo regarded Andre with cold speculation. "I'm not sure what I believe anymore, Andre."

Andre stood and wagged his finger at me. "It's all your fault. You saw someone who you *think* looks like Alberto or Emilio or me, and because of your ridiculous theory about family members and close friends being first on the suspect list, you've turned Eduardo against us."

I looked at Eduardo and shook my head. I was not going to dignify that accusation with a reply.

"Andre, I'm so very disappointed in your attitude and behavior," Eduardo replied in a quiet tone. "Brandon saw what he saw. And so far as the family members and close friends being first on the suspect list, that is not his theory; it's a police theory. I advise you to sit down and try some self-control. You've made a fool of yourself more than once today."

Andre sat down without another word, but he continued to glare at me. He wasn't much older than my senior students. I'd love to take him across my knee and whack him a few times. I had a feeling Eduardo would enjoy that exercise as well.

The sound of a doorbell caught everyone by surprise. I had a feeling that Jimmy Taylor had arrived.

I stood. "Do you have a doorbell at the kitchen door?" I asked Eduardo.

"Yes, and that doorbell has a different ring from the front doorbell. That ring came from the kitchen."

"Then I believe it could be my student, Jimmy Taylor. I'll go check."

When I reached the kitchen and opened the door, I discovered it was indeed Jimmy. He was wearing a green tee shirt and tan shorts and carrying a plastic bag.

"Hey, Jimmy. Come on in."

"Hello, Mr. Sterling. I brought the white shirt and shorts like you said."

"Thanks." I took the bag and pulled out the contents. "These are similar to the ones the assailant was wearing. They'll do just fine."

The door opened and the captain walked in.

"Captain Delaney, this is my senior student, Jimmy Taylor. He's agreed to be in the re-enactment."

The captain held out his hand. "Glad to meet you, Jimmy. Thanks for helping us out."

Jimmy grinned. "I'm happy Mr. Sterling called. I'll have something to tell my friends on Monday."

"I tell you what, Jimmy. If you could wait until Mr. Sterling or I give you the go-ahead, I'd appreciate it if you'd keep it quiet at this time. We're trying to keep the media and busybodies at bay for a few days if we can. Okay?"

"Sure. And I haven't mentioned it to anyone since Mr. Sterling called."

"That's great, Jimmy," I said.

"The Feds are checking on those phone numbers Eduardo gave me plus the family member's backgrounds," the captain told us.

"They are especially interested in the whereabouts of everyone yesterday. They have so much technology at their fingertips, I don't think it will take too long."

"Good," I answered, glancing at my watch. "It's almost time for the re-enactment. Shall we go to the living room and give a rundown of how we're going to set things up, Captain?"

"Yes, we'd better. By the way, did anything of importance happen while I was gone?"

"Yes, Eduardo received another breathing-only phone call. I expect the caller was using a throwaway cell. Afterwards, sweet, adorable Andre accused me of turning Eduardo against his family with *my* theory about family members and close friends always being first on the suspect list. But Eduardo basically told him to sit down and stop making a fool of himself."

"Good for Eduardo!" the captain exclaimed. "Well, let's go. I'm sure there is going to be a lot of moaning and groaning by Emilio and Andre, so try and keep your cool."

"If I've made it this far, I think I'll do okay."

Chapter 9

Addressing the group in the living room, Captain Delaney explained how the re-enactment would be carried out. Andre, Emilio, Alberto, and Jimmy would take turns wearing the white shirt and shorts Jimmy brought along in his bag, don sunglasses, and run down the porch steps.

I would be standing and facing the ocean until I was given the word *turn,* then I'd give a quick glance towards the cupola steps as I'd done yesterday, then exit the gate. Of course, I would not know which order the four young men would be running down the steps. I would remember each one by the numbers one, two, three, and four.

"Are there any questions?" the captain asked. When no one answered, he said, "Okay, Sterling, you can go on out and stand by the gate and face the ocean. When the guys are ready to run down the steps, I'll give you the word."

I nodded and headed for the door wondering why no one had bitched and complained. I had a feeling Eduardo had lectured them about good behavior. I also had a feeling that I would have a difficult time picking out the guy who looked most like the one I'd seen yesterday.

The re-enactment was over. Everyone was seated in the living room. I glanced around the room at Andre, Emilio, and Alberto. With their faces etched with worry, they were staring at me. Except for Alberto, who had fully cooperated in every way, I would have liked to prolong the moment just to make them squirm a bit longer.

I cleared my throat, wishing I had a drum roll to make my announcement. "The only person I can eliminate as being the person I saw running down the steps, is number four who appeared thinner than the man I saw yesterday."

Captain Delaney smiled. "As everyone in this room knows, number four is Jimmy Taylor."

"I couldn't tell the difference between numbers one, two, and three," I told them.

"So what does that mean?" Eduardo asked.

"I suppose it means we still have three suspects that don't have airtight alibis," I answered. "Right, Captain?"

"I couldn't have said it better myself," he replied, pulling out his ringing cell phone. "Excuse me while I answer this."

"So where do we go from here?" Emilio growled.

"Captain Delaney will have to answer that," I said. "I suppose when the Feds arrive tomorrow, we'll have a better handle on the situation."

The captain returned with an enigmatic expression. He shot Fernando one of his mean looks. "That call was from the FBI. Why did you lie about where you were yesterday, Fernando?"

Fernando's face grew ashen. He glanced furtively at his dad. "It's a long story, and it has nothing to do with what happened to Rosalia."

Captain Delaney did not try to conceal his displeasure at having caught Fernando in a lie. "We have plenty of time to hear your long story, Fernando."

Fernando, seated next to his mother, stood and folded his arms across his chest. "As you know, Dad and Mom, I've been interested in marine biology since I was in high school. Actually, I've had a passion for the subject, and it's grown through the years. Last week, I made an appointment with the dean of Dobb's college in Orlando. It has the best marine biology department in the U.S. I enrolled for the fall term, Dad. I was going to tell you when I returned home tomorrow. I know you're hurt and disappointed about my decision to leave the company, but I thought long and hard about the situation, and I feel I must make the move. There are many people who would fill my position better than I. I'm sorry you had to find out in this way and especially since you've gone through so much already this weekend."

Eduardo's first look of amazement had vanished. He now appeared crestfallen and shook his head slowly. "There have been too many shocks this weekend. We'll discuss this later, Fernando.

Right now, Rosalia's problem is the only thing that's important."

Captain Delaney said, "Okay, Fernando, you'll need to answer some questions. Let's go to the kitchen."

The room had grown eerily quiet. I felt like tiptoeing as I followed the captain, Fernando, and Jimmy Taylor from the room.

"Sit down, Fernando," the captain instructed when we reached he kitchen. He held out his hand to Jimmy. "Thanks, son, you've been a great help. But remember to keep a lid on it until we let you know. Okay?"

"No problem, Captain. See you in class, Mr. Sterling."

"Great job, Jimmy," I told him. "Enjoy the rest of your weekend."

The captain opened his notebook and turned on his recorder. "So Fernando, your visit to the college yesterday can be substantiated, but where were you at five-thirty?"

"Since I have a love for marine biology and was in Orlando, where do you think I would be?"

The captain's eyebrows climbed towards his hairline as he looked first at me, then back to Fernando, then back to me. "Well, now...it appears that Fernando wants to take up our time with guessing games. Would you like to venture a guess, Sterling?"

"Well now, let me see...he could have been at a movie about dolphins or other sea creatures; Jacques Cousteau perhaps? Maybe he went to Disney. Are there sea animals there?" I figured he was talking about Sea World, but I decided to play dumb.

The captain glared at Fernando with smoldering eyes. "Okay. Why couldn't you have just told us you were at Sea World?"

Fernando pulled in a deep breath. "I'm sorry. This horrible situation with Rosalia and then my dad finding out about my visit to the college before I was prepared to discuss it with him has put me into a terrible mood I guess.

"Yes, I was at Sea World where I spent most of the afternoon and evening. I was there when I received the call from Dad about Rosalia. Since he thought I was in New York and would be flying here today, I decided to wait to drive over here this afternoon. It all seems so ridiculous now, but I didn't want to upset him even more with my news of leaving the firm. I'm sure Dad was grooming me to take his place in the company when he retired."

"Would anyone be able to verify that you were at Sea World at five-thirty yesterday, Fernando? I asked.

"No, I was alone. I still have my ticket stubs, but they only give the date and not when I left. But look, the perpetrator has been identified as having blond hair. You can see my hair is dark."

"Yes," the captain answered, "but you could have worn a wig and given your sister an explanation of some sort if you popped over here yesterday. You're about the same size as the other three. It's a terrible thought that you or anyone else would kill their own sister, but I can assure you, Fernando, that kind of thing has been done. Since you don't have an airtight alibi, you've now joined the list of suspects."

"So what kind of explanation do you think I could have given my sister as to why I was wearing a blond wig?"

"You're a handsome man," I said smiling, "you might have told her you had been asked to model wigs for men who were losing their hair, and you wore it to get her opinion."

"And don't forget," the captain added with an obvious wink to me, "you could have mentioned you were wearing the blond wig because you heard that blonds have more fun! Have you heard enough, Fernando, or shall we go on?"

"I hope you're both intelligent enough to know that those are absurd and ludicrous accusations," he answered.

"Do you have anything more to say to this suspect?" the captain asked me.

"Yes, I've just thought of one. Perhaps you decided to dye your hair blond, Fernando, so you wouldn't be recognized, and then you dyed it back dark again when you knew you'd be seeing your family today."

I noticed a flicker of concern in Fernando's dark brown eyes after my remark. "You have the vivid imagination of a child," he said in a monotone.

"That's all I have to say," I said.

"Then you're excused, Fernando, after you write down your home phone, cell phone, and address," the captain instructed.

Fernando wrote down the captain's requirements, and without another word, he left, giving me a curious glance.

The captain switched off his recorder. "I don't think he was lying about his reasons for being in Orlando, and his visiting Sea World seems logical also. The theory of him wearing a blond wig or dying his hair is quite a reach, in my opinion."

"I agree with you, Captain."

"But I will hand over the interview tape to the Feds tomorrow."

I glanced at my watch. "It's six-thirty, and I have a date with my beautiful and patient girlfriend. If you can't think of anything else I can help you with, I'd like to be excused."

He grinned broadly. "Ah, I'm not so old that I can't remember those raging hormones! Of course, you can leave. But I'd like you to be back here around ten in the morning. The Feds should be here, and I'm sure they'll want to question you. Maria should be here also. Rosalia might have told her twin something that might help us with the investigation. Perhaps she knew a secret about one of our suspects. You told me that Alberto said the twins were very close."

"That's true. You have my cell phone number. Call me if you need me before then."

He nodded. "Have a good time, Sterling. As the golden oldie goes, *Enjoy Yourself; It's Later Than You Think.*"

"There's a lot of truth to that. I hope Rosalia lived by that philosophy."

The captain stretched. "And let's not give up hope that the poor girl might still be alive."

"A person should never give up hope," I answered, then turned to leave.

Chapter 10

Once again, I was happy to be leaving the ominous pink beach house. On my way to the car, I pulled out my cell phone and punched in Amberly's number.

"Hey, sweetheart," I said, when I heard her hello. "Get your glad rags on. Everything is on go for the Chart House."

"Great! We'll have time for a glass of wine before we leave."

"That sounds good to me. I'll be stopping at my house for a quick shower and to change into my one-and-only expensive, casual outfit. I'll be at your place in thirty minutes."

"I'll be waiting for you in my one-and-only expensive, casual dress," she answered chuckling. "Do you think we should start playing the lottery?"

"No, Amberly, I've been around wealthy people for most of the weekend. I'm quite happy with our lifestyle. Wearing expensive casual a couple of times a year is quite enough for me."

"And for me also, Brandon. See you soon."

I drove down the road, whistling the song the captain had mentioned which happened to be my grandmother's favorite tune: *Enjoy Yourself; It's later Than You Think.* I hoped it would not be a portent of things yet to come.

Thirty minutes later, after ringing Amberly's doorbell, I watched with delight when a vision of loveliness wearing a two-piece white cutwork dress with an ankle-length skirt, opened the door. She'd parted her hair in the middle and had fastened her long amber tresses with white clips behind her ears. Tiny white shells adorned the clips and matching earrings. I held out my arms. "Come here, you gorgeous thing," I said. "I want to kiss you to make sure you're not a dream!"

Amberly floated towards me, and after a tight embrace, I kissed her gently, then passionately. "Um-m, I'm glad you're not a dream," I told her pulling back. "You're wearing that expensive, divine fragrance that Rosalia wore, I might add. You'd better watch out or we might not make it to dinner."

"Oh, no, we can't let that happen, not after all the preparation I've been through. And speaking of fragrances, I came close to swooning when you kissed me, and I picked up the scent of your delicious aftershave."

"I'll be sure to take a little bath in it later on."

To my delight, Amberly continued with her compliments. "And I love your outfit; anyone would know it was expensive casual."

"Ah, yes, do you think we could pass for a rich honeymooning couple from the north with me in my light-blue, open-necked shirt, light beige pants and matching jacket and you making a fashion statement in elegant white?"

Her lilting laughter caused the room to light up even brighter. "We might pass for a rich couple, except your car would give us away. Perhaps we should have thought of a car rental for the valet parking." She handed me a glass of wine.

"We'll have to remember that next year when we make our annual pilgrimage to the Chart House." I held up my glass. "To Rosalie: May she be alive and well."

With a somber expression, Amberly touched my glass. "To Rosalie: God bless her, wherever she may be." She took a sip from her glass. "We have a few minutes, so let's sit down. I'm anxious to know how the re-enactment turned out."

She curled her petite, high-heeled, white-sandaled feet under her on the sofa. "Were you able to pick out the perpetrator?"

I sat down next to her and almost twirled my wine glass. I'd need to buy some brandy and two snifters. "Nope, but I did eliminate my student, Jimmy, because he seemed thinner than the other three. Emilio, Alberto, Jimmy, and Andre wore identical clothes and sunglasses. Of course, I was only able to give them a glance as I had done when I first spied the perpetrator coming down the stairs yesterday. And there's been a new development since Rosalia's brother Fernando arrived."

"Oh? Tell me about it."

I quickly described our interview with Fernando and said, "So that means he lied about where he was on Friday afternoon, but in my opinion he's at the bottom of the suspect list."

Amberly's expression was one of surprise. "Things are really getting complicated. What happened in the interviews with Emilio, Andre, and Alberto?"

"I'll tell you all about it at dinner. But I will say that now we have four suspects and none have airtight alibis." I drained my glass. "We'd better go. We don't want to lose our table. We'd look pretty silly eating at MacDonald's in our expensive casual, wouldn't we?"

Laughing, she headed for the bedroom. "I'll just get my purse."

Amberly and I were seated at a table next to the window at the well-known and atmospheric Chart House. We'd both ordered our favorite fish – pompano with crab-meat dressing. We were sipping our wine while waiting for our salads.

Amberly pointed to the sailboats tied to the docks. "Whoever thought of building a restaurant in the middle of a yacht basin had a marvelous idea, don't you think?"

"Yes, indeed. I hear this place has been here for many years and is considered the best restaurant in the county, though it's quite expensive. My dad and mom treat me to dinner here whenever they come. The next time, you'll be with us."

Amberly grinned broadly. "I look forward to meeting your parents. I want to tell them what a fine, upstanding young man they raised."

Grinning, I reached for her hand. "Please don't…don't stop!"

"I'd better stop before you get big-headed. Changing the subject, you still haven't mentioned how the interviews went with Alberto, Andre, and Emilio."

I heaved a sigh. "Emilio's and Andre's interviews were quite testy." I gave her a short version of the interviews then said, "Alberto's interview went well, as I had expected. He continues to have a great attitude. I keep hoping he is not the culprit."

I glanced up at the waiter who set our salads on the table. I noticed his nameplate. "Thank you, Mike," I said.

Amberly speared a piece of lettuce. "As you've mentioned before, you have four suspects with no airtight alibis. And except for a bit of deductive reasoning on the part of you and the captain, none of them have a clear-cut motive."

"I have confidence that the Feds will come up with a motive after their investigation, and I have a gut feeling that Rosalia had recently discovered a secret about one of the suspects. Maria is arriving tomorrow. It's going to be difficult talking to her unless a miracle happens, *and* we have word from the kidnapper telling us where to look for Rosalia, *and* we find her alive *and* in relatively good health. Maria is heartbroken, I'm sure."

She nodded. "She must be. I'm curious to know whether she's picked up any thoughts from her twin. And I know it will be so sad for Rosalia's family and Alberto, that is, if he's not the murderer, to gaze at Maria and see her twin."

I crunched on a crisp piece of celery and wondered if everyone in the room could hear me chomping. "I would not want to change places with any of them, especially if one of them is guilty."

"So now that we've got that discussion behind us, let's choose a place for dancing to finish off a lovely evening. What do you say, Detective Sterling?"

"I say let's go to The Blue Room. They have a great jazz pianist, I've heard."

"Then The Blue Room it is," she proclaimed. "I'll get to enjoy your sexy after-shave even more."

"And I'll get to hold your sexy body close to mine and gaze into your eyes divine and make a little rhyme."

She giggled then said, "Brandon, I hope we'll always enjoy being with each other."

"I'm sure we will, sweetheart, as long as you keep wearing that divine perfume."

She blew me a kiss. "I promise."

I had a feeling I'd remember this evening for a long time, and I'd better because it only happened once a year! Our next dinner would be at a more moderate establishment. But then it wouldn't matter as long as I was with the woman I love.

Hours later, I lay listening to Amberly's quiet breathing as she slept curled next to me. We'd made exquisite love, and I was still basking in the afterglow. Though I would have preferred to continue to think about our perfect evening, fragments of the day kept slipping into my mind. The faces of the suspects popped in one at a time. They were all scowling except for Alberto. I wondered why I didn't have a gut feeling about one of them being the likely murderer. I knew my desire for Alberto to be innocent was because I liked him so much, and it had nothing to do with evidence. I moved a bit closer to Amberly hoping to absorb her dreams, so I could stop thinking about the suspects. I was unsuccessful. My dreams were nightmarish visions of four young men all traveling at great speeds with a body wrapped in a garment luggage bag bouncing around in the trunks of their cars.

Chapter 11

Sunday was a beautiful day. Amberly and I had enjoyed a leisurely breakfast, walked on the beach, showered together – which led to more love making – and were now having a second cup of coffee. It was almost time for me to leave for the pink beach house. I didn't want to go.

"Brandon, you'd better get your things together," Amberly told me. "It's almost ten. But I want you to know that last evening was perfect." A wide grin spread across her lovely countenance. "I'll miss you tonight."

I made a face. "And whose idea was it that I only stay over on the weekends?"

Her eyes sparkled. "It's better for a number of reasons, as you well know. And haven't you heard of the old adage: 'Absence makes the heart grow fonder?' "

"I don't know about that, but it certainly makes me grow in other ways!"

Giggling, she got up, stood behind my chair, and gave me a good neck rub. "If you were here every night, I'd never get my lesson plans done or papers graded. We'd be exhausted from making love and not fit for class!"

I reached back and took her hands in mine. "You're right, sweetheart. So far, our arrangement has worked really well, but I always hate to leave you, and we're being cheated out of our Sunday afternoon."

"I know, but we have many more days to look forward to. By next weekend, I have a feeling the mystery will be solved."

I stood and held her in my arms. "That would be pretty quick to solve a murder, but I hope so, for everyone's sake."

"Be sure and call me when you get a chance."

"I will." I reluctantly pulled away and headed for the bedroom.

"Guess I'd better get my expensive, casual wardrobe together. Maybe Eduardo will take us all out to The Chart House." I was joking, of course. And even if Rosalia was found alive and he would want to celebrate, it wouldn't be the same without my sweetheart.

Once again I parked on the side of the road when I pulled up to the pink beach house. I noticed there was a black car with tinted windows. To me, it looked like the kind of vehicle I thought the FBI might use. I'd never met anyone from the FBI and hoped the guys wouldn't be seven feet tall with menacing eyes; that's the way I'd always thought of them when I was a kid.

I walked into the garage and rang the doorbell at the kitchen door. A few seconds later, Captain Delaney appeared and stepped out.

"Hey, Sterling. The Feds have arrived and are listening to the last taped interview."

"Any new developments, Captain?"

"Eduardo received another call about ten minutes ago – the same muffled voice instructing him to not contact the police or FBI. Like the second call, this one was obviously a ruse, because the kidnapper already has received the money in his bank in The Cayman Islands."

I nodded. "I agree. If the kidnapper is a family member, he'd continue to have his accomplice make calls, hoping to take the suspicion off him, since he would be present when the calls came in."

The captain gave a half laugh. "I'm convinced that one of those four young guys in the living room did the deed and thinks he's really smart."

"Did Maria arrive last evening?" I asked.

"Yes, she arrived around ten. Naturally she was tired and distraught, so I told her I'd talk with her this morning. Eduardo came into the kitchen just before you arrived and fixed a tray to take to her room. The Feds said they would sit in on the interview with Maria. I thought I'd give her about thirty more minutes."

I pulled in a deep breath. "The poor girl; she must be going through hell."

He nodded. "I would say so. Let's go on in. The Feds should be through listening to the tapes by now."

We entered the kitchen and, to my surprise, the men sitting at the table were not seven feet tall with piercing eyes. So much for my childhood impressions of the FBI!

"Ted Whelan and Jack Heywood, I want you to meet Brandon Sterling. He witnessed the attack and has been a great help to me," the captain said, as we walked over to the men.

I held out my hand half expecting a bone-crunching handshake. "Nice to meet you."

"Nice to meet you, too," both men replied.

Their handshakes were strong but not bone-crunching. I was feeling a bit less intimidated.

"Let's sit down," Ted said. "I'd like to discuss the interviews."

We pulled up our chairs to the table.

Ted glanced at a few of the notebook pages and said, "Captain, which one of the suspects are you leaning toward?"

Captain Delaney glanced at the ceiling for a few seconds then shook his head. "I've looked at my notes and listened to the tapes several times, and I can't make up my mind. I don't even have a gut feeling about any of them, which is unusual for me. I will say that Fernando is at the bottom of the list. As you heard on the tape, he would have had to be wearing a wig or had dyed his hair which sounds rather remote. Though he lied about where he was on Friday afternoon, he was close to his sister and his motive for shoving her from the cupola would have to be unbelievably strong."

A semblance of a smile turned up the corners of Jack's mouth. "After talking to you yesterday, Captain, we took a copy of Fernando's drivers' license to the hotel in Orlando where his secretary said he was staying. The hotel desk clerk said the photo looked like Fernando except the guy had blond hair. He also mentioned that the man in question had spent most of the evening in the hotel bar."

With a face lit in triumph, the captain turned to me. "Well, how about that, Sterling?"

I was in shock. "As you heard on the tape, we were simply making cracks about how he'd need to have been wearing a wig or have dyed his hair to resemble the suspect. I'll be really interested to hear his reasons for doing that!"

Ted nodded. "And according to his interview on the tape, his father called him early in the evening on his cell phone, thinking he was in New York. If he was so close to his sister, don't you think he would have been in his hotel room waiting anxiously for a call from his father and not sitting in a bar?"

"I know I would have reacted that way," I told him, "but as Captain Delaney says, people don't always react the way you would. Perhaps he was so upset he wanted to get his mind off his worries."

"That could be, Sterling," Ted answered.

"I think it's time for another interview with Fernando. I suppose he's in the living room with the family. Would you find him and escort him back here, Brandon?" the captain asked.

"Sure," I answered.

When I entered the living room, I noticed empty cups and plates sitting on the coffee table. I wondered who'd gone to the bakery this morning. All the family was present except for Eduardo. I figured he was upstairs with Maria.

"Good morning," I said.

Estrella's eyes were swollen and red. "Good morning, Brandon."

I sat down on the sofa beside her. I lifted her hand and kissed it. "I can't imagine how difficult all this has been for you, Estrella, but I think we'll be making good progress now that the Feds are here."

She gave me a tentative smile. "I hope so. God, how I hope so."

I squeezed her hand and glanced towards Fernando who was sitting in a chair opposite the sofa. "Fernando, the Feds want to ask you something. Will you come with me, please?"

His questioning expression held a trace of fear. "I don't suppose I have a choice, do I?"

"Good luck, Fernando," Emilio said with a smirk. "Don't let those guys try and trip you up."

"It's my impression that the Feds are trying to find Rosalia," I retorted. "They are in the business of helping instead of trying to trip people up." I'd had enough of Emilio's sarcasm.

Emilio gave me one of his "you're a moron" looks. "Well, now, I expect that would depend on whether you are a suspect or not."

"You do have a point, Emilio," I answered. "But if you have nothing to hide, no one can trip you up."

Emilio's eyes shot flares at me, but he said nothing.

I kissed Estrella on the cheek. "Hang in there, sweet lady." I stood. "Let's go, Fernando."

In the kitchen, the captain introduced Fernando to Jack and Ted then pointed to a chair.

Jack went first. "We've listened to the tapes of your interview, Fernando, and we have a few questions. I'm sure you remember the captain and Brandon jokingly discussing the possibility of your wearing a wig or dying your hair to perhaps disguise yourself in case anyone might see you, that is, if you came over to see your sister Rosalia with intentions of murdering her. On the tape, you said the suggestion was ludicrous. I'm sure you never thought a FBI agent would be checking you out at your hotel in Orlando. By the way, we got your hotel information, along with your flight, from your secretary in New York. When we showed your photo around, which came from your driver's license, the hotel personnel identified you but said you were blond. So the captain's and Brandon's discussion of the possibility of your dying your hair or wearing a wig wasn't so ludicrous after all, was it?"

Almost imperceptibly, Fernando's shoulders seemed to slump. He shifted in his chair and stared into space as if he were gathering his thoughts. "I know my explanation is going to sound ridiculous. As you heard on the tape, I want to start a new life away from the company. When I made the decision to go back to college and become a marine biologist, I felt a huge weight had been lifted from my shoulders. After I registered at the college, I got this silly idea to dye my hair blond to…you know…well…I guess I felt something like a person might feel after a divorce. I thought dying my hair would change my persona, and it did. I felt young and free and full of hope. Of course, that was before I received the horrible phone call from my dad. I went downstairs to the bar to drown my troubles. I sat there thinking that while I'd been rejoicing in my newfound freedom my sister had been presumably murdered and then kidnapped. And I'd been caught in a lie, because my dad thought I was in New York. I wanted to get into my car and run over to the beach house and comfort my family, but I couldn't. I didn't want to reveal what I'd been up to because I knew it would add to their burdens. So after I'd had more than a few drinks, I trudged into my room and dyed my hair back to its natural shade. And you know the rest of the story."

He looked first at the captain and then to me. "I'm sorry I acted like an asshole, but you can imagine how strange I felt when you started throwing out those remarks about my wearing a wig or dying my hair. Though I can't prove it, I swear to all of you that I never came to the beach house on Friday, and I most certainly did not push my sister from the cupola. I loved Rosalia. Everyone did."

"You're right about one thing, Fernando; you can't prove any of it. And as you must know by now, if you've told any more lies, we'll find out," Ted commented in a stern tone.

"Yes, I'm quite aware of that, sir. And when my dad finds out about the hair-dying scenario, he'll most likely be happy that I resigned from the company."

I wondered what was going on inside Fernando's head. Was he really remorseful, and most important, was he at last telling the truth?

"That's all for now, Fernando," Ted said.

"Would you check on Maria and see if she's available to talk with us?" the captain asked.

"I can do that. I'm sure she's suffering from jet lag. Eduardo brought her a tray upstairs. They've been talking for a while now, so perhaps she's more fully awake."

We all watched as Fernando exited.

There was a long pause before the captain said, "Quite a story, don't you think? His explanation is so way out it's almost believable. But as we all know, killers can tell whopper lies."

I let out a long sigh. "I'm aware of that."

"Do you have any ideas about motive?" Ted asked.

"The captain and I believe Rosalia may have uncovered a secret about one of the suspects," I told him. "The kidnapping might have been done to make it look like an outsider committed the crime. But we could be dead wrong of course, pardon the pun, and it might actually be a business associate who hired a young blond male to do the shooting because he simply wanted the ransom. But we believe Rosalia must have known her killer since she was standing with her back to him as she looked through binoculars. We think she took him up to the cupola to show him the dolphins."

Ted tapped his pencil on the table. "Sounds like you two have summed up the situation pretty good. But there is also the possibility that the killer introduced himself as a friend of her dad's, or of some member of the family. After they talked, she offered to take him up to see the dolphins. It could be coincidental that he was a young, blond male."

"We've considered that," the captain responded. "But I'm leaning towards any one of those four young men in the house."

Jack crossed his arms. "Background checks are being done on those four as we speak. We'll find out even more about them as well as their whereabouts on the day of the murder. Of course, we may not be able to pinpoint exactly where they were at the time of the murder. Captain, you and Sterling have done a good job of placing them possibly in the vicinity of this beach house. When our crew finishes with a character study of their habits and so forth, we might get a better handle on a motive."

I was sitting in a position at the table where I could observe who entered from the hall. I could feel my eyes widen when a beautiful young woman, with dark hair pulled back into a pony tail, walked into the kitchen. She was wearing white shorts and a red, off-the-shoulder blouse. Gold loop earrings dangled from her ears. In spite of her swollen eyes, she looked fabulous. I knew I was gawking at Maria.

"I'm Maria Vargas," she said with a tentative smile.

Everyone at the table stood up. I wondered what they were thinking.

The captain pulled out a chair. "Please sit down, Maria," he instructed in a soft voice. He then introduced himself, the Feds, and me. "I know this has been a terrible ordeal for you, but please know we're doing everything we can to find the kidnapper and of course, your sister." He sat down next to her.

Maria covered her mouth with her fingers for a few seconds. I could see she was trying to gain control. "I'm sure you're doing your best."

The captain asked, "Did Rosalia give you any indication that she might have something on her mind that was worrying her?"

Before answering, she reached into her shorts pocket, pulled out a Kleenex, and blotted her eyes. "Rosalia and I talked several times over the phone this week. And yes, I could tell something was on her mind. I asked her if she was having pre-wedding jitters. She said that was not the problem. I told her I knew something was bothering her big time, and it might help if she confided in me. She said, 'I've discovered something about someone that would probably ruin his life. My conscience tells me I must do something about it, but my heart is holding me back. It's a decision I'll have to make on my own. Not you nor anyone else can help me. When I make my decision, you'll be the first to know, other than the person I'm telling you about. Try not to worry about it.' Of course, I told her I would be worried until she got back with me. And because I had a bad feeling about what she'd told me, I cautioned her to be careful. That was the last thing I said to her before I told her I loved her and hung up." Maria pressed her lips tightly together and blotted her eyes again.

I knew this beautiful young woman was in agony. "Maria, I've always been interested in twins and their close bond. I've read that often if one twin is feeling pain, sometimes the other twin will feel it also. Has that ever happened with you and Rosalia?"

She nodded. "It's happened many times. Once Rosalia picked up my toothache pain and had to go to the dentist with me. When the dentist gave me a shot of Novocain, we both stopped hurting! I think that experience was the most dramatic until late Friday afternoon around five-thirty, that is your time of course, I was asleep and was awakened sharply by a terrible pain in my neck. I sat up in bed, and just as suddenly as the pain had come, it disappeared. I tried to go back to sleep, but I was overwhelmed with a feeling of depression. I knew it had something to do with Rosalia. I tossed and turned for an hour or so and was about to get up and call her, when my phone rang. It was Dad. When he told me what happened, I felt she was dead or unconscious; that's why my physical pain went away and why I am feeling so depressed. I haven't told Dad, though, because I don't want my parents to give up hope just yet. False hope is better than no hope at all." She covered her face with her hands, but tears slipped from under her fingers.

I reached for my handkerchief and pressed it into her hands. She blotted her face and pulled in a deep breath. "Thank you," she told me. "I'm sorry. I'm trying so hard not to break down in front of Mom and Dad."

"No apology is necessary, Maria," Ted said kindly. "I wish we didn't have to ask you these questions. You've been very helpful; you've verified a theory that the captain and Sterling have come up with. They both feel your sister knew a secret or something that would ruin the life of the man who pushed her to her death. We know it's possible that her knowledge could have indicted one of your dad's business associates, but we strongly feel it's someone here in the family. I know this is a blow to you, but it could be Alberto, Andre, Emilio, or even Fernando. As your dad must have told you, Sterling here, witnessed the incident. The blond male he saw running down the steps fits the description of those four. Though Fernando has dark hair, he's just confessed that on Friday, he dyed it blond then re-dyed it. You'll need to ask him to explain that strange situation."

Maria appeared momentarily confused. She shook her head vehemently. "No, no! There is no way anyone in my family or Alberto or Emilio could have harmed Rosalia. They loved and respected her. It's just not possible."

I reached for her hand and held it. "But if this secret, or whatever information she knew, was about a business associate of your dad's, then why did she say her heart was holding her back? If the information was about someone she hardly knew, I don't think she would have made that statement, do you?" I squeezed her hand then released it.

"I understand what you're saying, and I've even thought of it myself, but I always come up with the same answer; it's impossible that Alberto, Andre, Emilio, or Fernando could have harmed her," she answered in a quavering voice.

I understood her anguish.

With a faint smile, she offered me my handkerchief. "I should launder this first."

I shook my head. "No, no. Please keep it. I have many more. Christmas presents from my students."

"I bet you are a good teacher."

"Thank you, Maria. I try to be."

"Does anyone else have a question for Maria?" the captain asked.

Ted, Jack, and I shook our heads.

"Thank you, Maria," the captain said.

Without another word, she left. I wondered if the captain had sown a few seeds of doubt about her brother being a suspect, but probably not. She seemed so sure of Rosalia's devotion to Fernando and vice a versa. But seemingly devoted people had murdered loved ones when the stakes were high enough.

The captain switched off the recorder. "So guys, what is your take on the interview?"

"The info she gave about her twin knowing something about someone she loved gives us the motive we've been looking for. Now we just need to find out what Rosalia knew. That might not be so easy," Ted interjected.

The captain held out his arms in a long stretch. "Let's take a break. I think it's time for a bite to eat." He looked at me and grinned. "It's been a long time since I've eaten my breakfast donuts."

"Why don't you two go and get something?" Ted commented. "You can bring us back a burger. We'll stay in case another call comes in from the kidnapper."

"I think I'll ask the group if we can bring them something. Okay, Captain?" I asked.

"Sure, why not?"

When I entered the living room I found a quiet group staring at the TV turned to a news program. I had the feeling that no one really knew what the newscaster was saying.

Estrella glanced up. "Hello, Brandon."

I walked over to where she and Eduardo were sitting on the sofa. "The captain and I are going out for a burger. May we bring something back for any of you?"

"That's most considerate, Brandon, but thank you no," Estrella answered. "Alberto and Maria are going to bring lunch for us."

"I guess we've pretty much taken over your kitchen."

"Not to worry, Brandon," Eduardo told me. "We have a very large dining room right through that door that opens into the kitchen. We can eat there. Don't give it another thought."

"Have Alberto and Maria already left?" I asked.

"I'm not sure. Alberto mentioned he needed to get his wallet, so they may be upstairs," Estrella commented.

"I just remembered I wanted to ask him a question about his garment bag luggage."

Estrella pointed towards the hall. "You can check upstairs if you wish, Brandon."

"Thanks, I'll do that." I glanced at Andre, Emilio, and Fernando, who were still staring blankly at the TV. They hadn't bothered to even look up. I'm sure they thought of me as enemy number one!

I ran up the steps wondering which bedroom Alberto would be in. I remembered where his clothes were hanging earlier and decided to try there. Once again, the heavily carpeted hallway muffled my footsteps. I reached the open door and stopped dead in my tracks, as the saying goes. I couldn't believe what I was seeing. Maria and Alberto were locked in a tight embrace and kissing passionately. I wanted to turn and run, but I was afraid my legs would buckle if I tried to take a step. I watched as the kiss ended, then hugging each other even closer, they both wept uncontrollably. I slowly backed away from the door and ran down the hall and down the steps. I felt as if I'd had a punch in the stomach from one of my boxing opponents. What the hell could that passionate kiss mean? I'd need to tell the captain, but I wanted to think about it first. I tried to pull myself together when I stepped into the kitchen.

"Estrella told me that Maria and Alberto were going out to get lunch for the group," I said. "And if you don't need me for anything else right now, I think I'll pass on lunch and get back to my apartment. I need to work on lesson plans."

"It's not a problem, Sterling, unless Ted and Jack want to ask you more questions," the captain answered.

Ted looked up from the Captain Delaney's notebook. "I think we've about covered everything at the present, so go ahead and do your thing, Brandon."

"The captain has my cell phone, but I'll write down my number for you and Jack. I'd like to be filled in on the background checks when they come in," I told him.

Ted pushed over a piece of paper and a pen. "I'd say by tomorrow at the latest, we'll have the information. The captain is right. You've been a big help, Sterling."

I wrote down my number. "Thanks. And if something comes

up and you need to talk with me, I'm usually up until eleven. Oh, perhaps I should get your number, Captain, in case I think of something."

"Sure," he said, handing over a card.

Just as I was about to turn to leave, Alberto and Maria entered. I prayed they wouldn't notice my neck pulsing at ninety beats per minute. I wondered if Estrella or Eduardo had mentioned that I'd gone upstairs to ask a question about the garment bag. I could see no evidence of them acting as if they knew I'd caught them in a compromising situation.

"Maria and I are going to get lunch for everyone. May we get you something?" Alberto asked.

I forced myself to act natural. "I'm going home and work on lesson plans, and the captain is bringing in a burger for Ted and Jack. But thanks anyway."

Alberto placed his arm around my shoulder. "Thanks again, for your kindness and consideration, Brandon. Will we see you tomorrow?"

"Yes, and perhaps before tomorrow if something comes up that I'm needed for." I was trembling on the inside from confusion, anger, disappointment, bewilderment, and I'd probably think of more reactions later. "I do have a question for you, Alberto. Do you or Rosalia have a garment bag as part of your luggage?"

A puzzled look crossed Alberto's face. "Yes, I do have one, but Rosalia didn't as I recall."

"Would it be too much trouble for you to go and check to see if the bag is still there?" I asked.

"Sure, I'll go check. It seems like I left it in the hall, but I'll check upstairs also. Why don't you wait for me in the car, Rosalia?"

Maria didn't look at all surprised at Alberto's mistake and didn't correct him. "Okay." She nodded at us and left through the kitchen door.

After Alberto exited, I said, "Since Rosalia is small, I have a theory that the abductor placed her into a luggage bag. It would be a good way to hide her and also keep blood and other DNA out of the car or truck."

"Alberto would be more aware of the garment bag than the others, don't you think?" Ted commented.

"That's true, but the other three knew that Rosalia and Alberto had flown, and at least one of them would most likely have a garment bag," I said.

Alberto returned, and with a perplexed expression he addressed me. "It's not in the hall closet or in the bedroom. My garment bag has disappeared. Brandon, did you suspect it was missing?"

"I have a theory that the kidnapper placed Rosalia's small body in that bag then put her into his vehicle. That's why your bag is missing."

Alberto placed his hand on his forehead as if to hold it up. He pulled in a deep breath. "That's a terrible image. It also means you feel sure she's dead. Right?"

"I'm afraid so, Alberto," I answered.

His face paled. "I'm not going to mention our conversation to anyone else just yet."

"That's up to you, Alberto," the captain said.

He nodded and left.

As if everyone was deep in thought, there was a brief pause before Jack spoke. "It must feel really strange to be in the company of the twin whose sister was killed. Every time Alberto looks at Maria, he must think about the woman he was engaged to and wishes it were his fiancée, don't you think?"

Okay, Brandon. That's your cue. Tell them what you saw. My conscience was urging me to speak up, but I just couldn't bring myself to do it.

"That's one way to look at it," the captain commented. "But perhaps her being there brings him a certain amount of comfort. If you noticed, he even called her Rosalia by mistake. But I wonder how different their personalities are."

"I saw a movie once where there was a good twin and an evil twin," Ted interjected. "The evil twin murdered the good twin, buried the body, and pawned herself off as the good one."

"Well, did she get caught?" I asked.

"Oh, yeah, don't you know that crime 'don't' pay?"

I tried to laugh with the others, but it was difficult. "I'm off. As I said, call me if you need me. I'll check in tomorrow after school."

I was glad that Maria and Alberto were nowhere in sight when I reached my car. I pulled out my cell phone and placed a call to Amberly.

As usual, her sweet voice soothed me. I tried to keep the concern out of my voice. "Hey, sweetheart. What are you doing?"

"I'm putting grades in my grade book. What are you doing?"

"I'm leaving the beach house, and I'm desperate to talk something over with you that just occurred."

"You're desperate, you say? I don't ever think I've ever seen you in that state of mind. Are you on the way over?"

"Yes, I should be there shortly."

"Has Rosalia's body been found?"

"No, it's nothing like that, but it's serious."

"You've really got my curiosity going. Have you had lunch?"

"No, have you?"

"No, I got too involved with my homework. I'll fix something right now. See you soon."

I was already feeling a bit better.

Before I had a chance to ring the doorbell, Amberly opened the door. I grabbed her and gave her my strongest bear hug. The sweet fragrance of her hair always acted as much like an aphrodisiac as her expensive, divine perfume.

She pulled back and smiled into my eyes. "You look more randy than desperate. I've got leftover pizza warming, and the salads and beers are on the table. Come on back."

I followed her into the dining room and sat down. I took a few swigs of beer and tried to get my thoughts organized.

She placed two plates of pizza on the table, sat down, and poured her beer into a glass. "Okay, now tell me what this is all about."

A re-run of the morning's activities crossed my mind. "I guess I should start with the interview with Alberto and Maria and then hit you with the bombshell."

Smiling and shaking her head, she crossed her arms. "Brandon! Can't you hit me with the bombshell first?"

I took another long swig of beer. "I'll try to make this short. Maria was called in for an interview. Incidentally, she is a clone of her twin. She said the afternoon that Rosalia was killed, she was awakened by a sharp pain in her neck, and then it disappeared. She believes that pain meant her twin is dead or unconscious. She told us that she and Rosalia were strongly bonded, and they often felt each other's physical and mental pain. Then she told us that Rosalia said she'd discovered something about someone that would ruin the person's life. Her conscience told her she must do something about it, but her heart was holding her back. But it was her decision, and she'd let Maria know when she'd decided what to do. Maria cautioned her to be careful."

Amberly stopped eating and laid down her fork. "So you were correct in believing Rosalia knew a secret about someone she was close to."

"Yes, and now for the bombshell."

She gripped the table with both hands. "Okay, I'm ready!"

"No, you'd better keep eating because I need to work into it."

She let out a long, exasperated sigh and picked up her fork. "Brandon, you do know how to make a long story even longer. Okay, then continue."

"I needed to ask Alberto if he or Rosalia had used a garment luggage bag on their flight. Estrella told me that I'd find Alberto upstairs getting his billfold, as he and Maria were going out to pick up lunch for everyone. I wasn't trying to eavesdrop, but I was wearing tennis shoes, and the carpet muffled my footsteps. I knew the bedroom he was occupying, so I went to that room. The door was open, and I caught Alberto and Maria in a tight embrace kissing passionately! When they drew apart, they held each other and sobbed."

The look of astonishment on Amberly's face was something to behold. "My God, in heaven! What do you make of that?"

"I'm not sure; that's why I want your input."

She propped her elbows on the table and lifted her glass, holding it with both hands. "Did they see you?"

"No, I backed away and moved out quickly."

"I take it you didn't mention what you'd seen to anyone."

"That's correct. I wanted to discuss it with you first. It could be really incriminating for them both. But of course, sooner or later I will have to expose them to the captain and the Feds. Oh, I forgot to mention that when they came through the kitchen, he mistakenly called Maria, Rosalia. She didn't correct him. Then Ted mentioned he'd seen a movie about a good twin and an evil twin. The evil twin murdered the good one and impersonated her. She was caught, and justice prevailed."

Amberly sipped her beer and put down her glass. "You're not thinking that Maria was the one who was murdered, and Rosalia and Alberto did the deed, are you?"

"I'd say it's in the realm of possibility, but not probable. Calling Maria by the wrong name was most likely a slip of the tongue, and she didn't think it necessary to correct him. It would be terribly complicated to make the exchange. Even though twins have the same DNA, I really think a mother and father would know which twin was which, don't you?"

"I would think so, but—"

"And after telling me he did have a garment luggage bag, Alberto checked and told me it was missing. So I strongly suspect Rosalia's body was moved in that bag."

She nodded. "I suppose somewhere down the line, Alberto and Maria had an affair but ended it because they didn't want to hurt Rosalia. They probably still have deep feelings for each other and feel extremely guilty now that they think she's dead."

I swallowed some pizza. "That makes sense, but there's a more ominous explanation. Alberto could have killed her so he and Maria could be together. Do you think that comment Rosalia made about discovering something about someone and her conscience told her she must do something about it but her heart was holding her back, could have been about Alberto and Maria's affair?"

"If Rosalia had discovered an affair, I believe she'd have let them know in no uncertain terms! That is, most women would have handled it that way, but that could be debated I suppose. I think the secret she uncovered had to do with business – something really dishonest, yet we really don't know anything definite at this point."

"Yeah, that't true."

For a few seconds, Amberly sipped her beer. "I think you should speak with Alberto and Maria about what you saw and ask for an explanation. Tell them you're duty-bound to tell the captain, but you wanted to give them a chance to explain. On the other hand, you could be placing yourself in danger if Alberto is the guilty party."

I was remembering Alberto's hand on my shoulder and his comment about my kindness and consideration. Was he really a con man? I still didn't want to believe it. "That's why I wanted to discuss the situation with you. You're the one who should be working with the police."

She smiled her thanks then turned serious. "I was just thinking about the Peterson case that was sensationalized on TV a few years back."

My stomach did a circus somersault. "I guess you mean the case where the soft-spoken, charismatic husband murdered his wife and unborn baby and dumped them into the bay in California?"

She sighed. "Yes, that's the one. He was well liked by everyone, so it seems, and many people thought he was 'Mr. Wonderful.' Though he never admitted to the murder, the experts proved he murdered his wife so he could continue his affair with another unsuspecting woman. Those experts believed he didn't get a divorce because he didn't want to destroy his 'Mr. Wonderful' reputation. Chilling isn't it?"

I pushed my plate away. "I guess you brought the case up because of Alberto's charismatic personality and everyone seeming to like him, including me! You are comparing Alberto to Peterson, aren't you?"

"Right, though I hope I'm wrong. I know you've formed a friendship with Alberto."

"But I lost respect for him when I saw him kissing Maria passionately. I can understand that he and Maria fell in love, but I can't understand why he planned to marry Rosalia."

Amberly's voice rang with sad reproach. "I refer again to the Peterson case. 'Mr. Wonderful' didn't want to ruin his reputation. In Alberto's case, he probably would lose his job with Rosalia's dad, and Maria would be looked down on as a terrible person to have stolen her twin's fiancé."

I reflected for a few seconds. "But if Alberto did the deed so he could preserve his and Maria's reputation, what about Rosalia's comments about discovering a secret that would ruin someone's life."

"Perhaps Rosalia found out Alberto had been doing something dishonest in the business. He thought he'd covered it up until Maria broke her twin's confidence and told him about her comments. Murdering Rosalia would serve two purposes; he could cover up his dishonesty and then marry the woman with whom he was having an affair."

I felt a sinking feeling in my chest. "Of course, Maria would know nothing about any of it."

"You're right. I don't think Maria would be guilty of anything but breaking her twin's confidence and having an affair with her fiancé, though that is quite enough!"

I finished my beer. "Should I talk to Maria in private first and ask her if she did tell Alberto about Rosalia's comments?"

Amberly nodded. "I think that's a good idea. I believe she'll come unglued when you tell her you saw them kissing passionately. Most likely she'll tell you the truth when you ask her if she passed Rosalia's comments on to Alberto."

"I do believe the murderer has to be employed by Eduardo. Since Rosalia was the company's auditor, she would be in the position of finding out if someone was lifting funds from the business."

With her eyes opening wide, Amberly sat up straighter. "Brandon, you never mentioned that Rosalia was the company's auditor!"

"Sorry. I guess it just never came up."

"I think that pretty much clinches it. Rosalia must have discovered someone had sticky fingers, and she was going to blow the whistle. As we've discussed before, it had to have been someone she knew and loved, since she made the comment about her heart holding her back."

"Yep, and that leads us right back to the four suspects – Alberto, Emilio, Andre, and even Fernando." My thoughts were shifting like a kaleidoscope. "I guess my next move is to try to work out a plan to talk with Maria by herself. Do you have any suggestions?"

"Hm-m. Let me think. If you had her cell phone number, you could call and ask her to meet you somewhere because you had something really important to discuss."

"Right. But I don't have her cell number."

"You could call the captain and ask for it. Tell him you need to talk privately with Maria, and he'd just have to trust you until you could reveal why you wanted to meet with her. I think he respects you enough to comply."

"Maybe. And if he doesn't comply, I'll just have to tell him everything we've just discussed here. Sooner or later I'll have to tell him anyway."

"That's true. Do you have the captain's cell number?"

I reached for my billfold. "Yes, I'll call him right away."

A few minutes later, after talking with the captain, I told Amberly, "As you would expect, the captain asked a lot of questions, but I convinced him that I would reveal all after I talked with Maria."

"Good. Why don't you ask her to meet you at The Black Cat Bar? It's not too far from the beach house."

"Good idea. I'll emphasize that she must come alone. I wonder how she'll manage that?"

Amberly grinned coyly. "Hey, you forget how smart women can be. She'll figure it out."

"Okay, here goes." I punched in the numbers wondering what Maria's reaction would be. When I heard her voice, I said, "Maria, this is Brandon Sterling. I need to speak with you alone. It concerns you and Alberto."

There was a long pause before she answered. "Okay. When and where do you want to meet?"

"Could you manage to meet me at the Black Cat Bar in say...fifteen minutes?"

"Yes, I know where that is. I'll see you in fifteen minutes."

When she hung up, I let out a sigh of relief. "She's going to meet me in fifteen minutes. I told her that it concerned Alberto and her. She didn't ask any questions."

Amberly nodded. "Since you put it that way, she didn't need to ask questions. She probably figured out real quickly that you'd seen the passionate kissing scene."

"I would think she'd be terrified. It will be quite interesting to hear what she has to say."

Amberly picked up the empty plates and started for the kitchen. "I can't help but feel sorry for her, that is, if she's innocent of her sister's murder."

"If she and Alberto are innocent of the murder, I feel sorry for them both."

Fifteen minutes later, I entered The Black Cat Bar. I spotted Maria sitting in a booth towards the back of the room.

I approached the booth and sat down. "Thanks for agreeing to see me, Maria." Just then, a waitress appeared.

"What can I bring you guys?" the pretty blonde asked.

"I'll have a glass of white wine," Maria told her.

"Make that two," I said and turned towards Maria. She'd changed into a jade cotton sleeveless dress, which brought out the green in her hazel eyes. She was indeed a beautiful woman. "Maria, I hate to strip-mine your personal life, but it's necessary. Before I talk to the captain, I want you to explain why I saw you and Alberto upstairs locked into each other's arms and kissing passionately."

She expelled a long breath and clenched and unclenched her hands which were resting on the table. "When Mom told me you had gone upstairs to ask a question about the garment bag, I had a feeling you'd seen Alberto and me. Thank you for allowing me to explain before you talk to the captain."

She paused when the waitress returned with our wine. After a sip, she continued. "The blame is all mine. As you may or may not know, most identical twins do not have the same character or personalities. Rosalia is mature and rather serious but with a good sense of humor, pragmatic, compassionate, and I could go on and on touting her sterling qualities. And I mean that sincerely. On the other hand, I've always been fun loving, passionate about anything I do or get involved in, playful to the point of tricking our teachers into thinking I was Rosalia on more than one occasion, and often jumping into something before I think of the consequences. In other words, I'm not as mature as my twin, I regret to say."

I had a good idea as to where her comments were leading.

She lifted her glass and drank more wine. "Last year, Alberto and Rosalia came for a visit in Spain. One afternoon, while Alberto was out shopping for things for his mom and dad, Rosalia had a call from the office here. From what she told me, I knew she'd be gone for a good while. I guess I was in a playful mood. I decided to put on one of Rosalia's dresses and fix my hair the way she was wearing it when she left. I thought it would be fun to see how long it would take Alberto to discover that I was Maria and not Rosalia."

She drained her glass then continued. "Alberto arrived around five with his arms full of bundles. I greeted him with a smile and a kiss and told him that Maria had been called in to work. I lit candles, poured wine, and pointed to the sofa. I asked him about his afternoon and held his hand. I continued to pour wine, and we continued to drink.

"After an hour or so he asked me when I thought Maria would be returning. I told him she'd probably not be back before nine or ten. Actually, that's when Rosalia said she thought she'd be back.

He reached over and pulled me into his arms and kissed me passionately. As I said, we'd both had a lot to drink. Before I knew it, he was unbuttoning my blouse and then kissing my breasts. I was so turned on plus being half looped, I didn't stop him. We made love and it was wonderful. While we were re-dressing he said, 'Rosalia, I guess we should always drink wine before we make love. I've never known you to be so passionate. That was superb lovemaking, don't you think?' Then what I had done hit me. I started to cry uncontrollably, and of course Alberto wanted to know what was wrong. When I finally regained my composure, I admitted, with guilt and terrible regret, the trick I'd played. I was sure he would hate me."

"But he didn't, did he?" I interjected.

"No, he just stared at me for a few seconds then said, 'I felt there was something not just right, but I couldn't figure it out. What you've done as a joke, will forever change our lives, Maria. Now I guess I'm in love with two women – though identical in appearance, quite different in the way they express themselves.' We were still half undressed, and he reached for me again. I didn't resist. We made love on the sofa again. This time, after our passion left us exhausted, we dressed, and I fell back into his arms. For a few minutes we said nothing. He was the first to break the silence. 'What do we propose to do about this situation?' he asked. 'Nothing. We can do nothing,' I answered. 'I will not break my sister's heart. I know you love Rosalia, and of course, you know how much I love her. After tonight, we must make sure we never are alone again.' And Alberto agreed with me."

"It did happen though, didn't it?"

"Yes," she answered with a deep sigh. "I found out Alberto and I are good actors. Rosalia never suspected a thing, so far as I know. Alberto was the first to call me, and I called him next. He made up some excuse to fly to Europe to check out some business in

France. I met him there, and we spent an entire weekend together, most of it in bed."

"Did Alberto ever consider breaking off his engagement to Rosalia?"

"No, he could not hurt her, and I wouldn't have wanted him to." Maria nodded to the waiter then ordered more wine.

"Did you ever make another vow not to see each other again?"

She gave me a tentative smile. "We made and broke many vows. We've both felt tremendous guilt, but it didn't keep us from our...our many rendezvous."

"It must have been rather difficult with you living in another country."

The waiter returned with two glasses of wine. Maria lifted hers and took a few sips. "If a person really wants to do something, he or she will find a way."

I nodded. "And more than one empire has fallen when a man and a woman felt great passion for each other."

"That's true enough. Alberto loved two women, but he loved me passionately."

"Rosalia didn't know about you, but you knew about her. Did it make you jealous knowing Alberto was making love to her also?"

Maria rested her elbows on the table and held her wine glass with both hands. "I never allowed myself to think about it. I tried to become interested in one of the male models, but it didn't work. It was a good thing that we lived so far apart. But I often wondered if Rosalia didn't suspect something. When she, Alberto, and I were together, I could hardly look him in the eyes. But she never said anything."

"Rosalia and Alberto were planning to marry in June. Did you plan to continue to see each other after the marriage?"

She shook her head. "We never discussed it. Perhaps he would have ended our affair. I'm not sure I would have been able to."

Out of habit, I twirled my wine glass. "And now you don't have to."

Copious tears ran down her cheeks. She fumbled in her purse and pulled out what looked like the handkerchief I'd handed her earlier. She cried softly for a minute or so then dried her eyes. "Beside the horrible guilt I've been dealing with, I'm now heartbroken. I loved my sister so much. I can't imagine my life without her. I would gladly give up my relationship with Alberto if she were found alive."

Even though she'd caused her own problems (don't we all?), I did feel sorry for Maria. "Maria, you must be honest with me. Did you let it slip to Alberto that Rosalia had told you that she'd discovered something about someone that would ruin the person's life?"

She peered into her wine glass as if to find the answer there. "I really don't remember whether I mentioned it or not."

"I'd think you would remember if you did."

She shook her head. "You'd think so. But I'm just not sure."

"How would you react if you found out that Alberto murdered Rosalia? He might have stolen money from the company so you could run away to another country, disappear, and continue your relationship. Rosalia could have found the discrepancy and finally faced Alberto with her discovery and threatened to expose him. Angry, when he realized he'd be ruined, he could have pushed her from the cupola. Deciding he could replace the money back into the company, he then cooked up the kidnapping as well. He'd then be able to marry you. Could you marry Alberto if you knew that he'd murdered your sister?"

Her eyes shot flashes of anger that threatened to burn me alive. "Brandon, you must think I'm the worst person in the world to ask such a diabolical question. If I thought Alberto had stolen money from the company and then murdered my sister, I think I'd kill him with my bare hands. But you see, I *know* Alberto is not capable of hurting anyone. He's as heartbroken as I am over Rosalia. You must believe me."

I patted her hand. "I really want to believe you, Maria. I really do. I know you believe in Alberto's innocence, but your affair does put him into a vulnerable spot. I'm in a spot also. If I don't tell the captain about your affair, then I'll be withholding evidence. You know how I feel about Alberto, and if he's innocent, we have nothing to worry about."

Once again, she clenched and unclenched her hands. "Do you need to tell my dad and mom about the affair?"

"That will be up to the captain."

She bit her lips as if to keep from crying. "I don't know how much my parents can take right now with Rosalia's murder and kidnapping. It doesn't seem fair."

"There are a lot of situations in life that aren't fair, Maria. Since I've come to know the captain better, I think he'll be sensitive to your family's feelings."

She reached over and grabbed my hand. "Thank you, Brandon. I hope you don't think too badly of me."

"My mom told me that a person shouldn't judge another person until they had walked in their shoes. That was not her original saying, however."

Maria stood. "My mother told me that one also. I hope she can follow her own advice when she finds out about the affair."

"Hang in there, Maria," I told her, more than glad that I was *not* in *her* shoes.

Chapter 12

Amberly and I were sitting on the sofa in her apartment. I'd just finished going over my entire conversation with Maria. I'd been watching her facial expressions as I'd given a play-by-play accounting of the incredible saga that held, in my opinion, an air of soap opera. Her expression had changed from serious to more serious.

She shook her head. "Amazing. Maria gives the word 'playful' a whole new meaning, don't you think?"

"A Shakespeare quote comes to mind—something about weaving and deceiving."

" 'Oh, what a tangled web we weave when first we practice to deceive.' "

I let out a long sigh. "Uh-huh. That's the one. Maria brought it all on herself, but I can't help feeling sorry for her. If Rosalia is dead, and I believe she is, and Alberto is found to be the murderer, I wouldn't be surprised if she found a way to do herself in."

Her eyes widened almost imperceptibly. "And think what that would do to Eduardo and Estrella."

"It would be an even worse tragedy than it already is. I guess I don't have any choice though. I'll have to call the captain." I glanced at my watch. "He may be eating supper."

Amberly reached over and pecked my cheek. "If he is eating supper, he'll tell you. I know you hate like hell to call him, but you might as well get it over with. As you told Maria, if Alberto is innocent, she doesn't have anything to worry about. If he's guilty, we need to find out and put him where he belongs."

I stood and stretched. "You're right as usual." I took out my billfold and pulled out the captain's card. Picking up the phone, I felt like I was giving Alberto a death sentence. Amberly was wrong about one thing, however. I had no desire to become a police detective.

The captain picked up after the first ring. "Hello, Brandon. How did your interview go with Maria?" he asked.

"I think we'd better talk, Captain."

"Okay. I'm at the station now. We've pretty much finished our business at the beach house. Come on down."

"All right, I'll be there in about ten minutes. Are you by yourself?"

"Yeah, the Feds have left. They said they'd be in touch after they'd checked out the whereabouts of everyone concerned."

"See you soon." I hung up, grateful that Ted and Jack had left. Perhaps the captain wouldn't feel it necessary to expose Maria and Alberto's situation just yet. But a federal auditor, if there was such a thing, would need to get into Rosalia's books as soon as possible.

I pulled Amberly up from the sofa. "Okay, kid, (another endearing term I'd stolen from Humphry Bogart) I guess this is good-bye until Friday. I'm liking this arrangement less and less." I gave her a passionate kiss and pulled her close.

After the kiss, she said, "When summer vacation comes, perhaps we can modify our arrangement a bit."

"Hey, I go for that idea!"

"Call me later. I'd like to know how the captain reacts to your interview with Maria."

"Will do. I miss you already."

"Take care. I love you, Brandon."

I squeezed her again. "I love you, too, sweetheart."

Chapter 13

I'd never been inside the police station. To my surprise, a policeman was sitting at a desk behind a glass enclosure. Guess I'd never thought about bad guys wanting revenge after they got out of prison. Just another reason I would not want to be in law enforcement.

The young, dark-haired policeman glanced up. "May I help you?"

"Hi, my name is Brandon Sterling. Captain Delaney is expecting me."

"Yes, he is, Brandon. I'll unlock the door, and you can go right in."

He held the door open and pointed. "Right this way."

When I entered his office, the captain was munching on a burger and gestured towards a chair in front of his desk. "Hey, Brandon, have a seat. I'm just finishing my supper. Have you eaten yet?"

"No, but you go ahead and finish."

"Would you like a cup of coffee?"

I grinned. "No thanks, I've heard that coffee in police stations is about three inches thick. I have a sensitive stomach."

The captain rolled his eyes. "You know, that's probably not much of an exaggeration. So, give me the low-down on Maria. I'm more than curious."

I pulled in a deep breath and began.

The captain's face remained impassive while he listened, finished his burger, and washed it down with what I presumed to be coffee. By the time I'd finished, he was leaning back in his chair with his hands locked behind his head. "Yep, I'd say Alberto is in deep 'doo-doo.' What a mess. So what do you think, Brandon? Have you changed your mind about your golden-haired boy?"

I stared at a spot over his head for a few seconds. "I'm still inclined to believe Maria when she said Alberto would not be capable of stealing from the company and then murdering Rosalia. But then, I know I'm inclined to be sympathetic towards someone I like. You've had experience to the contrary and can look at situations more objectively."

He nodded and said in a didactic tone, "I'll talk with Alberto tomorrow. I'd like you to sit in and see if there are discrepancies between his story and Maria's. Of course, they will no doubt make sure they are both on the same page, but there may be something that they may add or leave out that doesn't sound right to you."

I nodded. "I'll need to arrange for a substitute for my class. What time are you thinking about?"

"How about around ten here at the station? In the meantime, I'll get in touch with the Feds and make sure they're working on finding an auditor to check the company's books. I hope Rosalia didn't cover up the thief's tracks until she could figure out what to do."

"I don't think she would have done that, since no one was checking up on her."

"I hope you're right." He stood and held out his hand. "Thanks again, Brandon. You've got good instincts. I'll see you here at ten tomorrow morning."

I shook his hand. "See you tomorrow. And don't drink too much coffee! That stuff could burn a hole in your stomach."

"Yeah, you sound like my wife. Get out of here!"

I chuckled thinking how very much my feelings had changed for the good Captain Delaney.

Watching the captain eating a great-smelling burger had put me in the mood for one. I suppose nervous tension had caused my appetite to go bonkers! I stopped at a local burger joint, ordered a burger, fries, and a chocolate shake through the window. I ate, while parked, and I ruminated over the interview with Maria. If I was any good as a judge of character, I would say the young woman was experiencing a living hell, and everything she said was the truth. It would be difficult to make up a story like that. But if the culprit was one of the family or had close ties as we suspected, he'd probably know when to make his escape, and we'd never catch up with him. The captain and Feds would need to be very careful not to let anyone know they were checking Rosalia's books. I finished my meal, and as I drove out of the parking lot, I saw Emilio pulling into a parking space. Andre was sitting with him. They got out of the car and headed into the restaurant. It seemed everybody was in a burger mood this evening. I'd give a day's wages (which wasn't all that much) to have been invisible and walking with them. There was something about the two that repelled me. They seemed so smug and snobbish – not kind and considerate like Alberto! Then Amberly's voice echoed her previous message about a different "Mr. Wonderful" who murdered his wife and unborn son. I felt another sudden chill and thought, *With all the chills my body has been sending me, I might consider wearing something besides shorts!*

Chapter 14

The first thing I did, when I entered my apartment, was to call for a substitute. I told Mr. Red that I'd leave complete plans on my desk as usual. Mr. Red had subbed for me before and already knew the ropes and which students to look out for. He didn't let anyone take advantage of him. I was glad he'd been available.

I took a shower and then attacked my lesson plan book to make detailed plans for the sub. I'd need to run over to the high school early in the morning and set up the classroom. I would also check in with the secretary and tell her I needed a mental health day, which wouldn't be all that far from the truth. I'd forgotten to ask the captain when the media would be alerted. I figured it would be soon. Since I was asked to help out in police matters, perhaps the board of education would not count my day as an absence, sort of like jury duty. *Dream on,* I told myself laughing inwardly.

At nine p.m., my detailed plans were complete. I put down my pen and called Amberly.

When I heard her voice, I sang in my finest baritone, *"I just called to say I love you."*

She giggled. "Hey, I remember that song. My mom used to play it when I was just a tot."

"My mom used to sing to the tape. It's a neat number, and it expresses in a simple way how I feel."

I could feel her smiling when she answered, "I love you, too, Brandon. And I agree with you that it's getting more difficult to say good-bye on Sunday afternoons. How did your meeting go with the captain?"

I leaned back on the sofa and threw my bare feet up on the coffee table. "It went fine. He asked me to meet at his office in the morning around ten. He's going to set up an interview with

Alberto, and he wants me there. He's also checking with the Feds to make sure they are working on auditing Rosalia's books."

"So you've got a sub, I suppose."

"Yes, I have Mr. Red. I'm hoping the media will be informed tomorrow, and I fervently hope this case will be solved soon. It's taken over my life!"

"Brandon, I'm proud of you. When the story breaks in the newspaper, your students will think you're a hero!"

I could picture banners with "Our hero, Mr. Sterling," and confetti falling from the ceiling. "I doubt that, but it's a nice thought. Hey, I'm going to hang up and let you get some sleep. And I've got to get up early and get my plans over to the school. I'll call you tomorrow, after your classes are over."

"Sleep well, Brandon."

"You sleep well too, sweetheart." I hung up already missing her.

I tossed and turned for an hour after going to bed. I finally got up, turned on the light, and picked up an unfinished novel I'd been too busy to read. I read the same page over and over then realized there was no way I could concentrate. Snatches of conversations with all the participants in the beach house drama were playing through my mind. I couldn't turn them off. I lay back down and closed my eyes. When I finally drifted into a fitful sleep, I dreamed Rosalia, with a worried expression, was pointing at one of the four suspects, but I couldn't make out which one.

Chapter 15

The alarm went off at seven. I shut it off and slowly pulled myself to a sitting position. I felt like I'd not slept at all, and I was moving in slow motion. I padded to the kitchen and made coffee. After a semi-cold shower and a cup of coffee, I was slowly coming alive. I threw on a shirt and long pants, chug-a-lugged another cup of coffee, grabbed my plan book, and headed for my car.

Driving towards the high school, I glanced into my rearview mirror and noticed a blue, older-model truck. Suddenly, I felt a cold fist closing over my heart. *Now that's strange. I wonder why that old truck brought on that eerie sensation.*

At eight-fifteen, I'd finished my school business and pulled out of the parking lot. Hungry as always, I decided to pick up coffee and a pastry from the grocery store and park where I'd parked on Friday afternoon.

A bit later, I was enjoying my delicious junk-food breakfast and the view of the ocean when I had a sudden desire to turn around. Lo and behold, the same old truck was slowly passing behind me. This time I got a better look. The dusty vehicle was rusting around the bottom of the doors and fenders. I didn't recognize the young-looking male driver with long hair, but once again I got an eerie sensation. Usually, the mesmerizing sound of the waves relaxed me, but not this morning. Suddenly, Amberly's voice entered my conscience. "Brandon, be careful, you're the only witness." I tried laughing it off. "Brandon, you fool," I muttered, "No one is going to harm you in broad daylight." Then I remembered Rosalia was shoved from the cupola during the daylight hours. I pulled out of the parking lot and headed home to change into my shorts. I looked carefully in my rearview mirror before turning into my apartment space. No one appeared to be following me. I hoped my witnessing a murder had not caused me to become paranoid.

I entered my apartment and for the first time in daylight hours, I put on the safety latch. As I changed my clothes, I peered out of the window and thankfully didn't see the dusty, old truck.

I glanced at my watch and noted it was 9:30. It would take about ten minutes to get to the station, so that left me twenty minutes. I headed for my computer. I'd use those twenty minutes to work on the murder mystery I'd started writing a few months ago. While going into my documents, I wondered if I could use some of the experiences I'd encountered during the past few days in my novel. *Sure, if you want to be sued. Go right ahead!*

Chapter 16

At ten o'clock, Alberto and I were at the police station sitting across from the captain. Even though the office felt as cold as a wintry day in Alaska, I noticed beads of perspiration on Alberto's forehead. Both of us were dressed in shorts and tee shirts and were sitting directly under the air conditioning vent. I hoped my teeth wouldn't start chattering. I did mental pushups hoping to warm myself up.

The captain leaned back in his chair and crossed his arms. "Alberto, I'm sure Maria has told you about her meeting with Brandon, where she confessed to an affair with you. You must know you're now in a vulnerable position. However, we'd like to hear the story from your viewpoint."

Alberto's voice sounded thin and strained when he began. "As Maria told you, our affair began in Spain. Rosalia and I had gone for a visit. While I was out shopping and thinking Maria and Rosalia were having a sisterly chat, Rosalia was called to the office on business. Maria, being the fun-loving sister who had always enjoyed tricking people, decided to see if she could fool me into believing she was Rosalia. When I returned from my shopping trip, Maria greeted me dressed in one of Rosalia's outfits.

"She poured us both a big glass of wine and asked me about my day. On my third glass of wine, I remember thinking that Rosalia had always stopped at two glasses. The wine made me a bit fuzzy headed so I didn't dwell on the reasons Rosalia might have taken a sudden love of wine. I have no idea what we discussed after our third glass, but for me, after two or three glasses of alcohol I start feeling quite…quite romantic. I reached over and kissed Maria passionately, still thinking she was Rosalia, of course. Feeling even more turned on, I remember unbuttoning her blouse and kissing her breasts. I asked her when Maria would be returning, and she told me not until nine or ten. We made love there on the sofa. Rosalia was far from frigid, but Maria was wildly passionate."

I cut in. "Alberto, it's difficult to believe that as intimate as you'd been with Rosalia, you didn't notice something different with your first kiss with Maria."

The muscle beneath one of his eyes twitched. "If I'd kissed her passionately before I drank three large glasses of wine, I believe I'd have noticed something different. When your mind is fuzzy, and you're consumed with passion, you're not going to think about anything except the present moment, or at least that's the reason I've come up with."

"I think that's a reasonable explanation," the captain commented.

His face grew pensive. "As soon as we finished making love, I pulled her into my arms and told her I loved her. I also told her that I'd never known her to be so wild and passionate and perhaps we'd better drink more wine the next time we had sex. As I'm sure Maria told you, she burst into tears and told me how she'd tricked me. Shocked, I told her that now I was in love with two women. Still half drunk, I reached for her again. I don't remember how many times we made love before Rosalia returned. Of course, we promised each other we'd never put ourselves in a compromising situation again. And of course, we broke our promise. Though we felt tremendous guilt, we still continued our affair."

"Do you think you'd have continued the affair after you and Rosalia married?" I asked, remembering that I'd asked Maria the same question.

His eyes were misty. "I wish I could say we would not have continued to see each other, but I can't. However, at this moment, I'd swear never to see Maria again if Rosalia were found alive."

I glanced at the captain but his face was impassive. He pursed his lips and said, "If what you say is true, I'd like to turn Maria over my knee and give her a sound spanking for starting this…this regrettable love triangle. But you had some responsibility also."

"Yes, I'm fully aware of that, Captain. I can say nothing in my defense. I must be a weak person, and I've lost respect for myself. I've performed self-flagellation over and over and especially since learning about Rosalia's kidnapping and probable murder."

"Guilt and self-flagellation have never changed any situation for the better, Alberto," I told him.

The captain nodded. "That's true I suppose." His sympathetic voice suddenly took on sternness. "I don't think it's important to reveal your affair at the present time, Alberto. But when it does become necessary, I'll let you and Maria know so you might tell Eduardo in your own words."

"That's all we could ask for, Captain. Thank you for your understanding."

The captain's eyes were fixed on Alberto with a level stare. "Don't think you're not still on the suspect list. As I mentioned earlier, your affair with Maria has cast even more suspicion your way. You may go now." He turned to me. "I want you to stay, Brandon."

I stood and patted Alberto on his arm. "Hang in there," I said.

He nodded. "Thanks." With his shoulders slumped, he walked out of the office like a condemned man.

The captain glanced at his watch. "The sergeant and I have a little plan, and we want you to be part of it."

"Oh? Why am I thinking that this plan is surreptitious?"

The captain's grin reminded me of the famous cat's grin in my childhood favorite, *The Cat in the Hat*. "You definitely should be in law enforcement, Brandon. You have excellent gut reactions. The sergeant and I are going to put on our civilian clothes and take a little ride over to Kissimmee. I'll drive my personal car so we won't attract attention. We want you to come along with us. We'd need to get a warrant from the district attorney then take it to the judge to have it signed, and we don't want to bother with a search warrant at this time. So we want you to go into Emilio's cabin and do a little search for us."

I swallowed, trying to pull my thoughts together. "Oh, you do, huh? How much time do you think I'll get for breaking and entering?"

The captain rolled his eyes towards the ceiling. "Since you told me you have a clean record, you might get off on probation. I'm kidding, of course. You'll be in no danger of getting caught, and you might help catch a killer."

"Captain, I thought you said the Feds were going to investigate all the suspects."

"I did and they are. I just don't know how long it's going to take. In the meantime, the perp could take off in the middle of the night, and we could lose him."

I could feel a few goose bumps blossoming on my arms. I wasn't sure if it was from cold or anxiety. "I thought you might want to consider having someone stationed somewhere close to the beach house in case one of the suspects decided to do just that!"

"I'm planning to ask the Feds if they can spare a man to do that job."

The phone rang, and I decided to take a break from the air conditioning. On the way out, I nodded to the desk sergeant and said, "Tell the captain I'm standing outside."

He grinned. "So the captain froze you out, huh?"

I rubbed my arms numb with cold. "Yeah, you got that right!"

"I keep telling him he needs to ask a doctor why he's so damn hot all the time."

I opened the door and sucked in some hot, humid air. "Perhaps he's in male menopause," I said over my shoulder.

Leaning against the warm building, I thought over my conversation with the captain. It had not been the first discussion we'd had about search warrants. The first discussion occurred when we entered the beach house to see if the murderer was lurking inside. The captain had me to open the door since he didn't have a search warrant. At that time, we both would have been surprised to know I'd once again be involved in breaking and entering to help with the investigation.

The desk sergeant poked his head out of the door. "The captain wants to talk with you. Are you warmed up?"

"Not much; I must remember to bring a sweat shirt and long pants the next time I come down here!"

He opened the door for me. "Yeah, I wear an undershirt under my uniform. It helps."

I entered the captain's office and sat down. "What's happening?"

He leaned back in his chair. "The call was from Ted. Some of his men in Miami have searched Andre's house."

I raised an eyebrow. "Did they have a search warrant?"

"Of course, they did. You wouldn't catch anyone in the FBI not going by the book!"

I didn't know whether he was joking or not. "So what did they find?"

"The house seemed to be in pretty good order, considering a male college student lives there. But they found a couple of interesting things. First, there was a family photograph album lying on his bed. It was mostly filled with pictures of Andre and one of the twins; we're assuming the twin was Rosalia. His bedroom walls were filled with large posters of some of the pictures of Rosalia and himself taken from the photo album. In other words, it appears Andre was obsessed with his stepsister. As we've discussed before, if he declared his love for Rosalia and she turned him down, he could have pushed her from the cupola because of his rage from being rejected. He'd also be extremely jealous since she planned to marry Alberto."

"That's certainly possible."

"The Feds are coming up to get a piece of Rosalia's clothing to take back to Miami. They'll have the canine squad check out Andre's fenced-in back yard."

I shuddered as I envisioned yapping dogs sniffing around Andre's yard. "Perhaps we can ask Maria to bring some of Rosalia's clothing down here. I'd hate for the parents to know about the dogs. It's seems so gruesome."

"Sure. We can do that. We can use some of the clothing for a canine search around Emilio's cabin and also for the stretch of vacant land south of the beach house, if the dogs don't turn up anything at Andre's place. If and when we find her body, we should also find the perp's DNA."

"I guess there's no hope that Rosalia is still alive."

"If her neck was broken from the fall, and she was unconscious, she could also have a concussion. So far as we know, all the suspects are at the beach house. No one is giving her medical attention or even water and food, so I can't see as there is any chance at all."

"What about the guy who made those phone calls telling Eduardo not to call the police. Could he be taking care of her?"

He sighed wearily. "That's possible of course, but I don't think she could live for three days without being hospitalized. And she's definitely not in any area hospital."

"I have to agree. But if I were the parents, I'd have to hope that her neck had not been broken, she'd regained consciousness, and someone was looking after her."

"I'd probably do the same, Brandon. Oh, I forgot to mention, the Feds checked Andre's VISA account and found he'd charged gas on Friday afternoon in Ft. Pierce. The time would coincide with the time line that could put him here around five-thirty. When we return from our trip to Kissimmee, I'm hauling his ass in here. The little twerp should know we could check up on his VISA."

"Yeah, that wasn't too bright. Would you like me to call Maria about the clothes?"

"Sure. While you're calling her, I'll change into my civvies. Sergeant O'Grady should be here shortly."

I walked back outside into the warm sun to make my call to Maria. I told her why we needed the clothes, and she said she'd bring them down to the station immediately. I heard a catch in her voice as she was talking.

A few minutes later, Sergeant O'Grady caught my attention as he drove up. I noticed he was removing civilian clothes from the car. I had an image of the captain and sergeant, out of uniform, taking off and leaving me stranded when the owner of the cabin dropped by to check on his cabin.

The captain approached. "Okay, Sergeant, go change your clothes. I'd like to get going."

I was wondering what I was about to get myself into. My involvement seemed to be getting more whacky with each passing day. I was about to make the suggestion that perhaps we really should get a search warrant, when my thoughts were interrupted by the sergeant, obviously a quick-change artist, who returned dressed in civilian clothes.

It would be an understatement to say that I climbed into the back seat of the captain's tan Chevy with trepidation.

Chapter 17

Forty-five minutes later, the captain parked his car a half block from the cabin. Emilio had correctly described the place when he told us he was at the end of a bumpy road in a secluded area. As we approached, I noticed the cabin was surrounded on both sides by palmetto bushes and tall pine and palm trees with a grassy area in front and back. The grass needed mowing. No flowers or flowering bushes had been planted. I spotted a large lake in the back with a short fishing pier. I estimated the cabin had two bedrooms, one bath, an eat-in kitchen, and living room. The one-car garage, minus a garage door, was not attached to the cabin. I was curious to know how much the cabin rented for. Since Emilio said his plans had been to return to New York and meet Rosalia and Alberto at his parents' home on Sunday, then he must have called the owner of the cabin and told him he needed an extension.

"I'd say this would be a perfect area to hide or get rid of a body," the captain said walking towards the garage. "My bet is that lake is infested with alligators. If he dumped the poor girl into the lake, the alligators would have no trouble tearing the garment bag to shreds. I don't want to think about what one of those prehistoric reptiles would do to Rosalia or anyone else for that matter!"

I wished he hadn't made those comments. I, for one, was not planning to walk down to the lake and investigate. It was beyond me how anyone could be so cruel as to throw someone into an alligator-infested lake. I followed the captain into the open garage and spied an older-model blue truck covered in dust and rusting around the bottom of the doors and fenders, standing in the middle of the garage. I instinctively placed my hand over my heart to warm the cold hand inside my chest.

"Captain," I said, "you may think me paranoid, but I swear to you that someone in this truck, or one exactly like it, was following me this morning."

"What are you talking about, Brandon?" the captain asked in obvious astonishment.

I explained what I'd observed earlier. "I thought I was being paranoid but not anymore. I wish I'd written down the license plate."

"Brandon, there must be dozens of old, blue rusty trucks in Florida. I don't think you're paranoid, but maybe you're overreacting just a bit, unless it was Emilio driving the truck," the captain commented condescendingly.

"No, as I told you, the male driver had long hair." I placed my hand on the truck over the engine. "The engine's still warm."

"Maybe the owner came over and used the truck for some reason," the sergeant suggested.

I didn't want the two men laughing at me, so I didn't mention my eerie sensations. "You're probably right," I answered, but I was not at all convinced.

The captain donned a pair of latex gloves and picked up a shovel that had been standing like a sentry waiting to be found. After examining it, he said, "There's dirt here. If Emilio is the perp, he could have used this to bury her. Of course, the dirt could have come from someone digging for fishing worms."

"If Rosalia's around here, I hope we find her in the ground and not in the lake," I said quietly. The horrible image of alligators tearing into the garment bag had not left my imagination.

The captain frowned. "For everybody's sake, I hope so also." He peered into the back of the truck. "There's dirt and dust but nothing else. We'll send the Feds over and have them check out the shovel for prints and the back of the truck for DNA."

We walked around the garage and saw fishing poles, glass jars, a hammer and nails, a ladder, empty paint and oil cans along with other garage paraphernalia, but nothing that would be of interest towards solving the case.

We exited the garage and the captain reached into his pocket and handed me a pair of latex gloves. "Okay, Brandon, put these on. First you try the front and back doors, though I'm sure they're locked. Then see if you can open a window. If you can't, the sergeant will give you something to help you jimmy the window. We'll stand beside you and direct you."

"Good," I said slipping on the gloves. "If you assist me, then we'll all go to jail! Do you guys know how to play pinochle?"

"You're funny, Brandon," the captain said grinning. "If I thought there was any chance of getting into trouble, we wouldn't be here. Trust me now, okay?"

I pulled in a deep breath. "I've come this far, so I might as well finish the job, I guess. We'll try the back door first."

As we trudged to the back of the cabin, I wondered if the sergeant and captain were feeling as anxious as I. I kept a close look out on the lake hoping an ugly, ten foot alligator wouldn't make an appearance. I was feeling really sorry that I'd accepted this assignment. I tried the back door, but as expected, it was locked.

"Okay, let's go to the front," the captain said. "I'd be surprised if that door was not locked. But sometimes people can be careless, especially if they have something on their minds."

"Yeah, like murdering someone and trying to cover it up, I thought grimly. We reached the front quickly, and once again we found a locked door.

"We'll get in through the window in the back, which is probably the kitchen," the captain instructed.

So now I had the anxiety of being torn to shreds by an alligator creeping up the embankment or sent to jail for breaking and entering! I'd never thought of myself as a coward, but at that moment I wanted to cut and run!

The cabin window was low to the ground, so at least I didn't need a ladder. I tugged off the screen and, much to my surprise, the unlocked window came up without any problem. "I hope you guys are coming in with me," I said, climbing through the open window.

"Of course," the captain said, "after you unlock the back door for us."

The kitchen I found myself in was furnished with a round wooden table and four chairs, a stove, refrigerator, and a small microwave. The wall and cabinets were made of varnished pine, and the floor was tiled in brown vinyl. A few blown up photos of men fishing from piers and in boats were scattered about on the walls.

I traipsed to the back door and lifted the latch for the captain and sergeant.

After surveying the room, the captain opened one of the cabinet doors. "I'm just checking to see if Emilio has any peanut butter, as he said. And it looks like he was telling the truth on that point."

I peered into the refrigerator and noticed a quart carton of milk, a few beers, an egg carton, a half loaf of bread, and a jar of strawberry jelly.

"Nothing much of interest in here," the captain commented, leading us into the living room.

The living area was as void of personality as the kitchen. The floor was tiled in brown vinyl with a brown area rug covering most of the floor. A brown leather sofa, two, brown leather chairs with ottomans, an end table with a brass lamp, and a widescreen TV completed the furnishings.

"I don't believe the owner's wife had anything to do with these depressing decorations," the sergeant commented.

The captain nodded. "I should think not. He probably thought only men would be renting the cabin, and they wouldn't care one way or the other. Of course men with discriminating tastes, like us, would be offended."

I chuckled. "I wonder if the bedrooms will be more colorful."

"Let's check them out," the captain replied.

We entered the hall that led to the two bedrooms. As I had expected, the first bedroom appeared just as bland and uninteresting as the kitchen and living room. The walls were tan, the floor the same brown vinyl with a tan scatter rug, the maple double bed was covered with a tan bedspread, and a maple dresser stood against the wall. Tan blinds hung in the windows with a small, air conditioner in one of the windows. A few black-and-white Florida photos were hung on the walls.

I peeped into the empty closet. "Nothing here except a few rusty coat hangers. I guess Emilio used the other bedroom."

The second bedroom was a bit of surprise. Perhaps the owner's wife had insisted on decorating this one. The walls were painted cornsilk blue, the brass double bed was covered in a blue-and-white comforter over a white bedspread, the brown vinyl floor was covered in a blue area rug, and the oak dresser appeared to be an antique. A large brass mirror hung on the wall behind the bed, and several large, colorful watercolors were hanging on the walls. Blue blinds adorned the two windows, and an air conditioner had been placed in one of them. A large, closed suitcase was sitting on a straight-backed oak chair.

"Voila'," I shouted. "Finally some color. I had the feeling I was playing a part in an old sepia-colored movie."

"Oh, and 'looky-here,' " the captain exclaimed. "Let's see what Emilio has in his expensive piece of luggage." He carefully pulled out polo shirts, shorts, good-quality long-sleeved shirts and pants, underwear, and casual, expensive shoes. "The man has good taste," he said, as he carefully returned the items to the luggage.

I examined the handle of the suitcase, noticing that Emilio had not removed a luggage tag that gave the destination as Nice, France. "Looks like Emilio enjoys expensive vacations."

"How about that Monte Carlo place?" the sergeant asked. "You know, the place where all the rich and famous go to gamble. An American movie star was married to the prince who owned the palace and casino, but they're both dead now."

"You mean the beautiful Grace Kelly," I responded. "She was married to Prince Rainier who ruled that principality. It's a very small area in the south of France. I've seen several movies that were made there. I guess if you wanted to fly, you'd need to land in Nice, which is fairly close. Monte Carlo is too mountainous to have an airport."

The captain appeared deep in thought for a few seconds. "Perhaps Emilio likes to gamble. He travels a lot in Europe for his company, and he may have gotten in the habit of stopping by Monte Carlo at the gaming tables."

While the captain had been talking, my brain jumped into overdrive. "If Emilio had experienced some bad moments at the gaming tables and got into bad debt, what do you think he would have done?"

The captain leaned against the dresser. "Emilio appears to be a smart man, and sometimes smart men outsmart themselves. Perhaps he cooked his company books in Europe, planning to replace the money with a better night at the tables, but lady luck eluded him. Rosalia discovered what he'd done, and because he is her fiancé's brother, she didn't want to turn him in until she talked with him. That could be what she meant when she told Maria she was wrestling with a problem. When she approached Emilio about what she'd discovered, he panicked and shoved her from the cupola."

"That's brilliant," I said, admiring his efforts at deductive reasoning. "It will be interesting to hear what Emilio has to say when you confront him with your theory. And when the Fed's auditors check out Rosalia's books, we might have the motive we've been looking for, unless she didn't uncover the discrepancy because she wanted to talk to Emilio first. Of course, Alberto and Fernando would also have a chance to cook the books. That would give Alberto another motive besides the one he might already have – like being in love with Rosalia's twin." I hated to bring that up.

"From my understanding of auditing, the Feds will certainly be able to uncover the mistake if Rosalia had found it," the sergeant interjected. "They should be just as smart as she is, don't you think?"

The captain gave the sergeant a thumbs up. "On the other hand, we may be totally on the wrong track. We haven't had our second interview with Andre to ask him why he lied about buying gas in Ft. Pierce. As we've discussed before, as a spurned lover, he could have done the deed also."

I opened the closet door. "Rosalia's remarks to Maria about discovering something about someone that would probably ruin his life may have not been the motive for the murder; that is, if Andre is the perpetrator."

"True enough," the captain answered, his expression thoughtful. "So what have you found in the closet, Brandon?"

I glanced at two expensive jackets and a pair of trousers hanging next to a garment bag. "Not much here but it does appear that if Emilio had planned to fish, hike, or go for a boat ride, he forgot to pack the right clothes." I closed the closet door. "But then the rich and famous might have a different opinion of what to wear on a fishing-camp trip. I've never seen a designer's catalog for fishing clothes!"

"That's funny, Brandon," the captain said. "Even though I could explain the situation, we don't want to be caught inside this cabin, so we'd better get a move on."

I felt my muscles tensing and walked briskly to the kitchen. "Hurry up you two," I told them as I rushed them through the door. I locked up, and by the time I scooted out of the window, the captain was holding the window screen in readiness.

With the captain huffing and puffing, we all jogged down the driveway and headed for the car. Luckily, we were only a few feet from the car when a truck passed us. Watching with baited breath, (I can't resist a fishing-camp pun) the truck, with a lawn mower perched in the back, turned into the cabin driveway.

"Damn," the captain said. "That truck driver could very well be the owner, or else he's the lawn-cutting guy. If we'd stayed one minute longer, we might have been forced to hide in the closet until he left!"

Jumping into the back seat, I laughed raucously at the image of three grown men hiding in a closet. "That should teach you not to con innocent people like me into compromising situations, Captain!"

He turned on the ignition. "Aw, shut up, Brandon," he said with a chuckle. "It's good for you to get your heartbeat up once in a while."

Bumping down the dusty road, I was thinking that we did learn something for our trouble. Emilio had visited Nice and, therefore, most likely Monte Carlo. And he didn't bring any fishing clothes to the fishing camp.

"So, Captain," I said, "if you send the Feds over to check out the shovel and the back of the truck in the garage, you're going to need to tell them about our little excursion aren't you?"

"If you're worried that the Feds will question us about breaking and entering, you can relax, Brandon. I'm sure they have better things to do than worry about how we got information about a truck, a shovel, and a luggage tag!"

I chortled. "That's a relief. So what's next, Captain?"

"The sergeant here is going to call Andre on his cell phone and tell him to meet us at the station in an hour. You can stick around if you want. I'm anxious to see his face when we tell him we know he gassed up in Ft. Pierce."

"That should take him down a notch or two," the sergeant said, pulling out his notebook and cell phone.

"Yes, indeed," I answered, watching the passing landscape dotted with palm trees, pines, and palmettos. I suddenly felt immensely grateful that we hadn't stumbled on a big, fat rattlesnake or a sharp-toothed alligator while we were up to mischief.

Chapter 18

The captain and sergeant had changed from their civvies back into their uniforms. The three of us were in the captain's office waiting for Andre. As usual, I rubbed my arms to keep the chilly-bumps from appearing. I decided to sit closer to the wall to avoid the polar air blowing down my back.

I plopped down into my chair. "I wonder if Maria came in and left some of Rosalia's clothing."

The captain nodded. "Yes, she did. I asked the desk sergeant about it a few minutes ago. He's probably getting in touch with the Feds as we speak."

The desk sergeant popped his head in the door and told us that Andre had arrived.

"Tell him to come in," the captain said with a sly smile.

With a surly expression, Andre walked slowly into the room without greeting anyone.

The captain pointed to a chair in front of his desk, directly under the air conditioner. I wondered how long it would take for Andre to start rubbing his arms.

"So Andre," the captain began, "I'll get right to the point. At our last interview, you told us that last Friday, the day of Rosalia's disappearance, you spent the day and evening in the Miami area. Is that correct?"

His eyes narrowed, and there was annoyance in his voice. "Yes, that's correct."

For the first time I noticed a slight French accent. I suspected that when Andre became nervous he would slip back into his childhood accent. I watched the captain lean back in his chair and place his hands behind his head. I had no doubt he was getting ready to make Andre do a little squirming.

The captain spat out his words slowly and contemptuously.

"You lied, Andre."

Andre stuck out his chin defiantly and shot the captain a smoldering look. "What are you talking about? I didn't lie."

"You think you're so smart, don't you?" The captain's lips curled in disgust. "The Feds checked on your VISA and discovered you'd charged gas in Ft. Pierce around three o'clock in the afternoon this past Friday. That would have placed you at the beach house around four. As we discussed in our last interview, we know you were obsessed with your stepsister. We believe you tried to talk her out of marrying Alberto, and when you were rejected, you were so hurt and angry you shoved her from the cupola."

His face etched in desperation, Andre covered his eyes with his hands and sobbed uncontrollably.

Shrugging, Captain Delaney looked at the sergeant and then to me with a questioning look.

I walked over to Andre, pulled out my handkerchief, and placed it under his fingers. I seemed to be losing a lot of handkerchiefs that way. I prepared myself for a tearful confession.

Andre swiped at his eyes and sat up straighter. "I did not push Rosalia from the cupola. Yes, I loved her, and I'll always love her." He paused, apparently to pull himself together. "I did lie about coming to see her on Friday afternoon. I spoke to her on the phone earlier last week. When she mentioned Alberto would be in Orlando on Friday afternoon, I decided to come and talk to her. I made a complete fool of myself when I grabbed her and forcibly kissed her. When she pulled back in complete surprise, I confessed I'd been in love with her for years. I actually got down on my knees and begged her not to marry Alberto."

He paused, dabbing at his eyes for a few seconds. "Rosalia stared at me with pity. I was still on my knees, and she got down on her knees and looked squarely at me. She told me that I meant the world to her, and she couldn't love me more than if I were her own flesh and blood. She said she loved me dearly as a sister loves a brother, but she could never love me in any other way. She said she was sure there were many young women who would jump at the chance to discover the wonderful person that I was."

His face was flushed as he continued. "I felt sick with embarrassment. I got up and pulled her up from the floor. She placed her arms around my neck and gave me a sisterly hug and whispered, 'We'll forget this ever happened, Andre.' I didn't bother to answer. I simply bolted out of the door and left. I'm not sure of the time, but I believe it could have been around four-thirty. I'm sorry I lied, but I was too ashamed to tell you the truth."

His arrogance had dissipated. We were looking at what I believed to be a young, brokenhearted man. I wondered if the captain was as touched as I was at his confession, but I doubted it.

The captain's expression was indiscernible, but his voice was strong. "Well, Andre, I hope you've learned at least two things from this interview. First, it's not smart to lie to the police or to the Feds, because more than likely you'll get caught in the lie. Secondly, if you've been caught lying, even if you tell the truth, the police may not believe you. Do you understand what I mean, Andre?"

He nodded. "Yes, I understand perfectly, Captain." He raised his right hand. "But I swear to you, I'm telling the truth. I could never hurt Rosalia."

The captain folded his arms and gave him a hard look. "I hope for your sake that you are telling the truth. If you aren't, we'll find out."

Andre appeared contrite. "Yes, Captain, I'm sure you would." His eyes filled and threatened to spill.

"Oh, I forgot to mention that the Feds will be using canines to search your backyard. But if you're as innocent as you claim, you have nothing to worry about," the captain told him.

"The canines will find nothing, but I do have something to worry about. I'm worried that Rosalia's last image of me was one of me making a fool of myself."

I cleared my throat. "Andre, that's a rather self-centered statement. You should be happy that Rosalia loved you as much as she did, even if it was sisterly love."

"You're right, Brandon. I guess I have some growing up to do."

"If you have nothing else to add, you may be excused, Andre," the captain said.

With his shoulders slumped, Andre walked towards me holding out my handkerchief. "Thanks, Brandon."

I shook my head. "Just keep it. As I told Maria, I get all the handkerchiefs I need from my students Christmas presents."

His smile was tentative. "Goodbye then."

As soon as he opened the door and left, I turned to the captain and sergeant. "What do you think of his story? As I recall, we predicted he came to see Rosalia to beg her not to marry Alberto."

The captain pulled his arms up in a long stretch. "Yes, we did predict just that, except we added that in his fury from Rosalia's refusal, he shoved her from the cupola."

"Is that still your opinion?" I asked.

"I'm reserving my opinion at the moment. He could be telling the truth, but as I told him, once a person is caught in one lie, it makes it difficult to believe anything he or she tells you."

"What's your opinion, Sergeant?" I asked.

The sergeant got up and walked to the window. I assumed it was to keep his teeth from chattering.

"I'm inclined to believe his story, but not totally. The captain makes a good point about lying. What do you think, Brandon?"

"I believe his story about ninety-nine percent."

The captain grinned. "Stick with us a few more weeks, and we'll harden you up, Brandon."

"I wouldn't argue that point," I answered.

The captain lifted his phone. "I think I'll check in with the Feds. I'd like to see how those names Eduardo gave us checked out. I also need to talk to them about checking out the shovel in Emilio's cabin and DNA in the back of the truck. One of the men will need to pick up Rosalia's clothes for the canines to sniff out the vacant lots south of the beach house, the backyard in Miami, and the area around the cabin in Kissimmee."

I nodded. "Okay, I'm going outside. Call me if you need me."

The desk sergeant glanced up as I approached the exit. "Going out for another warmup?" he asked.

"Yeah, I bet the captain has obtained a few confessions from felons just so they could escape to a warm cell!"

"I wouldn't be at all surprised."

Glancing at my watch, I leaned against the warm building. It was five o'clock. I knew I should get home to make detailed lesson plans. Preparing for a substitute was almost as hard as teaching all day. I hoped the captain would not need me tomorrow. But first I'd check in with Amberly. I pulled out my cell and punched in her number.

"Hey, how was your day, sweetheart?" When I heard her sweet, sexy voice, I responded in my usual way.

"Hey, Brandon, my day went well, thank you. I had to send my unruly student, Paul, to the office. But other than that everything went smoothly. I've been thinking about you. What's happening?"

I briefly filled her in.

"I must say your day was far more exciting than mine, Brandon. But I'm not sure I like the idea of someone following you this morning, and I bet your cabin adventure unnerved you! You don't have professional experience, and your life could be in danger. I think the captain is taking advantage of you."

"Not to worry, sweetheart. I feel perfectly safe," I fibbed.

"Well, please be careful. Make sure all your doors and windows are locked."

"Okay, Mother," I said laughing.

"Brandon, I love you. I don't want anything to happen to you."

"I know that, and I love you, too."

I switched off the phone and headed back into the building. I hoped the captain would be through with his call to the Feds. He was hanging up as I entered.

"What's the scoop?" I asked, heading for my chair next to the window.

The captain leaned on his desk with his elbows. "Everyone who had Eduardo's unlisted number at the beach house checked out with solid alibis. The Feds will be picking up Rosalia's clothing in a short while to take to the canine squad. Ted was somewhat intrigued with our findings at the cabin and especially our suspicions about Emilio's Monte Carlo visits. Someone is now checking into his credit and bank account to see if he's in debt. In the meantime, an auditor is going over Rosalia's company books very carefully."

"Looks like they're really moving," I commented. I stood up and leaned against the wall. "I don't suppose Eduardo has received a phone call from the kidnapper today, has he?"

"No one has called. I don't think there will be any more calls. The perp has probably notified his fellow conspirator that the police and the family members suspect the calls are a ruse. Oh, I forgot to mention that the Feds are sending in a man to keep a close watch on the beach house in case someone tries to make a getaway."

I nodded. "Just in case the perp decides to…to do me in, you could still proceed with the case, couldn't you? You'd still have those interviews and my statements. Right?"

I was leaning against the window not only to keep warm but also to support myself. My knees were threatening to give way. Talking about my early demise was having an effect on my physical being as well as my psyche.

"Oh, yes, we could continue with the case, but it just wouldn't be the same without you, Brandon," he said sardonically. "But don't worry, I've never lost a witness yet. You can count on it."

I was tempted to say there was always a first time, but I didn't want him to think I was afraid. A man must hold on to his male pride no matter what the cost. I glanced at my watch and noticed it was now five-twenty. "If you don't need me for breaking and entering anymore today, I'll grab a bite and head for home. I need to stop by my school and check out what my sub did today."

His eyes crinkled mirthfully. "Brandon, when this case is closed, I'm going to miss you. Are you sure you don't want to go into law enforcement?"

I shook my head. "I believe I'd rather take my chances in the classroom dodging spitball missiles rather than to join forces with the police."

"If you ever change your mind, come and see me. In the meantime, I'll give you a call when something develops."

"Please do." I gave a salute and headed for the door.

Chapter 19

After I left the station, I dropped by the school and picked up my lesson plan book. My sub had left a note saying all went well.

I returned to my humble, one-bedroom apartment, which had been furnished by my parents when I moved in five years ago. Since they'd been so generous, I told my mom she could select the furniture. She'd chosen rattan with foam-green cushions. Mom is a watercolor artist, and she framed some of her seascapes and hung them around the apartment. My bedroom, also furnished in rattan, is fairly large, so I had placed my desk and computer there.

I'd been working on my lesson plans for a while when suddenly I felt ravenous. I stood, stretched, and headed for the refrigerator.

I reached for a frozen spaghetti dinner and placed it in the micro. I whipped up a salad, and warmed some rolls. It wasn't exactly a gourmet dinner from The Chart House, but I'd learned that when you're really hungry almost anything tastes good.

I'd just switched on the TV and was making coffee when the phone rang. I picked it up, expecting it to be my honey, but if it was Amberly, she must be giving me the silent treatment. No one spoke. Perhaps the perp wanted to frighten me by the old breathing-into-the-phone trick! I slammed the phone down and disconnected it. Amberly, my folks, and the captain had my cell phone number. If the caller was the guy in the truck, how had he gotten my phone number – unless the murderer had given it to him? Sure, that was it, the guy, asking for ransom, and the guy following me could be the same person. He'd be working with the murderer. And if that was true, then the murderer must be Emilio, since he has been staying at the cabin where the truck is parked.

I pulled out my dinner from the micro and placed it on a tray. I thought if I watched a TV program while eating, maybe it would get my mind off of my scary thoughts.

For once, my anxiety stalled out my appetite, and the TV program failed to get my attention. I threw my half-eaten dinner into the garbage and headed for the bathroom, hoping that a hot shower might relax me.

Since I was exhausted, I figured I'd go to bed early. But thirty minutes later, after tossing and turning, I gave up on the idea of going to sleep. Crazy ideas kept me awake. If I heard someone breaking in, what would I do? I didn't own a gun, and the thought of plunging a butcher knife into someone's gut wasn't at all appealing. Finally, I dozed off.

Later, I woke up and glanced at my illuminated clock. The hands pointed to one-fifteen. I had a sudden urge to go to the bathroom. I kept a nightlight on in the bathroom, so I had no need to switch on the overhead light. Standing in the middle of the bathroom, I heard a noise coming from the direction of the living room. It sounded like someone was trying to open the front door with a key. My first thoughts were that someone had gotten the wrong apartment, and they'd leave as soon as they realized their mistake. The key-fiddling noise stopped, and I heard the creaking of the door as it opened. Then a replay of the captain's voice entered my conscious, telling me that if the beach house door was locked, Sergeant O'Grady could jimmy the door. I knew it wasn't Sergeant O'Grady jimmying the lock. *It must be the guy who was following me in the old truck,* I thought with panic. *What the hell can I do? There's no phone available unless I run to the bedroom, and there's no lock on that door. I guess I'll hide in the tub behind the shower curtain.* With that last thought, I sneaked into the tub. Thank goodness, the shower curtain was pulled halfway so I didn't make any noise. Feeling like an idiot for hiding in such a ridiculous place, and scared out of my wits, I pulled in long breaths to calm myself.

Since the living room, hall, and bedroom were carpeted, I couldn't hear where the intruder was going. I prayed he didn't have to take a pee! It seemed like a year, but it was probably less than a minute before I peeked around the shower curtain and saw the rays of a flashlight shining down the hall. A few seconds later, I heard two muffled shots in the bedroom. I felt like a trapdoor had opened in the bottom of my stomach! The intruder must not have shone his flashlight on my bed, or he would have realized I wasn't in it! I heard a rustling of clothes and watched the rays from the flashlight as it moved quickly down the hall. Then I heard the front door open and slam. My heart was racing like the lead car in a police chase.

I jumped out of the tub and ran to the living room. Breathlessly, I switched on the lights and called 911. After giving the operator a brief summary of the terrifying events, she told me she'd send someone immediately. I then called the captain on his cell. He said he'd just received the 911 call, and he and the sergeant would soon be on their way.

Waiting for the police, I stood next to the door with horrifying thoughts. If I'd been asleep in my bed and not in the bathroom when the murder attempt was made, I could very well be dead. That moment of truth caused eerie sensations that far surpassed the sensations I'd felt that morning.

The wail of sirens were the sweetest sounds I'd ever heard! I threw open the door to greet the police. Down the hall, I could see a few heads poking out of opened doors. I saw the older couple, Alice and Dan, who lived directly across from me, staring at me oddly. Alice's eyes were enormous, and she covered her mouth with one hand. I had a fleeting thought that she was trying to keep from laughing. Dan glared at me with a menacing frown. I wondered what they were thinking. I breathed a huge sigh of relief when I recognized the captain and sergeant running towards me.

"Good Lord, Brandon," Captain Delaney said with a concerned look. "What the hell is going on? Did the perp steal your clothes?"

I suddenly realized I was standing there stark naked, as I always slept in the nude. "Damn," I exclaimed, feeling myself flushing from head to toe. "Come on in and close the door behind you. I'll get some clothes on."

I could hear them laughing as I rushed to the bedroom to put on my shorts and tee shirt. In spite of my embarrassment, I started laughing, too. No wonder my neighbors were looking so astonished. I'd probably never live it down, and the captain and sergeant would never let me forget it either.

I returned to the living room and then, while leading them into my bedroom, I detailed what had happened.

The captain and sergeant examined the bed but could find no

bullet holes.

"Hey, Captain, look up here," the sergeant exclaimed, pointing to the wall behind the bed.

The captain examined two bullet holes in the wall just above the bed. "Well, I'll be damned. Someone was either a terrible shot, or he deliberately shot into the wall just to scare you, Brandon."

"If his intention was to scare me, then he did a hell of a good job!"

"What is your opinion, Sergeant?" Captain Delaney asked.

"Were there any lights on in the room?" the sergeant asked me.

"No, there was only a faint nightlight from the bathroom, but remember he had a flashlight. I figure he didn't shine the light on the bed, or he would have noticed that no one was there!"

"I believe the intruder only wanted to scare you," the captain replied. "All the suspects seem to be intelligent, so I can't understand why they think that threatening the witness would change anything – unless you get a call saying that if you don't change your story you'll be killed."

"Guess what? The phone rang tonight, but no one spoke. Perhaps it was to find out if I was at home."

"Maybe you'll get a second call. That one will be a threatening one instructing you to change your story," the sergeant interjected.

"That makes sense," I answered, not feeling a bit better at probably having solved the mystery of the two bullet holes above my bed.

The captain frowned. "Brandon, I guess the Feds will have to put you into the witness protection program."

I could envision myself in a dingy motel in Oregon or another distant state watching soap operas day after day on an old black-and-white TV. "No, I don't think so. Don't you have any extra men that you could pull to be my bodyguard?"

"Yeah, we could do that, but our budget is short. The Feds have more money than we do, Brandon," the captain replied.

"Hey, how about finding someone in security who works for Walmart or somewhere? I'll pay him myself, even if I have to borrow from the Teacher's Credit Union. *So what do you need the money for, Mr. Sterling? Oh, you want to pay for a bodyguard? Gosh, the classroom situation must be more dangerous than I thought. Perhaps you'd better change careers. Sorry, your request is denied.*

"Let me work on it, Brandon," the captain suggested. "I believe we can come up with the money. I'm certain we'll solve this murder soon. In the meantime, you'll need to get a substitute until we do. You don't want to bring any danger to your students. You can stick with the sergeant and me in the daytime, and we'll find someone to guard you at night. What do you think?"

"I can handle that plan." *But I'd need to remember to bring long pants and a sweatshirt to the captain's office.*

He glanced at his watch. "It's two fifteen. You know the sergeant and I were at home in bed when you called. We can't do anything else tonight, so I'm going home and hit the sack. Even though I'd be surprised if the intruder would return tonight, I'd like the sergeant to sleep on your sofa for the rest of the evening. I'll give you the morning off, Erin."

"Sure, no problem," the sergeant replied obligingly.

Captain Delaney headed for the door. "Okay then, both of you try and get some sleep. After you take care of your school business in the morning, come on down to the station, Brandon."

I nodded. "Thanks for everything, captain."

After he left, I offered my bed to the sergeant and told him I'd be happy to sleep on the sofa. He declined but made me promise I'd sleep with some clothes on!

Chapter 20

The alarm went off at seven. Sleepy-eyed, I padded to the kitchen to make coffee. My overnight guest sat up when I approached. "Sorry, Sergeant, I had to set the alarm so I could call my substitute. The coffee will be ready in a few minutes."

Sergeant O'Grady put both feet on the floor and rubbed his eyes. "Not to worry, Brandon. The captain gave me the morning off, so after I leave here I'll head on home and go back to bed."

I opened the freezer door and pulled out some sweet rolls. "I'll thaw these in the micro, and we can have a bite before you leave. But first I need to make my call."

"That sounds good, Brandon. In the meantime, I'll wash my face in the bathroom."

"Were you able to sleep on that sofa?"

"I slept just fine."

"Good." I picked up the phone and called my sub. I told him I would probably need him for the rest of the week, and I'd leave my weekly plans on my desk. I'd explain later why I needed to be absent. He said not to worry, as he was familiar with my routine and students.

I placed the sweet rolls, plates, and cups on the table and was pouring two cups of coffee when I heard my guest approaching. "Have a seat," I said, sitting down in front of him. "It would be great if the captain chose you be my nighttime bodyguard. That way you could make a bit of extra money. And you said the sofa wasn't bad. Of course, your wife might not like the idea!"

The sergeant grinned and reached for a sweet roll. "My wife is used to my strange hours, and we could use the extra money. I'll mention it to the captain."

"Good." I liked the good-natured sergeant and would rather have him around than a stranger.

After leaving my lesson plans in my classroom, I drove directly to the police station. Before I could open my door, my cell rang. "Hello, sweetheart," I said when her number appeared. It was the first time she'd ever called me early on a school morning.

"Brandon," she said, her voice anxious, "I just got a call from Emily, and she said your sub was there again. What's going on?"

Emily was Amberly's best friend and taught French at my high school. "Amberly, it's complicated, and I know you don't have much time before your class starts. Why don't you call me during your planning period?"

"I switched planning periods with another teacher. I have thirty minutes right now while the students are having P.E. I've got a terrible feeling your being absent has to do with the police. Right?"

"Right." I gave her a brief summary of my scary ordeal. "So, not to worry, luv, I'm being protected both day and night."

Her voice had a troubled undertone. "I wish I could believe that, Brandon. Naturally, I've been thinking a lot about the case. I know we've discussed this way-out theory before, but I believe we should discuss it again. Suppose Rosalia did find out about Alberto and Maria's affair. "I'm sure you've heard the truism: 'Hell hath no fury like a woman scorned.' Perhaps to get even, she talked Maria into changing places with her. She could have said it would be a fun to see if Alberto could tell the difference. Maria would have been shocked at her suggestion, since she'd already tricked Alberto before, but of course she couldn't tell her twin. If Rosalia did talk her into it and told Maria it would only be for a day, Maria could have arrived on Friday, while Alberto was in Orlando at a meeting. Rosalia could have hired a young, blond hit man who resembled Alberto, and in that way Alberto would be blamed for murdering Rosalia – who in reality is Maria. Rosalia would get even with both of them that way. Maria would be dead and Alberto would get the blame."

"I can see where you're coming from, but the beach house is in an almost deserted area. It was just a fluke that I just happened to witness the incident. And wouldn't Alberto know that he was kissing Rosalia, and not Maria, in the bedroom? I mean; he'd been fooled once. I don't think he'd be fooled twice!"

"Perhaps not, but if he did have suspicions, he couldn't well reveal them.

If you hadn't been there, the hit man would have made himself noticeable in some other way, or he'd have left some kind of clue pointing to Alberto. By you being there, he didn't need to do that."

"I suppose that's possible. But what about the statement Rosalia told Maria that she knew something about someone that would ruin his life?"

"Brandon, that statement would be a perfect ruse for her plan. Naturally, the police would suspect someone in the family."

"I was told that Rosalia was the sweet, compassionate, mature twin. I can't believe she'd have her own twin murdered no matter how angry she was; that is if she did find out about the affair."

"Brandon, who told you about Rosalia's sterling qualities?"

I searched my mind. "Alberto and...and the last person who raved about Rosalia's superlatives was Maria."

"If Maria were the twin who was murdered, then it would have been Rosalia telling you how wonderful she was. Rosalia may have possessed sterling qualities until she found out about the affair. Shock and rage can change people overnight."

My thoughts were kaleidoscopic. "I can't say your idea is not possible, sweetheart, but in my opinion, it sounds too dramatic to be true, you know, pretty much like a movie script. Though it could be the reason Rosalia would want Maria's body to disappear. But what about asking for ransom? She wouldn't need the money."

"It could be another ruse. And the person taking a shot at you last night could be a ruse so you'd think the suspect didn't want a witness. Of course, Rosalia would want a witness!"

"It's an intriguing idea, Amberly, but I still can't believe a twin would have her own sister murdered and her fiancé framed for the murder. She'd have to be truly evil to want revenge in that way. She'd also be aware of how much pain it would cause her parents. And as I said, I still can't believe Alberto could be deceived yet again. Remember he said he was pretty tanked up when he was deceived the first time."

"That's true, Brandon, and as I said, perhaps he became suspicious but didn't know how to handle it. He couldn't very well say, 'Are you Rosalia or Maria?' I agree with you that it's a way-out theory and one we've touched on before. But anything's possible. Right?"

175

"Right."

"Please call me this evening, Brandon. My anxiety won't go away until this murder is solved. I love you."

"I love you, too, Amberly. I'll call this evening."

After I switched off my cell, I grabbed my sweat shirt and headed for the captain's office. All the talk about the twins changing places was as confusing as hell. I hoped I could keep our conversation in my head.

Sergeant White, the desk sergeant, greeted me with a smile. "Hey, I see you came prepared for the ice box."

I returned his smile. "I hope it's enough."

The door to the captain's office was open, so I peeked in. "Good morning, Captain."

"Come on in, Brandon. I'm glad to see you remembered to put on your clothes!"

I'm sure my expression was sheepish. "I hope you haven't spread the rumor that I'm an exhibitionist."

His eyes twinkled like a Norman Rockwell Santa painting. "I haven't mentioned it to a soul, but I did have to include it in my report. Don't worry, most of the people who read my reports won't know who you are. Have a seat."

I moved the chair to the usual spot next to the window, knowing he was stifling laughter. "My girlfriend, Amberly, has presented a theory to me. It's a really, far-fetched theory, but I thought I'd better run it by you anyway."

Ten minutes later, I rested my case.

The captain had listened attentively without interrupting. "It's a far-fetched theory, all right, but in some ways it makes sense. Even though identical twins have the same DNA they do not have the same fingerprints."

"Alberto told me that he, Maria, and Rosalia attended Greenwood University in Greenwood, New York. I know most colleges now require students to have their fingerprints taken."

"Then there should be no problem in having the college fax the prints. I'll ask Joe to check on it right away. When Maria arrives here, I'll take her prints and compare them with those from the college. Shall we take a ride over to the beach house?"

"Sure. I've rather missed Alberto, Eduardo, and Estrella, but I can't say I've missed the others." I pulled off my sweat shirt and hung it on the back of the chair."

Chapter 21

Fifteen minutes later, the captain and I pulled up to the beach house. The gate was open, so we parked inside the gate. I rang the kitchen doorbell. A few minutes later, I was happy to see that it was Alberto opening the door.

"Come on in," he told us. "Everyone is in the living room as usual. Are you taking a sabbatical from high school, Brandon?"

I laughed. "No, it's a bit more complicated than that." I expected the captain would inform the group about my frightening experience with the intruder, so I didn't attempt to explain why I was taking off another day. We followed Alberto through the kitchen and down the hall.

Eduardo and Estrella were sitting in their usual places on the sofa. Eduardo stood when he saw us. "Please sit down." He pointed to two chairs in front of the coffee table and sofa. "I hope your visit means you have some news."

The captain nodded but didn't answer.

I noticed Maria standing by the window, but Andre, Emilio, and Fernando were absent.

Looking beautiful as usual, Maria, wearing yellow Capri pants and a yellow, low-cut cotton blouse, walked over and stood by Alberto. "In case you're wondering, Andre and Fernando are walking on the beach. Emilio has gone grocery shopping for our lunch and supper. He enjoys cooking and considers himself to be a fairly good gourmet cook."

"However, that is a debatable subject," Alberto added, smiling slightly.

I walked over to Estrella and squeezed her hand. "How are you doing, Estrella?"

She gave me a tentative smile. "As well as can be expected, I guess."

I turned to the captain waiting for his lead. "There has been a rather unusual development," he told them. "Last night someone broke into Brandon's apartment and fired two bullets over his bed."

I noticed the looks of astonishment amidst murmurings.

"My God, what do you make of that?" Eduardo exclaimed.

The captain explained in more detail, but thankfully he omitted the "exhibitionist" scenario.

"That's why I'm not teaching today," I said. "The captain wants to keep a watch on me. And I'll have police protection tonight as well."

Eduardo's expression was one of dismay. He shook his head. "I'm sure you're wishing you'd never gotten mixed up in this dreadful affair, aren't you, Brandon?"

"No, not at all, Eduardo, if my witnessing will help solve the case and bring you closure."

Estrella burst into tears. "Will this nightmare never end?"

"The FBI is checking in some areas that will help us prove the motive for the kidnapping," the captain replied. "Once we find the motive, then we believe we'll find the perpetrator."

I felt grateful the captain didn't reveal how the canines were searching for the body. Whether it was Maria's or Rosalia's body was up for question, but surely the captain would not expose that wild theory to Eduardo and Estrella.

The captain turned to Maria. "Maria, we have a few more questions we'd like to ask you at the police station."

Her eyes narrowed speculatively. "Oh? You can't ask them here?"

"Actually, no. I'll explain when you come to the station. It would expedite matters if you could come right now."

She shot Alberto a questioning look. "Well…I think I can arrange that. Is it okay if Alberto comes with me?"

The captain smiled faintly. "Certainly, he can, as long as he waits for you in the car."

Maria paused a few seconds. "Of course, if that is necessary, Captain." Her voice sounded expressionless.

Eduardo's face appeared haggard with worry. "Captain, I don't suppose you can tell us why you need to question Maria alone, can you?"

"No, but try not to worry; it's just routine. If you remember, I've questioned everyone alone."

I could see that Eduardo was not consoled.

Maria bent to kiss her parents. "I'm sure this won't take long."

Captain Delaney and I arrived at the station a few minutes before Maria and Alberto. The captain stopped at the front desk.

"Sergeant White, did you receive the fingerprints for Rosalia and Maria Vargas?"

"Yes, sir."

"Good. When Maria arrives, send her right in."

I followed the captain into his office and took a seat in my usual spot next to the window. I retrieved my sweat shirt and pulled it over my head.

"Brandon, you remind me of my mother. She's always cold and wears a little shawl," he informed me with his old sarcasm.

"Captain, if your mother sat in this office as much as I have, she'd no doubt be wearing long underwear and her winter coat. There's nothing wrong with me; you're the one with the problem. It must be all of forty degrees in here!"

The captain shook his head. "You exaggerate like my wife."

"I don't think we should reveal our way-out theory to Maria, unless her fingerprints prove she's Rosalia."

"I quite agree, Brandon. No use putting her through any more pain. I'm sure she's feeling bad enough as it is from her affair with Alberto—that is if Maria isn't Rosalia!"

"Well, we'll soon find out." I'd just finished my sentence when the desk Sergeant popped in.

"Captain, Maria is here."

"Send her in, please," the captain said, standing.

I wondered if I should offer Maria my sweat shirt, but then if she got cold enough she might confess to almost anything. I was becoming more convinced by the hour that the deep freeze treatment was the captain's means of torturing his suspects into confession!

Captain Delaney pointed to a chair in front of his desk. "Have a seat, Maria. I'm sure you're wondering why I brought you in. I need to take your fingerprints."

Her beautifully arched eyebrows shot up. "My fingerprints?

181

What on earth for?"

"I'd rather not say just yet, Maria. I'll tell you after we take the prints."

Maria's frown equaled my worst school-teacher's frown. "Captain, I refuse to allow you to take my fingerprints until you tell me what this is all about!" Her voice rang with reproach.

"Okay, Maria, legally, I have the right to take your prints, and I think you'll be sorry you insisted on knowing my reasons for taking them. We've come up with a diabolical, way-out theory, which I'm going to lay out to you. But I'll tell you upfront. I hope it will remain just a theory instead of the truth."

Maria seemed surprised and a bit fearful. "Okay, you've got my attention."

As the captain leaned back in his chair and began, I kept a close watch on Maria's facial expressions. If I'd been watching her act in an old silent movie, I'd have believed she was first perplexed, then shocked, and then extremely angry. By the time the captain finished with his narrative, Maria had defensively crossed her arms and was glaring belligerently at her accuser.

She spat out her words. "If you think I could be Rosalia, then you must think I'm a monster. I'm not Rosalia. How many times do I have to tell you that Rosalia is or was as perfect as you could expect anyone to be. She was an angel – maybe that's why she left us – she was too good to live here on this less-than-perfect planet! And if that's the best theory you can come up with, you'd better hand over the case to someone else!" Supporting her head in her hand, she wept uncontrollably.

A feeling of déjà vu swept through my psyche when I jumped from my seat and handed over my handkerchief. "Just keep it," I mumbled, sparing her the student Christmas present story. On my way back to my seat I glanced at the captain and shrugged.

"Maria," the captain said gently, "as I said, I hope this improbable theory turns out to be just that…an improbable theory. However, we do still need to check your fingerprints. Please come with me."

As the captain escorted Maria from the room, I was thinking that if the young woman we'd observed was indeed Rosalia, she had put on a performance every bit as grand as Alberto's – that is, if Alberto turned out to be the murderer.

I followed the grim-faced twosome to the desk. "Would you please fingerprint this young lady?" the captain instructed Sergeant White.

As I watched the procedure, I was filled with as much tension as an expectant father. I was hoping with all my heart that the twin standing next to me was Maria. I hoped it as much for her parents as I did for her.

The captain looked at Maria's prints, and then at the copy of the prints of the twins that Sergeant White handed him. He smiled at Maria. "You're off the hook, Maria, and I must say, I'm quite relieved."

Maria glared at all of us. "I think you all have been watching too many evil-twin movies." Without another word, she stomped out the door.

"Do you think she's going to tell her folks about our theory and that we fingerprinted her?" I asked.

"I don't know, probably not. She knows it would only upset them."

"Yeah, I know what you mean," I answered. "But Maria shouldn't have insisted we tell her our unlikely theory before we fingerprinted her." I was feeling a bit guilty for having put her through more torment.

The captain squared his shoulders and changed the subject. "Well, let's move on. If the Feds don't call me soon, I'm going to call them."

Five minutes later, the captain and I were taking a break in his office. We were eating donuts and drinking coffee. The donuts were delicious, and the coffee didn't taste too bad, because it hadn't been sitting long enough to meld into diesel oil. The phone's sudden ring jarred me out of my ruminations.

The captain picked up, and from his conversation I knew he was speaking to Ted, the FBI agent. My mind backtracked to our conversation with Maria. I felt sure she told Alberto about the fingerprinting episode and our way-out theory. I wondered what his reaction had been. I was still feeling a bit sheepish about the way we handled it. I noticed the captain hanging up the phone.

He reached for his coffee cup. "That was Ted. They checked into all the suspect's bank accounts. There was nothing suspicious about the accounts except for Emilio's. By the way, he and Alberto make a little over two hundred thousand a year plus an expense account. Anyway, Emilio's account seems erratic. His checks are automatically placed into his account each month. Right now, he has a good balance, but a few of the months he has hit bottom. He has the type of account that keeps his checks from bouncing, and then the money is taken out when his next check comes in.

"Ted checked with the airlines and found his bottoming out has occurred at the times he was visiting Nice. So it appears that Emilio must be a big gambler and has lost heavily. It's possible he's been diddling around with the company's accounts. If that's true, and Rosalia discovered the discrepancy and threatened to tell Eduardo, then we have a good motive for murder."

"I'm sure you remember your interview with him when he got all mixed up with his going-to-the-grocery-store story."

He nodded. "And Alberto told us that when he called Emilio to tell him about Rosalia's disappearance, it sounded like he was driving an old clunker. The time line would fit also."

"Captain, if Emilio is our man, how do you think he found his accomplice, the one who broke into my apartment?"

"Go to the seedy part of any town and look for someone who needs drug money."

I grabbed another donut. If I didn't get back to my classroom soon, I'd need to buy a larger wardrobe. "But wouldn't Emilio, or anyone in that circumstance, be setting himself up for blackmail by his accomplice?"

"Possibly, but as the saying goes, when you've killed once, it's easier to kill twice."

"Emilio would have to be a sociopath." I was finding it difficult to see any of our suspects in that light.

Once more the phone rang, and when the captain picked up, I left for the bathroom. Too much coffee. But at least I was warm.

When I returned, the captain was hanging up the phone.

He glanced up and said, "The call was from Ted again. The canines found nothing in Andre's back yard or in the empty lots south of the beach house. This afternoon the Orlando police are bringing their canine squad over to the area around Emilio's rented cabin. The FBI auditors are still working on Rosalia's books."

"Have they finished looking into Alberto's, Fernando's and

Andre's checking accounts?"

The captain nodded. "Yes, and everything looks normal there. I'm surprised. I really thought Alberto had the strongest motive because of his affair with Maria. But we haven't proved anything yet. Just because Emilio has a gambling problem, it doesn't mean he's a criminal."

I started to reach for another donut but thought better of it. I didn't want "love handles" like the captain. "I suppose the Feds are watching the beach house closely, huh?"

"Yes, someone is on duty twenty-four hours a day now."

"Hey Captain; Hey Brandon," Sergeant O'Grady said, walking into the office. "I just noticed a blue, rusty truck that looked like the one we saw parked in the garage in Kissimmee. Looked like a young dude with long hair driving past here as I was getting out of my car."

The captain stood. "Okay, then get back into your car and see if you can find him. If you do, stop him and ask for his license. If he's an accomplice, at least we'll have his name. Be sure you check the license plate, and we'll see if it's the same truck as the one in Kissimmee. Why don't you go with him, Brandon? That way you can see if it's the truck that was following you the other day."

That's a good idea," I replied. I was ready for a change of scenery, anyway.

With me by his side, the sergeant had driven up and down many streets, but to no avail.

"I have an idea," I told him. "Let's drive by my apartment. Since he knows how to jimmy my lock, maybe he's returned and left me a present.

Ten minutes later, the sergeant and I entered my apartment. I'd been left a present, all right! I felt sick all over at the sight of total disarray – turned-over chairs, books thrown on the floor, and drawers emptied and piled high. I pulled in a deep breath. "Looks like I've had a visitor," I said, trying to remain calm and not doing a good job of it.

"Damn, I bet you'd like to get your hands on the twerp, wouldn't you?"

"You got that right," I answered, with a vision of my hands

throttling his no-good throat. "And I bet he left me a calling card in my bedroom. If he's trashed my computer, I may end up in jail myself because I'll find and kill the son of a bitch!"

"I wouldn't blame you, Brandon."

We entered my bedroom, and I breathed a sigh of relief. Though drawers had been emptied on my bed, the computer appeared okay. A sheet of paper had been taped on the back of my headboard with these words: THOSE SHOTS OVER YOUR HEAD LAST NIGHT WERE A WARNING. IF YOU WANT TO STAY ALIVE AND WELL, YOU'D BETTER CHANGE YOUR DESCRIPTION OF THE PERSON YOU SAW RUNNING DOWN THE STEPS. SINCE YOU ONLY GOT A GLIMPSE OF HIM, IT COULD BE THAT HIS HAIR WAS GRAY OR WHITE MEANING HE WAS AN OLDER MAN.

I'M WATCHING YOU!

I turned to the sergeant. "So that's why he gave me warning shots instead of aiming at the bed. Does it strike you that the trashing of my apartment and the note appear to be rather dramatic and amateurish? All the suspects at the beach house seem to be more intelligent than to pull a stunt like this!"

"I have to agree, Brandon. Maybe the kidnapper hasn't communicated real well with his accomplice. He could have given instructions to scare you into changing your story, but his hired help could have taken it on himself to do the shooting, apartment trashing, and note writing!"

"That makes sense. I'd better report this to the captain."

I could feel my shoulders sagging as I walked to the living room. I picked up the phone trying not to think of all the work it would take to get the mess cleaned up. When the captain picked up, I explained the situation.

"That's too bad, Brandon. Perhaps some of your students will help you with the cleanup. In the meantime, I want you to stay in a motel tonight with a bodyguard."

"You don't have to talk me into it, Captain. How about Sergeant O'Grady?"

"No problem. You two come on back to the station. I'll call the Kissimmee police and see if someone can go out to the cabin to check on the blue truck. If it's not there, I'll ask them to be on the lookout for it. I'm relatively sure the truck that you spotted in town is the same as the one at the cabin which of course points to Emilio."

After hanging up, I turned to the sergeant. "The captain wants us back at the station." I glanced around the room at the total mess. "And I'm ready to get the hell out of here!"

On our way back to the station, I glanced into the rearview mirror. My heart revved up like a souped-up hot rod. "You won't believe this, but I believe that rusty old blue truck is directly behind us."

Looking into his mirror, the sergeant answered, "I think you're right, Brandon. Why on earth would that stupid kid be following us? I'm going to pull over and let him pass. Then we'll follow him, if it's who we think it is."

The sergeant pulled over, and as soon as the truck passed he shot back into the street. We were still in a thirty-five mile zone, but the blue truck took off at a high speed. We took off right behind him with the blue light turned on and the siren blaring!

"I can't believe anyone could be so dumb," the sergeant retorted shaking his head. "Chasing someone down the street could cause an accident. I don't want to take a chance on an innocent person getting hurt."

He reached for his mike and called the station. "Captain, we're giving chase to a punk in a blue truck. We think he's the guy we've been looking for. We're on Berkeley Street, heading east towards A1A. Okay, the truck is now heading south. I don't want to give a high-speed chase that would cause an accident. See if another car can intercede and head him off. I'm not letting him out of my sight."

I was excited, somewhat frightened, and on an adrenaline rush that equaled the first time I'd ridden a roller coaster. An unexpected feeling of importance boosted my ego when I noticed cars pulling off to the side. The truck continued to speed down the highway. I didn't want to do or say anything that would cause the sergeant to lose his focus. I kept silent.

I watched breathlessly as two more police cars joined the chase. Finally, the blue truck pulled off the road. The sergeant pulled off behind the two other police cars parked behind the blue truck. I decided to wait in the car.

The punk finally had a name. According to his license, his name was Billy Winstead. He was five-foot-ten and weighed two hundred pounds. His address: Kissimmee, Florida.

I'd been allowed to sit in on his questioning, and as I observed him, I noticed how badly he needed a good shower. Also his scraggly, longish-blond hair was in need of a good shampooing. His dingy jeans and black tee shirt with "Shit Happens" written across the front, appeared filthy. Perhaps...no, I won't go there!

He denied breaking into my apartment, firing two shots over my bed, and then returning the next day to leave a big mess and a note. As we had expected, Billy was not one of the brightest bulbs in the chandelier, which would probably be the undoing of the person who had hired him. His unregistered gun was found under his seat. We were sure the bullets in his gun would match the ones found in the wall over my bed. The truck was registered to the owner of the cabin in Kissimmee. Billy was in big trouble, but he would not "squeal" on the person who had hired him. He demanded a lawyer. As expected, he said he couldn't afford one, so the county would have to provide one. As badly as I wanted to throttle him, I decided to let the law inflict the punishment.

"Since Billy boy was driving the truck connected to the cabin in Kissimmee, and since Emilio is renting the cabin, I think it goes without saying who our prime suspect is now," the captain said, glancing at the sergeant and me, then back to Billy.

Billy crossed his arms and glared. "You can't prove nothing."

The captain's grin was wicked. "Perhaps you'd like to call your boss and let him know how much trouble you're in, Billy. Since he's a rich man with a million dollars in ransom money, he'd be able to hire a big-time lawyer for you."

Billy's longish chin jutted out further. "You can't trick me."

"We wouldn't dream of such a thing, Billy, mainly because we don't need to," the captain informed him.

After Billy was led to his jail cell, the captain phoned Ted and filled him in with the morning's activities. "So what's happening over there at the cabin? Any luck with the canines?"

"Nothing yet, but we have a lot more territory to cover. I'll get back with you if we find anything, and I expect we will since Emilio is now the prime suspect."

The captain hung up. "We don't want to bring Emilio in until we find the body. It may take awhile. The feds have two men watching the beach house, so I don't think he will get too far when he makes his move."

"Hey, I have an idea," I said. "I'll pick up something from the bakery and take it over to the beach house. While I'm there, I'll tell them that you caught the man who broke into my place. I won't mention that he was driving the truck that belongs to the owner of Emilio's rented cabin. I'll act like I don't know much about it. If Emilio is there, I'll watch his expression carefully. And I'll bet he'll make his move shortly after I leave."

The captain seemed to be mulling over my suggestion for a few seconds. "Okay, I'll go along with that plan, although I did want to wait until we found the body. But we actually have enough evidence to bring him in anyway. It will be interesting to see how long it takes him to take off when you tell him we've got his not-so-bright accomplice. Be sure you mention his name, Billy Winstead."

"Oh, I won't forget that. I'll report back here after I leave."

Chapter 22

My mouth was watering for the delicious-looking chocolate cake I'd just purchased. Driving towards the beach house, I was hoping Estrella would offer me a piece. My donut sugar high was dwindling. I felt so bad for the lovely woman who was soon to find out her daughter was no longer alive. Of course, we couldn't be one hundred percent sure until her body was actually found. But I didn't think there was even a slim chance that she would have survived the fall and the kidnapping.

I parked my car, grabbed the cake box, and rushed towards the house, wondering who would answer the door. My answer came in the form of Emilio. I noticed his frown when he saw me.

"So, Brandon," he said, "what are you up to today? Are you playing hooky again?"

"Sort of, I guess. I've been working with the police."

He smirked. "Oh, I forgot you've been deputized. Well, come on in."

I followed him down the familiar hall. Neither one of us engaged in any small talk.

Once again, I entered the living room. This time everyone was present and watching the news on TV as if they expected to hear something about the kidnapping.

Eduardo was the first to notice my entrance. "Hello, Brandon. Do come in."

"Thanks, Eduardo." I walked over to the sofa and held out the cake box to Estrella. "I hope you like chocolate cake."

She peeked into the box. "How nice of you, Brandon. It's my favorite, and it was Rosalia's favorite, too." Her eyes took on a wounded look.

I reached over and squeezed her arm then sat down next to her. "I thought you might be interested to know that we caught the guy who took shots over my bed. He also trashed my place this morning."

"How do the police know that guy is the one who broke into your apartment?" Emilio asked with a pained expression.

I was enjoying Emilio's discomfort. "It's complicated, but his name is Billy Winstead. The strange thing is, he was driving an old, blue, rusty truck that was parked in the garage of the cabin you rented in Kissimmee, Emilio."

Emilio appeared bewildered. He bit his lips for a few seconds. "I guess I must have forgotten to take out the keys when I drove it last. It's a deserted area and easy to steal things, I suppose."

Obviously perplexed, Eduardo directed his question to Emilio. "But why would someone randomly pick out Brandon's apartment and shoot over his bed, then trash his place?"

A bead of perspiration popped up over Emilio's lip. "I have no idea." He turned to me. "Are you sure he's not one of your old students trying to get even for a bad report card?"

If I told the group about the note Billy left over my bed, it would be obvious that the not-so-swift young man had been hired by Emilio. Though I was tempted, I kept quiet about the note.

I smiled. "No, I'd never met Billy until the police caught up with him."

Estrella sat up straighter. "I wonder if Billy is the kidnapper's accomplice. If so, and since you, Brandon, are the only witness to Rosalia's accident, then his visits to your apartment may have been to frighten you into not telling what you saw."

Alberto spoke for the first time. "I think you're on to something, Estrella."

I nodded. "And there's more evidence concerning Emilio's cabin, but I'm not at liberty to reveal it at this time."

Eduardo's voice was just above a whisper. "Do you mean the police are getting close to finding Rosalia and who abducted her?"

Though I was facing Eduardo, I could see Emilio out of the corner of my eye. He was turning as red as one of Amberly's lipsticks. "Yes, Eduardo," I answered, "I think the Feds and police will have some answers very soon."

Estrella was staring into space as she spoke, "I'm not sure I'm ready to hear the answers. As long as I don't know anything for sure, I can remain hopeful."

His expression grave, Eduardo placed his arm around his wife's shoulder. He said nothing.

I kissed Estrella's cheek. "I must be going. Is there anything I can do for you before I go?"

"No, dear Brandon," she replied. "Thank you so much for the lovely cake. We'll have it for dessert. Emilio is cooking us a gourmet dinner tonight. Why don't you stay?"

"I appreciate the invitation, but I have things I need to do. I'll check in with you tomorrow." My chocolate cake might be the only thing on tonight's menu. I was sure Emilio would not be around to serve his gourmet meal. I figured he'd bypass the cabin and high tail it to the nearest airport, unless he needed to pick up his passport. The group would no doubt wonder what had happened to their chef.

Chapter 23

As soon as I slid into the front seat of my car, I pulled out my cell phone and called the captain. I quickly told him of my conversations with the group. "My bet is Emilio will be running out of the garage and jumping into his car in the next ten minutes. I hope the Feds won't lose him. Those expensive sports cars can go pretty fast."

"You needn't worry about anyone keeping up with Emilio," he replied in a confident voice. "Even if they lost him, which is doubtful, they have the description of his car and license plate, so every police vehicle in the state of Florida will be on his tail. I'm hanging up now and alerting the two Feds covering the beach house. Come on back to the station. You can monitor the action from here."

"Over and out," I said grinning, remembering when my buddy and I used to play "Calling all Cars."

I pulled out of the driveway and headed for the station. I wouldn't have been at all surprised if Emilio's sports car had passed me.

I entered the captain's office just as he was hanging up the phone. I took a seat next to the window.

"They've found Rosalia's body, Brandon."

Though I knew I'd eventually hear those words, I wasn't prepared for the chills that ran up and down my spine. I felt strangely semiconscious.

"Brandon, did you hear me? They've discovered Rosalia's body!"

Surprised at my reaction, I fought back threatening tears. "Yes, I heard you, Captain. Where did they find her?"

They dug her up about two miles south of Emilio's cabin. The canines found her. She was buried about three feet under the ground zippered into a luggage garment bag. You were right about that. At least he didn't toss her into the alligator-infested lake."

While a vision of the gory scene played through my mind, I pulled in a deep breath trying to calm myself. "Captain, on cases where you've had time to meet and talk with the family and have learned something about the victim, after all these years, are you still emotionally affected?"

He nodded. "Of course, I'm affected. I'm not a robot. I especially feel bad for Rosalia's parents and Maria and Alberto who will carry a certain amount of guilt around with them for most of their life, I suppose. I'm sure Fernando and Andre are heartbroken also. But I don't feel anything but anger and disgust for Emilio and his sidekick, Billy Winstead."

I pictured myself in the ring with those two calloused jerks while I beat the hell out of them both. Before I could comment, the phone rang.

The captain picked up, and I knew right away from his conversation that he was speaking with Ted and that Emilio had made his move. He hung up and smiled.

"Are they going to bring him in here or take him to Orlando?" I asked.

"They're bringing him here. He only got a mile down the road before they closed in. When they got the message that Rosalia's body had been found in the area of the cabin, they didn't need to wait any longer. I'm sure they'll find Emilio's DNA on the garment bag and body."

"I don't think the family will be too surprised, since I told them about Billy Winstead driving the truck that belonged to the owner of the cabin. From a few of the comments the family made, it was evident they thought there had to be some connection between Emilio and the lame-brained Billy."

Sergeant O'Grady poked his head in the door. "Two Feds have just driven up with someone in the back."

"Tell them to bring in the perp, Sergeant, and you come in with them."

Captain Delaney stood and folded his arms across his chest. I remained seated.

Two men I hadn't seen before accompanied Emilio, wearing

handcuffs, into the room.

"Good work, boys," the captain said. He pointed to a chair in front of his desk. "Sit down, Emilio. As you already know, we've got Billy Winstead locked up. The Feds just discovered Rosalia's buried body a few miles from your cabin." He read him his rights and said, "Do you have anything to say?"

Emilio stared at a spot over the over the captain's head. "I have nothing to say except that I want a lawyer."

The captain smirked. "No doubt you can afford a good one with one million dollars stashed away in a Cayman bank."

Emilio's eyebrows shot up, but he didn't answer.

"I'm getting ready to go to the beach house to inform the family of the situation, Emilio," I told him. "Is there anything you'd like me to tell them?"

He glared at me and clamped his jaws shut.

"Perhaps you'll think of something by the time Eduardo and Estrella visit you in jail," I replied. *If Emilio has an ounce of compassion in his body, he'll find it as difficult to face his brother and Rosalia's family as it will be to face his jail cell,* I thought.

Emilio remained mute and stone faced.

The captain nodded his head towards the Feds. "Okay, men. Let's take this fine specimen of manhood to the interrogation room." He turned towards me. "Sorry, Brandon, but you're elected to break the news to the family. I'm tempted to drag Emilio to the beach house and make him stand in front of the family while we tell him he's being indicted for the murder of his brother's fiancée."

After the captain's last words, Emilio closed his eyes for a few seconds. I wouldn't have wanted to change places with him for all the banks in the Cayman Islands.

The captain placed his arm on Emilio's arm saying, "Okay, Emilio. Let's go. You can make your call for a lawyer at the desk up front." He glanced at me. "You know what you have to do, Brandon. Check back here when you finish."

I pulled through the gate of the beach house wondering how many times I'd visited the pink beach house since last Friday. It had only been five days since the murder and kidnapping, yet it seemed more like five months.

My feet felt like lead when they hit the pavement. Informing the family of Rosalia's death would be the most difficult thing I'd ever done. I said a silent prayer as I entered the garage and rang the kitchen doorbell.

Maria opened the door. When she saw my gloomy face, she must have known what was coming. "Come in, Brandon. Emilio ran out of the living room without saying where he was going. Then we heard a siren. Is he...he the one?"

I nodded. "I'm afraid he is, Maria. They found Rosalia's body a few miles from his cabin. I'm so very sorry."

Watching helplessly when she began sobbing, I reached out and pulled her into my arms. I patted her back and wished I could do something to make her feel better.

Looking over her shoulder, I could see Eduardo entering the kitchen.

He let out a strangled cry. "Oh, my God! Have they found my daughter, Brandon?"

Maria pulled away and fell into her father's arms. "Yes, Dad, they found her buried close to Emilio's cabin," she sobbed almost incoherently.

Eduardo held his daughter tightly and said in a voice just above a whisper, "That's a double blow. After you told us, Brandon, about the possible connection between Billy Winstead and Emilio, I had some suspicions, but I just couldn't bring myself to believe he could murder his own brother's fiancée.

I watched Eduardo's shoulders heaving as he sobbed and tried to gulp air. I came very close to breaking down but tried desperately to control myself. The worst was yet to come when I would face Estrella and the rest.

A few minutes later, which seemed like an eon, Eduardo finally pulled himself together. "Thank you for coming, Brandon. Please come into the living room. I'm sure everyone will have questions."

When Estrella looked up, she burst into tears. No doubt she guessed the worst when she saw our expressions. Eduardo took her in his arms and they cried together.

"What's happening, Brandon?" Alberto asked, walking over to Maria.

I pulled in a deep breath. "Rosalia's body was found buried close to Emilio's cabin. Emilio is in custody."

Fernando's eyes were filled with grief and anger. "I knew it. I knew it when you indicated there was a connection between Billy Winstead and Emilio. And then when he left suddenly, I was sure. God, how could he do such a thing?"

Andre's face was drained of its color. "That bastard, I'd like to tear him to pieces."

"Okay, let's allow Brandon to tell us what he knows," Eduardo said with an uneven voice. "There will be plenty of time for us to rant and grieve. Sit down here in front of us," he said pointing to the chair in front of the sofa.

I sat down. "I really don't know that much, but I can tell you that the police found a piece of luggage in Emilio's cabin with Nice, France on the tag. The captain developed a theory that Emilio's finances may have been in trouble because of a gambling problem. Rosalia may have discovered that he'd been taking money from the company's accounts. That theory would fit into the statement she made to you, Maria, when she said she'd found something about someone that would probably ruin his life, but her heart was holding her back. Then when Billy was picked up in the old truck that belonged to the owner of Emilio's cabin, the police thought Emilio had most likely hired him as his accomplice. I'm sure Emilio rues the day he ever hired an accomplice, especially a not-so-bright person like Billy. The Feds and police believe Emilio thought having someone call the house, while he was in the house, would make him appear innocent. But Emilio wasn't thinking straight either."

"Do you think he planned to push her from the cupola, or could he have been so angry at her for her refusal to help him, that he pushed her in a fit of anger?" Alberto asked softly.

I fidgeted in my chair. "No one knows yet, Alberto, but my gut feeling is he didn't plan to push her. As you know, I said I didn't feel any pulse when I examined Rosalia right after she'd fallen. I believe he felt no pulse either, and in his panic, he decided to pull the kidnapping stunt. That way he could cast suspicion on an outsider and also take the ransom money and replace it in his account. Part of his plan may have been to leave the country if he became the prime suspect, so the ransom would serve another purpose. He might have gotten away with all of it if I hadn't been a witness, or if he hadn't hired not-so-bright Billy Winstead."

Tears were streaming down Estrella's cheeks. "My heart is breaking, but Emilio's mother and father will feel deep grief as well. They will mourn not only Rosalia's death, but the anguish of having a son who is a murderer."

Alberto kneeled in front of Estrella and took her hand. "I'm so very sorry, Estrella. My heart is breaking, too. I wish…I wish–"

"My feelings for you have not changed, Alberto. You are not responsible for what your brother did."

"But Emilio and I look so much alike, Estrella. Every time you look at me you'll think of Emilio and what he did."

Estrella took his hand. "Alberto, at this moment, everyone here is full of anger and grief, but sooner or later we'll have to forgive Emilio, because if we don't, our anger will destroy us."

Alberto buried his head in her lap and wept.

Andre headed for the hall. "I've got to get out of here. I'm going for a walk on the beach."

"I'm coming with you," Fernando said, following him.

I felt like I had to get out, too, before I lost it. "Is there anything…anything at all I can do for any of you?"

Eduardo stood and walked towards me. He held out his hand. "No, Brandon, but you've been a true friend from the start. You may not have realized it, but except for Emilio, you were the last person to see our Rosalia."

Well, that did it. I ignored his hand and hugged him tightly as my dammed-up tears finally broke. I wept with the family with whom I'd become so closely bonded in such a short while.

Chapter 24

Driving towards the police station, I pulled myself together. I felt a chapter of my life was over, except for the trial that was sure to follow. No doubt I'd be called as a witness. It would be good to start back to class again. I wondered how my students were going to feel when they watched the press conference that the captain would be giving soon.

I parked and walked into the station feeling like an old punctured tire. "What's happening?" I asked Sergeant O'Grady, who was standing by Sergeant White's desk.

"Emilio asked for a phone book and put in a call to a criminal lawyer. The lawyer hasn't arrived."

"Is he talking yet?" I expected his lawyer had told him not to answer any questions until he arrived.

He shrugged. "All I know is that they're still in the interrogation room."

"Please tell the captain that I've informed the family, and I plan to go back to my class in the morning. If he needs me for anything, he knows how to get in touch."

"Sure thing, Brandon."

"Oh, I guess you know that you don't need to spend the night with me tonight, since we have the bad guys locked up."

Sergeant O'Grady grinned. "Yeah, I'm sure you're relieved about that."

"Oh, I don't know, I rather enjoyed your company, but I am relieved that I won't be bothered anymore. Good night, you two."

Walking to my car, I thought that my relief hadn't brought any joy to the situation.

When I opened my apartment door, I was in for a shock. I'd completely forgotten about my trashed domicile! I was so emotionally drained, the last thing I wanted to do was start putting everything back together. I decided to take a long jog and face my dilemma when I returned.

Five minutes later, dressed in my running attire, I opened my car door and headed for the beach, but this afternoon, I would not go in the direction of the pink beach house. Perhaps it would be a long time before I could jog in that direction again.

Epilogue

As I said at the beginning of my tale, it's been a year since the incident at the pink beach house, took place. The captain and I have stayed in touch, and he's kept me informed.

He told me Emilio admitted to the murder but said it was not premeditated. Emilio said he waited until he knew Alberto would be in Orlando before he drove to the beach house that Friday afternoon. He begged Rosalia to give him time to try to get the money to replace the amount he'd lifted from the company to cover his large gambling debts. She refused. In a rage, he pushed her from the cupola. He was shocked at what he'd done, shocked to see me running into the courtyard, and shocked to discover that Rosalia was dead. The kidnapping occurred to him after he realized there was nothing he could do to bring her back to life. In a panic, looking for something to cover her, he rushed into the house and found a bag in the hall closet. He zippered her into the bag, placed her into his car, and raced back to his cabin. When he arrived at the cabin, he took her body from his car and laid it in the back of the truck along with a shovel. He was driving the truck and looking for a place to bury her when he received that call from Alberto.

He got the idea for an accomplice to make the ransom calls so while he was in the company of the family, it would appear that the kidnapping was done by someone outside the family. He searched around until he found someone who needed drug money. Billy Winstead had taken it upon himself to break into my apartment to do the shooting above my bed and the trashing of my apartment. Billy thought he was being smart when he broke into Emilio's cabin to take the truck keys so he could follow me and do the other foul deeds. I wondered if Billy had used the same window that I'd used to break into the cabin!

The trial is set for this coming December. The captain thinks Emilio will be found guilty for kidnapping and second degree murder. He'd no doubt spend many years in prison. I know I'll be called in as a witness, and I don't look forward to it. But at least I'll get a chance to see Rosalia's family again. According to Alberto, who has stayed in touch, the family hasn't had the heart to return to Florida since the murder, but I'm sure they'll be staying at the beach house during the trial.

Alberto told me he's grateful that the captain has not made his affair with Maria public. They are planning to marry sometimes within the year. The family thought it was only natural that they would be drawn together after Rosalia's death. He said that Maria has left her modeling job in Spain and is working for Eduardo in New York. Fernando has decided to stay with the company and not pursue his dream of becoming a marine biologist for at least a few years.

At the present moment, I'm standing on Amberly's patio grilling steaks while sipping a margarita. The sun has just set, and though I can't see them, I know that beautiful pink clouds are banked on the ocean's horizon directly in front of the pink beach house.

I've moved in with Amberly, and life is about as good as it can get. The money I'm saving from the rent of my former apartment is going into a savings account. When we marry this summer, we hope we'll have enough saved to make a down payment on a house of our own.

Last night we watched an old Bette Davis movie about an evil twin. Amberly and I discussed how glad we were that Rosalia had not changed places with Maria and murdered her twin. I'm not sure Eduardo and Estrella would have ever recovered.

I've talked a lot to my students about the consequences of rage and revenge. I hope they'll remember those lessons.

Well, that's my story and I'm sticking to it.

ABOUT THE AUTHOR

Kay Williamson, a former elementary school teacher and resident of Satellite Beach, Florida, is published in various literary anthologies and magazines. Her romantic suspense and murder mystery novels include: *Ghostly Whispers, Bridge to Nowhere, Listen to the Heart, Time After Time, Murder at the Starlight Pavilion, and The Mysterious Woman on the Train,* and *Murder on Star Route 1.*

Kay, a playwright and published songwriter, plays keyboard as Don, her husband, leads sing-a-longs at nursing homes in the Satellite Beach, FL area, the VA Hospital in Iron Mountain, MI, and the Golden Living Center in Florence, WI.

Also watercolor artists, the couple display their paintings in shows during the winter months in Florida.

Learn more about the author at www.kaywilliamson.com.

32313557R00115

Made in the USA
Columbia, SC
17 November 2018